GUNSMOKE MASQUERADE

Center Point
Large Print

Also by Peter Dawson and available from
Center Point Large Print:

Troublesome Range

**This Large Print Book carries the
Seal of Approval of N.A.V.H.**

GUNSMOKE MASQUERADE

A Western Story

PETER DAWSON

CENTER POINT LARGE PRINT
THORNDIKE, MAINE

This Center Point Large Print edition is published
in the year 2013 in conjunction with
Golden West Literary Agency.

"Gunsmoke Masquerade" first appeared as a
seven-part serial in *Western Story* (3/28/42-5/9/42).
Copyright © 1942 by Street & Smith Publications, Inc.
Copyright © renewed 1970 by Dorothy S. Ewing.
Copyright © 2009 by Dorothy S. Ewing
for restored material.

The text of this Large Print edition is unabridged.
In other aspects, this book may
vary from the original edition.
Printed in the United States of America
on permanent paper.
Set in 16-point Times New Roman type.

ISBN: 978-1-61173-638-0

Library of Congress Cataloging-in-Publication Data

Dawson, Peter, 1907–1957.
Gunsmoke masquerade / Peter Dawson.
pages ; cm.
ISBN 978-1-61173-638-0 (library binding : alk. paper)
1. Large type books. I. Title.
PS3507.A848G85 2013
813′.54—dc23
                                                2012038094

GUNSMOKE
MASQUERADE

Chapter One

The clump of giant cottonwoods by the spring at Agua Verde was the only spot of bright greenery along the whole vast sweep of the desert's eastern rim. Years back, the stage road had made a wide detour from its north/south line to touch at the springs. The station under the trees, now abandoned except for the corrals, had offered the traveler a pleasant spot to lay over and ready himself for either the northward or southward remaining half of the three-day journey across Dry Reach from Johnsville to Fort Sawyer.

When the high valley footing the lofty peaks to the east attracted settlers, another road came down to Agua Verde from that direction, and freighting wagons became even more numerous than the stages. A small town mushroomed along the foot of that east road close behind the cottonwoods, the buildings set far back from the wheel ruts out of respect to the dust. The town hadn't thrived for long, even though an occasional freight hitch still lumbered up the road out of the desert, for the heat along the wide street was close to intolerable except at night, and traffic went on through instead of stopping.

Still, the settlement didn't completely die. For the last several years it had remained in a suspended state of slow disintegration, the saloon and the hotel and one general store doing enough business to keep open, the stage corral still busy and boarding the teams and saddle animals of outgoing and incoming men from the east upcountry as it always had. And each mid-morning and late afternoon the townspeople, except for a few women, would drift toward the corral to watch the arrival of the stages as they had since the first adobe hovel was built on the town site. It was as though they awaited some happening, a summons to a less dreary life, perhaps, that never came.

This early evening the stage was an hour overdue. It finally made its appearance far out across Dry Reach, its progress marked by what looked like a lazy dust devil. Still, as that dust smear neared and the sun's brassy glare died with a faint breeze out of the eastward hills stirring the furnace-hot air, not a man or a woman came onto the street. They had good reason for staying indoors. Two hours ago a buckboard had rattled in off the east road. Its driver had pulled in at the hotel, tied his team to the rail there, and taken a chair on the wide portal fronting the low adobe building. His age was indeterminate, for his cornsilk hair and longhorn mustache gave him the look of an old man, while the lack of lines on his hawkish face, along with a springy yet awkward stride, were tokens of a saddle man in his prime. Boots cocked on the rail of the hotel verandah, he presently took a blackened brier from pocket, filled it with care, and began smoking. Those few townspeople already up from their *siestas* saw him and knew him to be Mike Sternes, foreman of one of the big upcountry outfits, and were incurious over his presence here.

He had barely got his pipe going when another traveler appeared at the head of the street, coming in from the same direction Sternes had. This second man rode a roan horse. When he first saw the rider, Sternes took the pipe from his mouth, knocked the tobacco from it against the heel of his boot, and returned it to his pocket. His face settled into cool impassivity as the horseman neared and, almost abreast the hotel, reined to a stop. By that time Sternes had his feet off the rail and was sitting straighter than before.

A brief and hostile glance passed between the two. Sternes's stare at length moved off the man, apparently ignoring him, yet not far enough so that he couldn't watch him out of the corner of his eye. The rider in the street smiled meagerly at the other's apparent disinterest. He was a tall and handsome man, young and with deep sorrel hair, and he sat the saddle with a carelessness that was cocksure, almost defiant. Shortly he said in a quiet drawl that, despite its low tone, carried to the other: "Want to settle this now, Mike?" His right hand lay carelessly against the inside swell of the saddle, within easy hand spread of the low-slung holster thonged to his thigh.

Sternes's glance swung directly on him again. "Not now, Dallam," was his slow answer.

That sparse exchange of words was overheard by three men watching from the saloon down and across the street from the hotel. By the time Dallam had put his horse to that side of the street and entered the saloon, those three had left by the back door. Within five minutes every soul in town knew that Pete Dallam and Mike Sternes were finally within shooting distance of each other. And one and all decided that it would be wisest to stay indoors, out of range of any stray lead that might fly at any moment. For the feud of these two upcountry men had long passed the stage of threats; neither would talk about the other; both had sought a final and deciding meeting. It looked as though this might be it.

The saloon remained empty except for a wary barkeeper whose anxiety must have showed on his face. For, as Dallam called for a bottle, he remarked: "Just stay set and you'll be all right."

The apron nodded but slopped a little whiskey over the edge of the shot glass as he filled it for his unwanted customer.

Dallam had three straight drinks before he sauntered back to the street door, went out, and leaned idly against the pushed-back window shutter. He looked across at Sternes, and there was a wicked deviltry on his handsome full face. He was this way when he drank, which was often.

"Changed your mind, Mike?" he called presently.

Sternes looked at him casually, then away, not bothering to reply.

"Why put it off?" Dallam taunted. "You've saved up enough to pay the undertaker."

This time Sternes completely ignored him.

With a low laugh, Dallam reëntered the saloon. As he came back to the stained pine counter, he told the bartender: "The old bird's hard to rile. I'll hand him that much."

"Yes, Mister Dallam."

"What's the matter, you scared?"

"So bad I can taste it!"

"I ought to be, too," Dallam said, and reached again for the bottle. The orange wash of the sun's last light was fading when the stage took the sharp rise up out of the sand and rumbled in toward the corral. By that time, Sternes had left his chair and was well down the street, almost to the arched gateway under the cottonwoods that marked the stage lot entrance. Dallam took a last quick drink, left the saloon, and rolled a smoke as he strode down the hard-packed dirt walk.

Sternes came up onto the corral's loading platform as the Concord's high door swung open. He took off his curl-brimmed Stetson, said—

"Cathy, you're a sight for sore eyes! Glad you're home."—and reached up to help a slim, raven-haired girl down off the step.

"You're not half as glad as I am, Mike." The girl gave Sternes her hand and a warm welcoming smile that let him know she meant what she said.

The sheen of her hair and contrasting light blue eyes would have made Catherine Bishop striking-looking even if she lacked any semblance of prettiness. But she was quite pretty. Her good looks weren't shallow, and, feature by feature, she wasn't beautiful. Her mouth was a shade too wide for perfection, but it made the face all the more expressive. Her slender nose had the hint of an uptilt, not flaw-less but adding to the vivaciousness of her quick and usually merry eyes. Her ridiculously small but becoming blue hat was powdered with dust, as was her puff-sleeved print dress, but in spite of this badge of her desert journey she looked remarkably well-groomed.

Sternes stepped back for a better look at her, his expression mock sober. "Are them doodads what they're wearin' back East these . . . ?" He broke off when he saw she wasn't listening. Turning, his glance following hers, he saw Dallam coming in the lot gate, and now his face turned genuinely grave. "I didn't know he was comin' or I'd have stayed away," he said in a low voice.

"Never mind, Mike," was the girl's quick

answer. "But promise you won't make trouble?"

"Ma'am, I been a saint ever since he showed up. Reckon I can hold out."

"Thanks, Mike."

She left his side then, going out across the platform to meet Dallam. Sternes watched until Dallam gathered the girl in his arms. Then he swung around irritably, quickly, intending to unload her things from the big mail coach's back boot.

His move brought him jarring against a stranger alighting from the stage. "Watch who you're pushin'!" he said angrily. The next moment he was looking closely at the man, his anger gone. The stranger laughed easily and said —"My fault."—as he turned away.

He was a tall man, heavy in the shoulders, and he had the look of a cowpuncher uncomfortable in his Sunday suit. As he moved away, Sternes noticed his dark-red hair. There were other things to notice about him—the ease with which he swung Cathy's heavy trunk down off the boot board so as to get at his own war bag, his Texan's drawl as he spoke a brief word to the hostler. Then Sternes's interest lagged, for Dallam and Cathy were approaching.

"You two are going to promise me you'll be gentlemen tonight," the girl said as she came up. "If you will, we can eat together before we start back."

"I'll get my feed across . . . ," Dallam began in a surly voice.

"Pete," Cathy cut in, "I'm asking you to do this for me!"

He shrugged, said—"Sure, I'll be good."—and left her side, stepping around Sternes to go to the coach's rear and reach for a suitcase in the boot marked with Cathy's initials.

In the act of lifting down the heavy bag, he saw the stranger and momentarily paused, eying the man carefully, a little surprised. He heard the stranger say to the hostler: "If you say I can make it tonight, I'll get started. Is there a place here a man can get a good meal?"

"Hotel up the street. We eat their grub."

"Then it's good enough for me," said the stranger, turning away. "See you later."

Dallam stood there, watching the man go out the gate. Then he asked the hostler: "Who is he?"

"Y' got me," was the reply. "He's hirin' a jughead to get up to Ledge. Want me to hang onto the lady's possibles till you get down to pick 'em up?"

Dallam nodded and walked off, his glance still on the stranger disappearing into the dusk upstreet.

The fact of the girl's being with the two upcountry men when they went up to the hotel somewhat eased the worry of the townspeople. Still, they were curious and a good majority of the men presently gathered in the obscurity of the walk awning fronting an empty store next to the saloon. From its protective shadow they could look straight across and into the hotel's shabby dining room and see something as unbelievable to them as it would be to most upcountry men when they heard about it. Pete Dallam and Mike Sternes were eating at the same table, and Frank Bishop's daughter was sitting between them. They watched closely every mouthful of food taken by those three across the way; they saw every unheard word spoken during that meal, and, by the sparseness of the two men's talk and the profuse-ness of the girl's, they sensed what a strained feeling held the trio. When she finally rose from the table and left them, someone in the group under the awning breathed: "This is it."

But it wasn't. Dallam and Sternes sat at the table coolly ignoring each other. Once it was apparent that they spoke. But even with that, neither made a threatening move. The watchers, knowing they were witnessing the unbelievable, took in every move of the two upcountry men.

At length, Dallam left the table to appear a moment later on the verandah, where he stood long enough to roll and light a smoke before coming out onto the street. He headed for the saloon. But instead of going in there, he went to his roan, untied his reins from the pole, swung into the saddle, and rode out the head of the street. The rhythmic *thud* of his pony's hoofs could be heard fading into the night's stillness out the road that led to the hills.

"That's that," a man in the crowd said, expelling his breath in eloquent relief.

"Sternes is drivin' her up in his rig," said another. "No use in Dallam hangin' around any longer."

Now the group began to break up slowly, a man or two drifting down the walk, a few more entering the saloon. But some stayed on. They saw the stranger who had come in on the late stage, who had also eaten in the hotel but left before Dallam, ride past on a horse they recognized as belonging to Hank Snyder, the stage yard hostler; it was a grulla gelding Snyder didn't often use himself, an animal gone splayfoot from age and neglected hoof care.

It was less than ten minutes after Dallam had ridden away that Sternes came out of the hotel and went across to the saloon. Now the last remnant of the small crowd left the walk, most of it going into the bar where they expected they would find Sternes and maybe get him to talk. But he wasn't there. The barkeep announced that Sternes had left by the alley door after a quick drink. He hadn't said where he was going.

Some time later, not long, the hotel owner came across to ask for Sternes.

"Gone," the barkeep told him.

"Gone where? The girl's across there's ready to go."

"He didn't say."

The hotel man glanced at the others. "Any of you see where he . . . ?"

The faint but sharp echo of a gunshot rode in out of the night. Every man in the saloon faced the door. Before anyone could move, four more quick-timed and muted explosions sounded. Then the night was still, the utter lack of sound strangely ominous.

"That came from over east," someone said sharply.

As though they had been waiting for the silence to end and release them, men made for the saloon's street door, hurried out onto the walk, and into the street. Gathered there, facing east, they listened again.

From across the street Cathy Bishop called: "Who was doing the shooting?"

The hotel man left the others and went across and onto the verandah where she stood. They heard him say: "We don't know yet, ma'am. Sternes is gone. No one seems to know where he went."

Two men left the crowd now and ran down to the stage corral after horses. The rest started up the street afoot, headed out the trail.

They found the bodies lying beside the trail less than a mile from town along a rocky hill

17

slope. It was gruesome enough without the light of the lantern someone brought along later. Sternes lay to one side of the trail, face down, his upper body and head hanging over a low shelf of rock and his .45 still clutched in his hand. The shirt along his back was torn and splotched with crimson where a single bullet had gone through him from the front.

They threw a coat over Dallam when they first looked at him by the light of the lantern. There was nothing left of his face.

Chapter Two

Pleasant City's jail was hot and dark, smelly, too. U.S. Commissioner Guilford stopped in the doorway as he took his first breath of the foul air. "Isn't there a window you can open in here?" he queried.

The fat sheriff, who had gone in ahead of Guilford and was now only faintly visible in the gloom between the cell rows, stopped and took the chewed stub of a cigar from his mouth. "I told you we was makin' sure of him," he said. "We bricked up the window."

"How does he get air?"

"The chimney." The sheriff indicated with a

jerk of his fat hand a hole in the roof just inside the jail office doorway, adding: "I'll leave that door open if you say."

"No. Close it when you go out." Guilford was curt, for he was beginning to dislike heartily this representative of the law. Now that his eyes had focused to the feebler light, he could see well enough. He noted with a dry inner amusement the way the sheriff stopped and drew his gun before approaching the end cell to the left.

"Inside or out?" the sheriff queried. "If you go in, I'll have to lock the door on you."

"I'll go in."

"You got a lot of faith in your luck." The sheriff unlocked the cell door and pulled it open. "Mathiot!" he bawled. "Here's a gent wants to see you." The commissioner knew then that the sheriff was afraid.

A shape stirred on the cot in the deep shadow of the cell's back wall. "Send him away," said a slow-drawling voice.

"Not this one, I don't," the sheriff told him. "This's a federal commissioner. Looks like Uncle Sam's interested in you, too."

Guilford had come in close behind the sheriff and now looked at the man on the cot and moved his head in a brief negative. He wasn't sure the prisoner understood until Mathiot said dryly: "You don't say. What's on his mind?"

"I'll let him talk." The sheriff motioned

Guilford on in, closed, and locked the door. "Sing out if he gives you any trouble," were his parting words as he turned and moved his ample weight back up the corridor and into his office.

When that far door was closed, Guilford looked down at the man on the cot and with an effort kept a straight face as he said: "This time you've really done it."

The prisoner stood up now, topping the commissioner's generous height by a full half head. He held out his hand. The smile that came to his lean, beard-stubbled face was infectious. "The devil looks after his own," he drawled.

Guilford ignored that remark and the other's proffered hand. "Sit down, Streak. We've got a lot to talk over."

Streak Mathiot sighed, but his grin didn't relax. He ran his hand through his thatch of curly black hair, the move drawing Guilford's attention to the mark that gave the man his name. It was a streak of pure gray hair patterning the black from the hairline on the forehead back over the top of the head. That mark of advancing age, belied by a young and bronzed face, had made most men who knew Mathiot forget his given name, which was Ned. Guilford himself wouldn't have known it but for having just seen it on the warrant in the sheriff's office. "Don't tell me you're here to try and reform me," Mathiot said. "First they sent in two deputies to try it. Then . . ."

"I know. One of them is still laid up," Guilford cut in.

Mathiot gave a brief shrug and went on: "Then the Baptist preacher. Wants me to join the church. Told him I never learned to swim."

"Streak, this is serious. Will you listen?"

Mathiot's smile faded. His face became sharp-planed and more mature. "I'll listen," he said.

"They've got enough against you to keep you here for years."

"I know. But I've figured a way to break out."

Guilford winced at this reminder of the other's capabilities. He decided to ignore it and went on: "You're being held without bail. The man you tossed around is still unconscious."

"Good. They hadn't told me. He was a cheap glory hunter. We were having a quiet game of cards when he came in and went on the prod because I packed an iron. Shucks, I could've drawn on him."

"Regardless of why you gave him that beating, he's the son of a very influential man here. In addition to assault and battery, they've got charges against you of willful destruction of property, resisting a peace officer, and illegal possession of a firearm."

"I didn't ask his *compadres* to tie into me and wreck the place. That possession of firearms is a laugh. Half those jaspers were packing irons and tried to use 'em on me. As for that hog-fat fool out

21

front . . ." Mathiot ended with an eloquent shrug.

"All right, I can appreciate your feelings. But you're in trouble . . . bad trouble."

"I'll get out of it."

"Break out?" Guilford laughed dryly. "They'll slap a reward on you."

"Then I'll drift. Always did aim to go up and look over that Wyoming country."

"No, Streak. Your only chance is to clear yourself legally."

"They won't even set bail. How can I?"

"There's a way," Guilford said. "But when you do get out, you've got to settle down and quit raising so much hell."

"I've tried, but something like this always seems to happen."

"You're too willing to let it."

"Maybe."

"Streak, will you take a job?" Guilford queried abruptly.

Mathiot shrugged. "I could use one."

"Not a riding job. One with me. As a deputy U.S. marshal."

Mathiot was incredulous. His blue-gray eyes opened wide. "Me a tin star?" He laughed softly. "And you want me to stay out of trouble."

"You'd have to be careful what trouble you got into. It would teach you how to use your head instead of your hands."

"Thanks, I'll stick with the hands."

"Then you're turning me down?"

"Correct."

"Think again. Take this job and I'll get you out of here. I have a blank warrant. I'll tell the sheriff you're wanted on a federal charge. He'll be glad to get rid of you. You need never see him or this town again."

"No dice, Guilford."

"You sided Ed Church for years. He was a deputy marshal."

"Is, not was. Ed's gone soft. Must be that touch of red in his hair."

"No, Ed *was* a deputy marshal," Guilford said quietly.

Something in his tone laid an impassive cast over Mathiot's face. "So you fired him?"

"No. And he didn't quit."

"He's . . . ?" Mathiot stopped there.

Guilford nodded. "I'm afraid so, Streak."

"How did it happen?" Mathiot asked tonelessly.

"Two weeks ago I sent him up into Peñasco County to investigate a sheep war. He was to report twice a week. I haven't heard from him since he started across Dry Reach."

All the pleasantness had gone out of Mathiot's face now. It was sharp-lined even with its three-day-old beard, almost threatening. "Ed had his own ways of operating. He may be hoping to wind up the job in a hurry before he lets you know how he came out."

"That couldn't be. His instructions were definite. He's either in trouble or . . ."

"Dead?"

"Dead."

Mathiot reached automatically to a shirt pocket, took out a sack of tobacco dust, and built a smoke. Then he automatically handed the makings to Guilford as he said: "I can go into that country without your law badge."

"You can't. That's the price I ask for getting you out of this. Either go in there to do a job for me, or break out of here and have the law hound you clear of the country. That way you'll never know what happened to Ed."

Mathiot smiled crookedly. "You make a close trade, friend."

"Admitted. But I send you in there with the authority to hunt down the man or men responsible for Ed's death . . . if he is dead."

"Why not go yourself?"

"I'm known there. This job calls for someone who isn't."

"You've got other men."

"Not the right kind. Not a one who knew Ed the way you did."

There was a moment's silence. Then Mathiot asked: "How much do I get to work on?"

"Nothing except the orders I gave Ed. He was sent in to check on giving a sheep outfit a permit to drive through a government cattle lease. A man by the name of Dallam is the one running the sheep. Frank Bishop, an old friend of mine, wants to keep the sheep out."

"That's all?"

"We know that Ed took the stage at Johnsville and headed across Dry Reach for Agua Verde. That was two weeks ago and no word from him yet. I was stumped on what to do until I heard they were holding you in jail over here in Pleasant City."

Streak took a pull at his cigarette. "Am I on my own if I take the job?"

"Completely. Maybe before it's over you'll wish you weren't."

Streak looked down at his smoke, dropped it, ground it under his boot heel. "It's a deal, Guilford. Get me out of here."

"Sheriff!" Guilford called.

Shortly the lawman trudged down the corridor.

"This is the man I'm after," Guilford told him. "I even got a confession out of him."

The sheriff's glance widened. "The devil you say. What's he wanted for?"

"Murder. He'll probably hang."

"Fine! Fine! You're savin' us the expense of doin' the same." The sheriff looked at his prisoner with gloating beady eyes. "Want to take him along now?"

"When does the westbound come through?"

"Right away. I heard her whistlin' the station just as I come in here."

"Then let's get a move on." Guilford turned to Mathiot. Taking a pair of handcuffs from his back pocket, he said tersely: "Hold out your hands."

Streak stood up and let his wrists be manacled.

"Better put a gun on him," the sheriff advised as he backed away from the door to let Mathiot out.

"I can handle him."

Guilford followed his pretended prisoner up the corridor and into the office.

They stopped there when Mathiot said: "You've got some things of mine, fatso."

Guilford looked at the sheriff, whose face colored at the name Mathiot called him. Going to his roll-top desk, the lawman opened a drawer and took out a wallet, a watch, and some small change. "Count it," he growled as he handed it to Mathiot.

"You've forgotten something, fatso." Mathiot nodded to the gun rack over the desk, pocketing his possessions.

The sheriff's color deepened. "Why, you . . ."

"Give it to the commissioner," Mathiot's quiet drawl cut in.

The sheriff reluctantly reached down a filled shell belt from which hung a worn holster sheathing a horn-handled Colt. "Thanks," was Mathiot's sparse word as the gun was handed to Guilford.

"We'll have to hurry. Thanks for your help, Sheriff," the commissioner said briefly. He pushed Mathiot out the street door and into the hot bright sunlight.

Chapter Three

The Agua Verde stage was late. It was dark when the two teams of Morgans, played out from the last twenty desert miles, hauled the heavy Concord into the stage lot. Hank Snyder, who came out to help the driver put the fresh relays into harness, carried a lantern.

Only one passenger was leaving the stage here. Because he had lost an hour in a sandstorm and would have to make up part of it on the next leg of his trip, the driver was in a hurry and let that passenger heave his baggage down out of the boot himself. It consisted of a sacked saddle and a war bag.

The driver was a little reluctant to lose this fare, for he had enjoyed the stranger's company and appreciated the help the man had given. During the bad blow out there on Dry Reach, for instance, the two of them had held the spooked teams easily where the driver alone would have had a tough time of it. Afterward, the stranger had ridden the top seat. It wasn't often the driver let anyone ride there with him, less frequent that he talked much when he had a seat mate. But he and the stranger had found a lot to say to each other. They'd had some good laughs, too, for the stranger had some tall tales and a dry wit and, best of all, didn't ask a lot of fool questions.

If the driver had been told that he had given his passenger an exceedingly accurate impression of the upcountry and its people, particularly as concerned the town of Ledge, he would have denied it indignantly, for he prided himself on being a close-mouthed man. Yet such was the case. The stranger hadn't put so much as one direct question. But in the hard ten-mile haul after the storm, while the going was slow and there wasn't much rein work, their talk had drifted into the details of a certain double killing that had taken place about two weeks ago near Agua Verde. The stranger had spoken of several shoot-outs he had witnessed or heard about. Not wanting to be outdone and hoping to impress his passenger, the driver had mentioned a sheep/cattle war that was threatening to flare out in the hill country near Ledge. The killing had resulted from that. Only trouble was, he had admitted finally, the war seemed to be petering out. For Pete Dallam was dead now, and Dallam had been the man bringing in the sheep.

So, before he ever saw Agua Verde himself, Streak Mathiot knew almost every detail pertinent to the happenings on the night Ed Church had reached the town. Not yet, however, did Streak know that the shoot-out and Church's arrival had taken place on the same night.

Now, finished with harnessing his fresh teams, the driver took the time to see that the hostler and the passenger he was losing got acquainted. "Treat him right, Hank," he told Snyder as he climbed to his seat atop the coach. He assumed, rightly, that Streak might be wanting to hire a horse.

As the stage rolled out the desert end of the street, the *rattle* of its iron-tired wheels fading into the distance, Streak mentioned his wants: "There'll be a moon tonight and I might as well go on. How much'll it set me back to hire a horse to get me up to Ledge?"

Snyder frowned. He was remembering the driver's parting word, and the driver was to be trusted. But Snyder had had a recent unfortunate experience that was too fresh in his mind to be ignored. When he answered, he made his reluctance plain. "Two dollars a day for the horse. Then you get as far as you're goin', turn him loose, and he'll find his way back. But you'll have to leave a ten-dollar deposit."

"Ten?" Streak drawled. He was surprised and showed it. It went without saying that they hung a horse thief here the same as they did on any other range. "Wouldn't four be more like it? Two days at the most. I'd turn your jughead loose and he'd be back sometime tomorrow. I'm only using him as far as Ledge."

"It ain't that I don't trust you," Snyder was

quick to say. "But a couple weeks ago a stranger come through here, hired a horse, and took it with him for keeps. It ain't that I lost much. The nag was an old grulla gone splay-foot. But I hate like thunder to have something like that put over on me."

Excitement flowed suddenly through Streak as he asked: "What did he look like, this stranger?"

"Not as tall as you. Easy-talkin', duded up a little. Said he was headed for Ledge, the same as you." Snyder's glance narrowed. "Why you askin'?"

Streak shrugged. "No reason. I heard 'em talking about a horse thief over across the desert. Only he was a sawed-off ranny missing a couple of fingers on his right hand, so they said. Must've worked for a railroad once."

"That wasn't him."

Snyder did some quick thinking then, remembering something that changed his idea on hiring the stranger a horse. Abruptly he said: "Come to think of it, I'll let you have a horse for nothin'. There was a killin' out east of here the same night that stranger got away with my jughead. Two men from over Ledge way shot it out and afterward we had the devil of a time findin' one of their horses. It was Dallam's roan. The horse showed up over at Two Forks a few days ago minus his hull, so they brought him across here for me to send up to Dallam's place. I ain't had

30

the time to take him yet. You could save me a trip by takin' him up to Ledge."

"Anything you say," Streak replied. "Where do I leave him?"

"The feed barn'll do. I'll send along a note for you to give to the man there and they can come in and pick him up. How soon you want to leave?"

"Soon as I can put on the feedbag."

Snyder nodded. "Four doors up the street on this side. The food ain't any too good, but it's fillin'."

He watched Streak walk out of the lot and up the street, still puzzled by his hunch that Streak's query regarding that other stranger hadn't been quite as casual as it was meant to be.

After taking a long interval making up his mind to something, Snyder went back around the corral to the harness shack and hung his lantern from a nail on a roof stringer. He spent a minute rummaging through the odds and ends in an old and dusty leather-covered trunk in the shack's far corner, finally finding what he wanted, the stub of a pencil, a sheet of paper, and a soiled envelope. Then he squatted in front of a small packing box and, in the light of the lantern, composed a brief message. He put a lot of thought to what he was writing, for he considered it important. Finished with it, he put the paper in the envelope and sealed the flap. On the envelope he wrote the name: *Tom Buchwalter.*

He was sitting beside his lantern at one end of

31

the big log watering trough when Streak came in off the street about twenty minutes later. Tied to the hitch rail a few feet away stood Pete Dallam's Fencerail-branded roan, wearing Streak's saddle.

"All set," the hostler said as Streak came up. He held out the envelope. "Leave this with the man at the barn in Ledge. He'll give it to Buchwalter. I've explained in there about Dallam's hull bein' lost. We may find it later."

Streak pocketed the envelope, thanked Snyder for the horse, and was about to swing up into the saddle when he hesitated. "About this horse thief . . . You say he came through the night of that killing?"

The hostler nodded. "Came in on the stage with the Bishop girl . . . Frank Bishop's daughter. The two men that shot it out, Dallam and old Mike Sternes, was down here to meet her."

"And this stranger just rode out and never came back?"

"Yep. I was out three days later tryin' to pick up his sign. But we'd had a blow meantime and the trails was pretty well sifted over."

Snyder waited for another question, sure now that he'd made a shrewd guess on this stranger's interest in the horse thief. He was glad he'd written Buchwalter that note. But Streak didn't have any more questions. He went up into the saddle easily, well seated before the roan, ornery from nearly a week in the corral, tried to pitch him off. Snyder, watching this big man top off the spirited animal, couldn't help but admire the ease with which the job was accomplished without the use of spurs or a heavy hand on the bit. Finally Streak reined over to Snyder, the roan well in hand. "Much obliged for the free ride," he said.

"Glad to help." Lifting a hand in answer to Streak's parting salute, Snyder watched the big man leave the lot and put the roan up the street. He grinned broadly when he began thinking of the favor he'd done Buchwalter, the late Pete Dallam's foreman. He wasn't exactly sure what that favor consisted of but, as an ex-Fencerail man, he'd followed out the instructions Tom Buchwalter had given him two weeks ago after the double inquest. He wondered just what sort of trouble this second stranger would run into in Ledge once Buchwalter got that note.

Chapter Four

Bill Paight rode down out of the westward hills a little after 11:00 that night, picking up the lights of Ledge in the valley trough close below. There were only a few at this late hour, made feeble against the light of the waning moon. The

33

valley stood out in clear relief, rugged, even the lower tiers of hills solidly timbered. The chill air had a bite to it on this midsummer night, giving a strong hint of the hard winters a man would find here. It bore a blending of fragrant pine scent and dust, the latter reminding Paight that unless rain came soon the haystacks in the pasture of the hill ranches would be a good bit smaller than in past years.

He never tired of the broad vista of the valley that lay before him at this point, a scant mile from town. There weren't many open places in these foothills where a man could get the proper perspective of the country. But here the twenty-mile breadth of the valley swept uninterruptedly from horizon to horizon. Westward, behind him, there ran a low line of foothills. To the east were mountains, gently rounded, broken at a point midway on the horizon by the broad saddle of the pass above Elbow Lake. Off to his left, close in the north, towered the sheer and jagged line of the Arrowheads, appropriately named because their harsh and sharply upthrust shoulders formed an impassable barrier to block that end of the valley. The whole bore an almost forbidding look; there was nothing soft about this country. And now Bill Paight again experienced the old feeling that had seven years ago prompted him to stay on here, a deep stubbornness, a feeling that the country offered man a challenge to wrest a living from it.

Well, he had made a living out of it. Not as a brand owner but as a top hand rider for an outfit that was itself involved in a grim struggle to survive. That outfit was the late Pete Dallam's Fencerail.

Had Paight been asked to explain his ride tonight, he couldn't honestly have done so. He had come down across Fencerail's meadow all of two hours ago, knowing only that he was too restless to sleep, even to sit idly by the bunkhouse with the others. He had been held by this nervousness ever since that day, now two weeks gone, when the news of Pete Dallam's death had reached the layout. So tonight he had saddled a pony and started out, feeling the urge to work off some of the nervous energy that was in him. He had swung off toward Prenn's place, then away from it at the prospect of being stumped for a reason for making the call on his neighbor. He guessed it was about time to move on to another country; the fiddle-footedness was on him again and that meant his days here were numbered. Yet he didn't want to go. He had found the valley a good place. He hadn't even minded this recent trouble or the fact that the outfit he worked for had gone over to sheep.

Bill wondered what had drawn him down here to town and, asking himself, knew the answer at once. It was Laura Dallam, Pete's sister, who had arrived a week ago. Buchwalter had sent him down to Agua Verde in the buggy to meet her and drive her to Ledge where she was to stay. Bill had spent a good share of each day since thinking back on that long thirty-mile drive with Laura Dallam that night. There had been a full moon and the country hadn't looked as dry in that favoring light as it was really. In fact, the night had been quite romantic.

He'd started out by telling her how sorry he was over what had happened to Pete. In a few words, she had accepted his sympathy and then tactfully hinted that she would prefer not to have the subject brought up again. There hadn't been any tears, even as much as a break in her voice, and she had spoken of Pete in a strange offhand way, in quite a contradictory way, for Bill had since found her to be sensitive in other things. So they'd just talked, talked of a lot of things and nothing in particular. Even now he couldn't define the girl's attraction. She was plain-looking, so much so that the prospect of the long ride with her had at first seemed more a chore than a pleasure. But she had shortly changed his mind. Once the first strangeness of their being together wore off, she became a wholly different person. She had been almost vivacious, and, when she laughed, it was with an abandon and a husky throatiness he found so pleasant that he had tried to think up ways of making her laugh again. He had found her strangely reticent about her past, but had assumed it was probably because so much of that past concerned Pete.

Since that night Bill had seen Laura only twice, both times briefly. But it hadn't been his imagining that changed her from her ordinary and distant self to a warmly attractive girl in his presence. Tom Buchwalter had noticed it, had even said: "You seem to get on better than anyone else with Pete's sister. So it's your job to handle any business we've got with her." Because he knew Buchwalter was speaking the truth, because he knew he had the power to transform this exceedingly plain girl into another person, Bill Paight was a little awed and even afraid. The truth lying behind all this recent restlessness in him was that he was on the verge of falling in love. He hadn't yet made that admission to himself.

Now that he was here, within a mile of town, he had a moment in which he felt exceedingly foolish. He couldn't, of course, see Laura Dallam at this time of night. Yet that hope had brought him here; the possibility that he might catch a glimpse of her, maybe sitting on the hotel verandah or even crossing the lobby toward the back hallway that led to her room, had been in his mind. But because he wouldn't admit to himself that she was the sole reason for his having ridden so far, he said aloud to his pony—"We could both use a drink, couldn't we?"—and tried to relish the prospect of a drink at the Pride's bar.

That brought up an unpleasant thought. Supposing some of Bishop's riders were in town and at the Pride? It was the middle of the week and Crescent B usually hit town on Saturday, but still there was the possibility that one or two of Bishop's riders might be hanging around the bar. Bill had made his feelings pretty open where they were concerned; he had that habit of speaking his mind. It hadn't yet reached the point where one of them would shoot at him on sight. On the other hand, he couldn't expect them to be friendly. "The devil with 'em," he muttered, and touched his pony with spur to go on down the trail.

It was the Pride he headed for when he rode down the crooked, narrow street. He passed the hotel, giving it only a brief glance that showed the verandah and lobby deserted and the night lamp already on.

When his glance went on down the street again, it was to see a rider on a vaguely familiar long-legged horse turning in off the street toward the ramp of the feed barn. As that rider came within the circle of light shed by the runway lantern, Bill recognized Pete Dallam's roan horse. Instantly a wave of wariness and curiosity threaded his nerves. He lifted his pony to a quick trot, calling out—"You there! Hold on!"—realizing too late how foolish he might appear in a minute or two. There must be some logical explanation for a stranger to be riding Pete's horse; still, the animal had been missing two weeks and Bill wanted to know why.

He was turning up the ramp, the stranger having paused near the head of it and turned the roan to face him, when at the outward limit of his vision he sensed the Pride's swing doors opening and someone coming into the walk across there. Bill forgot this last as he halted below the stranger. He was seeing a tall, solid-looking man with a lean and pleasant face, a man with a generous span of shoulder and a careless but sure way of sitting the saddle. It bothered Bill a little that he had to look up at the stranger as he queried, too sharply: "Where'd you get that jughead?"

The stranger's brows went up. Then he smiled, and with that assurance all the tension went out of Paight.

"You must be a Fencerail hand," Streak drawled, adding: "I got him down at the corral at Agua Verde. Here's a letter I was supposed to give to Tom Buchwalter. You him?"

"No," Bill said. "Where'd Snyder pick him up?"

Streak was about to answer when a voice said sharply out of the street: "Feelin' salty tonight, Paight?"

Bill Paight's head came around to face the voice. He saw Sid Riggs, Bishop's new foreman, and two other new Crescent B men walking slowly toward the bottom of the ramp. He knew at once that they had spotted him from the Pride and he knew what they intended.

He swung aground slowly, thankful for at least one thing: that he hadn't worn his gun tonight. And now, facing the prospect of a severe beating—they would make a good job of it—he felt a high recklessness, almost glad for what was coming. With a slap on his pony's rump that sent the animal on up the ramp and into the head of the barn's long runway, he faced the trio.

"Salty enough," he said, and narrowly eyed Riggs, the nearest.

Streak, witnessing this and only halfway understanding it, felt a growing admiration for the man who had accosted him so curtly a few moments ago. He didn't know who the three men, facing Paight, were but guessed they might be Bishop riders; he had talked with the hotel owner down at Agua Verde and completed a fairly accurate picture of the trouble that had been plaguing the Ledge range. His admiration of Paight's nerve was heightened when he saw that Riggs was a big man, almost as tall as himself and a good bit heavier, and that the other two were both of a size that would more than match Paight's spareness and medium height. Streak sensed something of the rashness that was in Paight, knew, too, what the outcome of this encounter would certainly be. Because he found he liked Paight, he looked down at Riggs and drawled: "Wouldn't one at a time make it more interesting?"

"You want to buy into this?" came Riggs's cool query. "You one of his sidekicks? If you are, climb down. We're invitin' all Fencerail takers."

"Stay where you are, friend," Paight said to Streak, and suddenly lunged in at Riggs, whose attention was still off him.

The solid *smack* of his knuckles against Riggs's jaw sounded in the stillness. Riggs stumbled backward a step, shook his head to clear it, and lifted his arms to guard his face. Then the others came in at Paight, one from each side, swinging for his face. He ignored the one on his right and, arms crossed to shield his face, went in headfirst at the other, driving in two quick stabs at his opponent's stomach. Streak heard the man grunt as those blows told. Then the other swung a boot, heeled Paight hard above the hip in the side, and threw him off balance. Both men hit Paight again as he fell sideways, and rolled in the dust.

Riggs had shaken off the effects of that first hard blow and stepped in as the Fencerail man went down and tried to roll clear. Riggs kicked out savagely, the toe of his boot driving into Paight's chest. Paight groaned and struggled to get up. Then Riggs jumped on him, knees in his back, driving him into the dust again.

As Streak vaulted from the saddle, he was sure Paight's back must be broken. He elbowed one

41

Bishop man aside, knocking him down. The other he ignored as he lunged in at Riggs, who was pounding Paight's head into the dust. Grabbing Riggs by the shirt collar, he hauled him back off Paight, his free hand swinging in a jab that caught the Bishop man hard on the ear. He didn't give Riggs time to come erect but pushed him into the third man, who was closing in now. The two went down together as Streak reached out and pulled Paight to his feet.

Paight seemed all right except for a bloody mouth and a hunch that betrayed a sore chest. He even managed a rash grin as he wiped the blood from his lips and growled: "I'll make it. Clear out!"

"And miss this?" Streak shook his head, matching the other's grin.

There wasn't time for more. Head down, Riggs lunged in at Streak. The man Streak had first knocked down rose and swung on Paight. Streak and Paight stood back to back, Paight ducking under the blow aimed at him, Streak lifting Riggs's head with a sharp uppercut. Streak had time to hit Riggs two more times, his knuckles grinding into the man's lips, before the third Bishop man dived in at his legs. Bending a knee, Streak caught the Bishop cowpuncher in the face with it. But he was driven off his feet. He threw his body into a roll, taking up the shock of his fall on one shoulder. As he came erect again, he saw

Paight's opponent go down from a solid punch to the jaw. Paight swung around just in time to face the other man. Then Streak was standing toe to toe with Riggs, a fierce and ecstatic excitement welling up in him as he swung time and again at the man's bloody mouth. He knew he was hit repeatedly but could feel no pain as he drove in to beat the other to the ground.

Riggs was backing up now toward the head of the ramp, still slugging, still full of fight. Then he and Streak were in the big maw of the barn's open doors, to one side of the wide runway's center. Finally Riggs stood, boots spread wide, head hunched down between his shoulders, almost under the lantern and with his back to the partition that closed off the livery office. Streak felt his wind going and knew he must finish this soon or never; Riggs's powerful blows were beginning to hurt. He sparred for an opening, repeatedly weaving aside to avoid a slashing fist. Suddenly he saw his chance. Riggs went a little off balance from missing a hard swing. Streak took a half step in at the man and swung from the level of his knees, a wide, fast roundhouse. His fist caught Riggs on the point of the chin, lifted the man's boots clear of the planks, and drove him backward. Bishop's foreman smashed into the partition, his shoulder driving through one board in a splintering crash. Overhead, the lantern swayed and suddenly fell from its hook. It smashed in a shower of breaking glass, spraying coal oil over the worn planks. A tongue of fire licked out from the unprotected wick and caught on a pool of coal oil. All at once a puff of leaping flame burst up the office partition. Riggs, caught there with his shoulder wedged in the broken wall, cried out as the flame scorched his face.

Streak reached out and pulled the man free, swinging him aside. Riggs was too weak to stand and he went down, rolled onto his face, and gasped for breath. The sharp burst of a gunshot racketed along the street. Streak heard a step behind him and wheeled to find Paight almost at his elbow.

"That's our one-legged law, friend," Paight said grimly. "We'd better make tracks. To hell with this blaze! Kelso can put it out."

Streak noticed a red-painted bucket hanging from the end of a two-by-four wall brace at the back end of the office. Running over there, he swung the bucket down to find it nearly full of water. As he emptied it against the wall and over the blazing puddle of coal oil, Paight spoke again, more sharply this time: "Your jughead's right there beyond the walk! Run for it! Meet you out the upper end of the street!"

As he snapped those words, Paight was catching up his own horse, which had gone halfway down the barn's runway during the fight. He swung up into leather, wheeled the animal around, and dug in spurs, heading for the barn's back door that let into the alley. Streak saw that the water had nearly put out the fire. He tossed the bucket aside toward where Riggs lay, hearing the *thud* of boots on the walk out front blend with the racket of Paight's pony as it pounded out the back end of the runway. He ran toward the ramp and saw the roan standing beyond its far edge. He was jumping from the ramp to the walk when he sensed a shadow closing in on him from the left. Wheeling toward it, he cocked his right arm. Then some-thing caught his leg and tripped him and he went down hard.

He lay there flat on his back, looking up into the bore of a .45 Colt backed by the steady blue eyes of a middle-aged face with a close-clipped gray mustache. A five-pointed sheriff's star sagged from the man's vest pocket. Deliberately Sheriff Fred Kelso unhooked the crook of his thick-stemmed cane from Streak's leg, hung it from his arm, and shifted his weight off his game leg as he drawled: "You be good now, stranger, and we'll get along fine."

Chapter Five

The moon was close to its zenith as Bill Paight rode up across the meadow and in on Fencerail. He slowed as he neared the clump of jack pine, flanking the trail a few hundred yards out from the layout.

As he drew abreast the first tree, a drawling voice, close by in its shadow said: "You turnin' into an owl, Bill? This is the second night straight runnin' you been on the prowl."

Paight drew rein, now making out the red glow of a burning cigarette end in the deep shadow of the trees. He ignored the query of the Fencerail guard and put one himself: "Anyone been in?"

"Not a soul. It's lonesome as the devil here. Like sittin' at the bottom of a well."

"Stay with it," Bill said, and went on up the trail.

Ordinarily he'd have swung over to the barn lot and the big corral. But now he rode on up to the low, weathered house and around its near side. He came out of the saddle stiffly, for the bruise on his hip was hurting. He limped away from his ground-haltered horse to a door in the house's side wall and knocked on it lightly. Shortly he heard a furtive sound from inside. Then, before he was quite aware of it, the door stood open and Tom Buchwalter was there, a gun in his hand.

"Oh, it's you," Buchwalter said. There came the *click* of the hammer catch as he took the gun off cock. He tossed it across onto his bed and came out the door, running a hand through his sparse gray hair and yawning. It was obvious that he had been roused from sleep. "Why didn't you sing out?" he asked.

"Didn't want to wake the others," Paight answered. He dipped a hand into pants pocket and brought out the letter Streak had given him, offering it to the older man. "A stranger rode Pete's roan into town tonight. I ran into him. Snyder sent this letter up with him."

"Snyder? So he picked him up, eh?" Buchwalter tore open the envelope. "Got a match?"

Bill flicked alight a match and held it over the paper. Watching Buchwalter, he was thinking as he had many times before that nothing could disturb this man's calm serenity. Buchwalter's voice was always gentle, always kindly, as befitted his looks. Even now, despite his bare feet, the fact that he was shirtless, his chest spare under a suit of gray flannel underwear, even with his rumpled white hair and the suspenders that hung down around his hips, Tom Buchwalter remained a distinguished-looking man. The hawkish cast of his face, his warm brown eyes squinted against the flare of the match, the neatly trimmed silver mustache, and the erectness of his bearing gave him an unmistakable dignity. If there lived a man who could replace Pete Dallam in holding the respect of a tough crew, Tom Buchwalter was that man.

When the first match died, Bill lit another. Buchwalter handed him the note saying in a strangely hollow way: "Read it."

Paight gave the older man a sharp look, warned by his odd tone that something had affected him powerfully. Then Paight's eyes fell to the paper. What Snyder had written in his halting but careful hand was:

You said to watch for a stranger asking questions about that horse thief. This is him.

Paight looked up from the paper, his glance puzzled in the dying light of the match. "Meaning what?" he queried.

"I wish I knew." Buchwalter's voice was once more gentle and a slow sigh escaped his flat chest. "What did this stranger look like? Did you get a good look at him?"

Paight laughed softly, without much amusement. "Good enough. He's big and he's tough and he loves a fight. I ran into some poor luck tonight, Tom. Riggs, Black, and Riling corralled me on the street there in town. They were all set to have my hide nailed up when this stranger steps in and pulls 'em off me." He went on to tell about the fight, the blaze at the livery barn, and how he had arranged to meet the stranger but had come on alone after waiting close to half an hour at the edge of town. "Just before I high-tailed, there was a shot out there on the street. I figured it must've been Kelso. So maybe this stranger's in the lockup. If he is . . ."

"If he is, it's just as well," Buchwalter cut in.

"Why? Didn't he pitch in and save me a beating? I don't get this, Tom, not at all."

"I should have told you before, Bill."

"Told me what?"

"About Pete and Mike Sternes."

Paight's glance narrowed. "What about 'em?"

Buchwalter was a long moment answering that query, seeming to pause intentionally to arrange his thoughts. Finally he said solemnly: "Bill, Pete and Sternes were friends, about as close friends as blackmail and bribe money can make two men."

As Buchwalter spoke, Paight caught his breath, caught it in much the same way he had there on the street two hours ago when Riggs landed that kick in his side. "You gone loco, Tom?" he asked finally.

Buchwalter shook his head solemnly. "No, I wish I could say I had. This makes about as much sense to me as it does to you. But that's a fact, Bill. Mike Sternes was double-crossin' Bishop, selling Pete what information he could whenever

Crescent B was set to make a move against us. Do you begin to see it now?"

"No. They killed each other, didn't they?"

"That's where you're wrong. They didn't. The day before they cashed in, Mike was across here and collected something like a hundred dollars for the last favor he did us."

"But, damn it, they're dead. You can't argue against that."

"Dead, yes. But they didn't kill each other, Bill. Remember at the inquest how Snyder told about their meeting the Bishop girl at the stage? How he mentioned a stranger who had come in on the stage with her?" Paight nodded. "There's at least part of the answer we're after," Buchwalter continued. "That stranger. You've heard that he never showed up again, that he stole Snyder's horse. Well, I've even figured out that part of it."

"How?" Paight was obviously beyond his depth in connecting the stranger, the horse thief, with the double shooting at Agua Verde.

"Remember first that Pete Dallam and Mike Sternes were friends, that Mike was being paid by us even though he pretended to hate Pete. Now go on from there. Supposing Bishop found out that Sternes was double-crossing him. Wouldn't he plan a way of getting rid of Sternes? Not only that, but wouldn't he also plan to get rid of Pete Dallam if he could? After all, Catherine Bishop was coming back home against his wishes,

50

coming back to marry Pete, a man Bishop hated with all his guts. What would you have done under those circumstances?"

"I'd have met Pete on the street and invited him to go for his iron."

Buchwalter gave a slow shake of the head. "No, Bill, not if you were Frank Bishop. He's a cold-blooded devil. He doesn't think the way you or I would. No, he'd plan it so both the men in the play against him would die without once involving him. That's exactly what he did."

"But it was all there for anyone to see," Paight protested. "Pete and Sternes had the whole town treed that night they went down there. They simply decided to have it out and left town to do it. Didn't those folks down there see 'em talk it over there at the table in the hotel?"

"That's the way it was meant to look. But in reality no such thing happened. Here's the way I say it happened. See if it doesn't make sense." The Fencerail foreman frowned, obviously concentrating on trying to recall each detail of the explanation he was about to give. "Bishop stumbled onto the tie-up between Pete and Sternes, maybe long ago. He didn't do anything about it right away. Then, with his daughter comin' home, he saw his chance. He knew Pete would ride down to Agua Verde to meet her. He knew he could send Sternes to bring her home. That gave him his idea. He looked around for a killer he could hire. He might even have gone across to Johnsville and hired one there. Remember, he was away a few days. Say he paid this killer half the money right then in a town across the desert, promising the other half when the job was done. So his hired killer rode the stage in across Dry Reach with the Bishop girl. He rented a horse and rode out and waited for Sternes and Pete. Then he went to work on his bushwhack, made it look like they'd shot it out. He . . ."

"*Whoa!* Not so fast, Tom," Paight interrupted. "There's where the whole thing falls to pieces. How could he toll Pete and Sternes out of town to do his job? Remember, they were waiting for the Bishop girl."

"All right, suppose this killer knew Pete. That's likely, for Pete kept in pretty close touch with most of the hardcases hereabouts, thinkin' he might sometime need 'em. This man could've spoken to Pete, maybe telling him he had some important information to tell him about Bishop. He might even have gone so far as to tell Pete to bring Sternes along to check on his story. He arranged to meet him away from town, where they wouldn't be seen. Does that make sense?"

"There's a lot of ifs, Tom."

"Naturally. There have to be. We may never know actually how it happened. But you've got to take my word on this Pete/Sternes business.

They were close, both satisfied with an arrangement that benefited each of them. I'm having to work on that fact alone."

"I believe you. Go ahead," Paight said.

The foreman gave a meager lift of the shoulders. "That's about all. This killer tolled them out from town, killed them, and came on up here to collect the rest of his money from Bishop. You can go on from there as well as I. What would you do if you were Bishop and had hired a double murder done?"

"Killed the bushwhacker."

"Exactly. Only Bishop made one mistake. He must have killed Snyder's livery horse, too, maybe thinking it was owned by the killer. He wanted this killer to disappear, absolutely and completely. He probably caved in a cutbank on both the man and the horse."

Buchwalter paused there, letting his explanation have its effect. He knew how deep that effect was when Paight asked flatly: "And this other stranger?"

"I don't know, Bill, and that's a fact." Buchwalter's look was harassed, or so Paight concluded, peering at the man in the faint light. "He's either a sidekick of this killer or he's hunting him for some reason. I had the hunch he might show up, and for a very good reason. If you were doing murder for a man, you'd know damned well you were running a big risk of not

53

coming out of it yourself. So what would you do?"

"You've got me, Tom. My brain doesn't work that way."

"You'd hunt up a friend if you had one. You'd tell him just enough of what you were doing to make him curious. You'd tell him to come looking for you if you didn't show up within a certain time. Maybe you'd pay him to do it, promising him more money when he found you. That, I think, is what this stranger who drifted in tonight is doing."

Paight was silent a long moment. Then he breathed explosively: "Hang it, I can't make head or tail of this business."

"Have you ever had any reason to doubt my word, Bill?" Buchwalter spoke gently, as always. His reminder steadied Bill's thinking a little.

"No, Tom, I've found you pretty square."

"Then get your own answers. But in the end, you'll have to believe as I do, that Frank Bishop hired the killing of Pete Dallam and Mike Sternes."

"Then why don't we gather up every man on this slope and go across there and wipe out him and his crew? Killing would be too good for him." Paight's voice was brittle with cold rage.

"We couldn't get away with it. The law would be on us. Bishop's law. We'll have to lick him some other way. Besides, there's Laura Dallam."

Paight nodded soberly. He had forgotten Pete's sister.

"We have to save as much as we can for her from this mess," Buchwalter went on. "And we're going to. We're going to bring those sheep in and turn this spread into one that'll make her a big profit in a few years."

"I thought she was to see Bishop in the morning about selling out to him."

"She'll see him, but I doubt if she'll sell. That's part of your job, Bill. His offer is only seven thousand . . . two thousand more than Pete owed the bank. You're to tell her not to sell for less than fifteen."

"Seven!" Paight snorted. "It'd be a steal even at fifteen!" Abruptly his look went grave. "But what happens if she doesn't sell to him? That note of Pete's is due in another thirty days. Bishop the same as owns the bank. They'll take over the layout."

"Thirty days is a long time, Bill. Enough time to find another buyer maybe." In the pause that followed, Buchwalter seemed held by the same gloomy outlook Paight took toward the situation. At length he shrugged it off. "Better turn in and get some sleep. All this worryin' won't help things any."

"This stranger," Paight said, more to himself than to Buchwalter, "what about him?"

"I can't see that he's involved in this as far as we're concerned. What do you mean?"

"Nothing . . . nothing," Paight drawled, a faint smile easing the hard set of his homely face. "Only he's a gent I'd admire to know. He about killed Riggs. Maybe we could hire him to work here."

"Maybe. We'll talk it over in the morning. See you then." Buchwalter stepped back into the room and was closing the door as Paight turned away.

Paight led his horse down to the corral, his thoughts more than a little disturbed. What Buchwalter had told him would have to be gone over again before he would be able to see its full significance. It was mighty lucky for everyone here, for every Fencerail man, that there was a man like Tom Buchwalter running things. Tom was a sheepman and had come less than a year ago, when Pete first got the idea of bringing in the woollies. Regardless of that, regardless of the fact that Paight and a few others had at first hated running sheep worse than they would have hated losing their jobs, Buchwalter had become to them one man in a million. He maybe didn't carry as big a chip on his shoulder as Pete would have liked, but he obviously knew what he was doing. Or did he? There were a thousand head of sheep waiting beyond the pass above Elbow Lake. As yet, Buchwalter had found no way of getting them into the valley and across to this west slope, nor was he likely to with Bishop's crew keeping an endless watch on the trails down from the pass. He claimed to be waiting for the arrival of a federal marshal who would look the situation over and probably issue Fencerail a permit to make a drive across the government lease below the pass. But the marshal was long overdue and Bill doubted that Buchwalter's hope of getting legal permission to bring in the sheep would ever bear fruit. Meantime, to the north, on the far slope of the Arrowheads, was the main band of sheep Pete had counted on eventually bringing in to stock his range and that of his neighbors. They had been there close to a month. Feed was running low. What was Buchwalter doing about that? Still, Buchwalter had been right about one thing. Now was no time to get riled and make a play against Bishop even if he had hired the murder of Pete Dallam. There was Laura to think of—Laura's future. Bill uncinched the saddle, turned the black into the corral, and carried his hull up to the wagon shed. He was tired now, his spare frame beginning to ache in spots other than the one Riggs had kicked him. He trudged wearily up to the bunkhouse and turned in.

Tom Buchwalter's door had opened when Paight was halfway to the corral. Buchwalter leaned there, idly watching Paight's vague shape move around down there. His expression was one of perplexity, for Paight hadn't reacted strongly enough to the story he had just been told of

Pete Dallam's death. Buchwalter was puzzled by the mildness in Paight until he rightly laid it to the hold the girl in town had managed to get on the man over the past few days. Perhaps he had been wrong in letting Paight see so much of Laura. Disappointment was strong in Buchwalter's face, and now, with no one to see, the gentleness left his expression and it became narrow and ugly.

When Paight's figure came up and disappeared in the bunkhouse, Buchwalter stood for several minutes, considering something, his somber mood prolonging that tight and hard expression on his face. Abruptly he decided something and swung back into the room to pull on the rest of his clothes.

Some five minutes later he was down at the corral, gentling a dun horse he'd had the good fortune to catch without the use of a rope. He worked quietly, tying the dun outside the corral while he went to the wagon shed for his saddle. In a little while he left the layout, striking northeast into the nearest higher tier of hills footing the Arrowheads.

He was back as the first faint smudge of false dawn's gray light filtered into the night-blackened sky over the pass to the east. The dun showed signs of having traveled far and fast during the past three hours. Buchwalter rubbed the animal down with a piece of gunny sacking he found lying near the corral gate. He circled two of the smaller outbuildings in going back to his room at the house, not wanting to run the risk of being seen by an early riser in the bunkhouse. His obscure errand had evidently had a satisfactory outcome, for less than a minute after he'd pulled the blankets up over him he was sound asleep.

Chapter Six

This was another jail, a clean and airy one this time. Too airy. It was cold. Streak stood with the cell cot's single blanket drawn about his shoulders as he peered out across the lower valley from the small and sashless window. He was wondering, but only idly, why he was so often attracted to jails. He'd been in more of them than he could remember, not from any criminal leanings, but because he was a big rash man who instinctively loved a fight.

He hadn't intended to land in Ledge's jail last night and wouldn't have but for his staying to put out the fire at the feed barn. Someone else could have done that as well as himself, he now realized. But the fact remained that he was behind bars again, that a cripple had arrested him, and that this morning he was to appear in court to answer charges of disturbing the peace. Sheriff Kelso

59

could have included more in his warrant—
assault and battery, for instance, or even arson—
but he had last night made the rather ominous
statement that—"The judge ain't so easy goin' as
he once was."—in explaining the outwardly
mild charge he placed against his prisoner.

Streak could do one of two things when he
faced the court. He could let the judge into his
confidence and show his deputy marshal's badge
and be promptly released; that, however, would
risk exposing his identity. Or he could plead guilty
and pay a fine. This last, he decided, was the
thing to do. He was after information about Ed
Church and the quickest way of spoiling his
chances, as he saw it, was to let these people
find out he was a federal officer. For all he knew,
Ed's being a marshal might have been the very
reason for his disappearance.

Looking out the window across the generous
wedge of the lower valley southward, Streak
gradually came to the conclusion that this country
was as tough as his brief acquaintance with its
people had shown them to be. The hills were more
like miniature newly formed mountains than
foothills, and he could see but few open meadows.
The sky was murky with clouds this morning,
giving the pine-mantled slopes a drab and
forbidding look. Appraising what he saw with a
stockman's eye, he wasn't much impressed. It
seemed poor grazing country.

The town lay below the jail, which sat on the shoulder of a rocky hill, up a side alley from the street. From here, the twisting thoroughfare, flanked by slab-sided, false-front buildings, wasn't a particularly pleasing one. Everything looked baked and parched, even the green of the pines. Streak suspected that more than one eye was directed hopefully skyward at the clouds this morning. Everywhere there was evidence of the lack of rain; the barrel under a downspout behind the nearest store showed loose staves, a big cottonwood at the street's far end was yellowed and losing its leaves, and the wash below the far side of the street, the creek, showed a dry and rocky bed.

Streak flexed the fingers of his left hand, wincing at the pain it cost him, and was reminded once again of the brawl on the street the night before. Kelso had told him enough to let him know he'd landed in the middle of the Bishop/Dallam feud. This Bill Paight, the man he had sided, was a Fencerail top hand. The one he had knocked through the wall of the barn office was Sid Riggs, Bishop's foreman. Riggs and his two crew men, according to the sheriff's story, had been laying for Paight for some time. Fencerail was a cocky outfit and needed a good trimming. It wasn't hard for Streak to see where the lawman's bets lay.

Well, it had been a good scrap, a good clean

one even for the gouging and the kicking a down man. No one had lost his head and gone for his gun. Riggs was a man to stay clear of, but for luck, Streak figured, he'd have taken a good licking. He'd been lucky to whip the man. Paight had been lucky, too. Streak hated to think what might have happened to the Fencerail man without help. Paight had been game enough. But remembering the way Paight had accepted Riggs's challenge still brought a smile to Streak's face. It had been too much like watching a banty tackle three tough barnyard roosters.

Hearing the *rattle* of the padlock on the outside door at the end of the corridor reminded Streak that dawn had been a good three hours ago and that he was hungry. The door swung open and Kelso limped in, leaning on his cane.

"It's about time," Streak drawled. "I'd decided you were going to let me starve."

"I am, for maybe another hour. No use in the county buyin' you a meal if the judge is goin' to let you off." Kelso added a dry laugh that left little to the imagination; the judge wasn't going to let Streak off.

Ledge's sheriff was a breed of man quite familiar to Streak. Lean, spare, his bad leg probably the result of a riding accident, Kelso appeared to be close to forty, his mustache and gray-salted brown hair making it hard to judge. Although his manner last night had been gruff and unsmiling, the warm brown eyes and the generous full-lipped mouth told Streak of a kindly nature. Against his instincts, which were backed by a distrust of the average law officer, Streak Mathiot was taking to Fred Kelso.

He watched the lawman's preparations for removing his prisoner from the jail with a strong amusement. First, Kelso took out handcuffs and snapped one steel loop around his own left wrist. Then, unlocking the cell door, he swung it wide and stepped back, drawing a long-barreled Colt from its worn holster on his good thigh. His cane hung in the crook of his gun arm. Holding out the hand from which hung the handcuffs, he said: "Put this on your right wrist, feller."

Streak grinned broadly. "Not taking any chances, eh?"

"Nope. I know what happened to Riggs last night."

They went down the steep slope of the alley side-by-side, Kelso holstering his .45 but keeping his hand well within reach of it. The other, the hand fastened to Streak's, held his cane. His walk was slow and labored. He seemed a little sensitive about his game leg, for as they stepped up out of the alley onto the walk and started down street, he growled: "Them clouds is nothin' but a joke. Shucks, if it was goin' to rain, I'd have felt it in my stump when I woke up this mornin'."

"Been dry, has it?" Streak asked, a little

surprised to find that the lawman's bad leg was a wooden one.

"Dryer'n the inside of a bake oven. Not a drop since the middle of July, more'n a month ago."

Streak only halfway heard this last, for he was looking down the street at four men who had just turned in off the street and were tying their ponies at the rail in front of the hotel. One of these he recognized as Bill Paight.

"There's Fencerail," he drawled.

"Yeah, and here's Crescent B," was the lawman's acid rejoinder.

Looking back over his shoulder, the way Kelso was, Streak saw three riders approaching from the street's east upper end. The horses would have held the attention of any man, let alone Streak, who had a weakness for fine horseflesh. One was a big, clean-limbed chestnut ridden by a man whose seat was ramrod straight. The rider alongside was smaller, slight of build, and the horse was a bay. Behind, the third man forked a white-stockinged black.

"There won't be no trouble today," Kelso said. "Paight's in to side Dallam's sister on a deal she's makin' with Bishop for . . ."

The brittle explosion of a rifle chopped off his words. Streak, his glance on the three Crescent B riders, saw the chestnut suddenly rear, slashing out with forehoofs. The smaller rider alongside bent low in the saddle, away from the frightened animal as it lunged closer. Then, as the bay, in turn, shied away, one of the chestnut's flying hoofs caught it alongside the head and the animal went suddenly loose-muscled and fell. The rider tried to jump clear and failed, one leg pinned under the writhing horse. The next instant the rifle sounded again. As a puff of dust marked the striking bullet less than a foot from the down rider's head, her hat came off and a mass of hair, black as a crow's wing, fell loosely about her shoulders.

Streak didn't reason in that moment, didn't notice that the rearing, plunging chestnut had been in line with the sound of the rifle and the girl at that second shot. All he knew was that the bullet had come close to killing a woman and that, instead of helping her, the people on the walk were running for the safety of the nearest store doorways. He took a sideward step and threw his weight against the handcuffs. Kelso, rooted to the spot by a paralysis of surprise, was caught off guard. His cane flew from his hand as the weight of Streak's sudden pull spun him around and hard into the front of the building at Streak's back. By the time Kelso reached for his gun, it was out of the holster, in Streak's hand. Streak drew the sheriff's arm across his lifted thigh, held the handcuff tight, and put the gun's muzzle to the chain between the two wristlets.

The sound of his shot blended with two others

65

from the street. Streak felt the handcuffs come apart and wheeled out and vaulted the rail beyond the walk, crossing the street at a run. He saw that the chestnut had bolted now. The third Crescent B rider was afoot, behind his horse, lining shots into the upstairs window of a store across the way with a Colt. Then Streak was alongside the girl.

One look told him that her horse was dying. His bullet through the bay's brain ended its struggles. He gripped the horn and lifted on the saddle, pulling on the girl's arm. Her leg came free as the six-gun, then the rifle, laid sharp racketing echoes along the cañon of the street. Streak picked up the girl, got her onto his shoulder, and ran for the walk he had left. He was breathing hard when he wheeled into the deep doorway of a store, stooped, and let the girl stand.

All at once the street was quiet. From the alleyway behind the buildings opposite came the echoed hoof *thud* of a pony breaking into a hard run. People left the shelter of the doorways; the Bishop man in the street was punching the empties from his Colt. The rider on the chestnut, the animal in hand now, was turning to come back up the street. The fight was over.

Streak looked down at the girl. Her face was as smeared with dust as was the right leg of her Levi's, the one that had been pinned under the wounded horse. The molding of that face was a pleasing oval, pretty but the good looks secondary to a certain acute aliveness that spoke of strong character. Blue eyes formed a startling contrast to the wavy black hair she now brushed back and gathered at the neck with a silvered bar pin.

She laughed softly, her voice touched with a trace of nervousness, and said: "You didn't waste much time about it."

"Did it lame you?" Streak asked her.

"No." Her hand ran gingerly along her right thigh and felt of the knee. "Not a bit," she added more certainly. "But heaven knows why. He fell like he'd been pole-axed."

People were crowding around now, a few who knew the girl asking questions and trying not to crowd too close. Streak liked the way she answered them, briefly, politely, even though he saw that her attention was on the chestnut's rider approaching along the street.

Abruptly Sheriff Kelso pushed in through the crowd. The broken handcuff still hung from his left wrist. In his right hand he held a gun—one he'd a moment ago unceremoniously borrowed from a man up the walk—and, as he hobbled to the inside of the circle, he lifted the weapon in line with Streak.

"Drop the iron, feller!" he said curtly.

Streak willingly let the sheriff's .45 fall to the planks where it hit with a solid *thud*. "Anything you say, Sheriff," he murmured, his lean face slashed with a grin.

Kelso's glance shifted to the girl, who was staring at him, wide-eyed. "Hurt, Cathy?" he asked.

"No. But what's this, Fred?" She nodded at the weapon in his hand.

Kelso hefted the gun a bare inch, still keeping it lined at Streak. "An arrest," he told her. "Him and me were headed for the courthouse when this busted loose. He grabbed my iron and shot the handcuffs apart. Lucky I didn't lose him."

Wonderment was in the girl's blue eyes now. "Is his arrest more important than a murderer's?" she asked, so low-voiced Streak doubted that anyone but himself and the sheriff heard.

Kelso frowned a moment, then gave a spare lift of his shoulders. "I sent a couple of men after the bushwhacker. He'll probably turn out to be a Fencerail hardcase."

"I'm not speaking of him," the girl said. "I mean my father."

Shock was strong on Kelso's face. "What about him?" He glanced toward the rider on the chestnut, now close. Streak knew then that the rider was Frank Bishop.

"He's the one who's keeping this fight alive," Catherine Bishop breathed, the glance she sent in her father's direction bright with anger and loathing. "He's caused the death of two men already. Now this. If he keeps on, he'll . . ."

"You don't know what you're sayin', Cathy!" came Kelso's harsh interruption.

"That's just it. I do! He the same as killed Pete. He's in town this morning to try and cheat Laura Dallam out of her inheritance. He keeps hiring men like Riggs and Nephews to keep the fight alive. I don't . . ."

She stopped speaking abruptly. For Frank Bishop now sat his horse beyond the near tie rail and the crowd had given way to open a lane between him and his daughter. Bishop must have sensed that he was being talked about, for, although he was beyond hearing, his cool and aloof regard briefly inspected the faces of those nearest him. Then his glance settled on the girl and he said tonelessly: "Come along, Cathy. We're already five minutes late." He transferred his look to Kelso. "I'll expect you to have the Fencerail man responsible for that shooting under arrest by noon, Fred."

Kelso gravely shook his head. "All I can do is try," he said. "But he got a five-minute start on us and he likely got away."

Bishop said nothing further, reining the chestnut out and turning down the street.

Streak had been watching the girl. Something had gone out of her as her father spoke and now there was no longer that bright anger in her eyes but a dull look of helplessness. She caught his glance and her face took on a quick flush, whether from embarrassment at his having seen beneath the surface of her emotions or in humiliation at what she had said of her parent he had no way of knowing.

She said, humbly, for him alone to hear—"Thank you for what you did."—and left them, going up the awninged walk.

Streak caught the proud tilt of her head, the graceful poise of her tall body and felt an emotion he couldn't define, a reluctance at having had to witness what the past two minutes had brought.

Alongside him, Kelso said: "She's dead game. But her thinkin's been all wrong since Dallam cashed in. She don't know how hard they're crowdin' Frank." He looked up at Streak. "You've got my thanks for draggin' her in off the street. But you're still under arrest, mister. Now come along. Judge Kleefus is hell on wheels when he's kept waitin'."

Bill Paight and his three companions had been crossing the hotel verandah to the door when the first rifle shot cut loose on the street. His glance whipped up there in time to see Cathy Bishop's horse go down and her father's chestnut bolt. When Scott, one of the new hands Pete had hired shortly before his death, reached for his gun and started for the steps, Paight said sharply: "Stay where you are, all of you!"

He didn't recognize the stranger who had helped him last night until Streak was halfway back across the street with the Bishop girl. Beside him, Scott's awed—"There's a gent with a set of cast-iron guts!"—eloquently expressed Bill's own feelings.

After it was over, Paight kept his men on the verandah for a purpose. He, like the others, was puzzled over the attempted bushwhack. He only half listened to their speculations over the identity of the rifleman as he watched what happened down the street, for he realized that Fencerail would be suspected of having framed that attempt at murdering Frank Bishop. But for Bishop's unruly horse, Paight had no doubt that the rancher would be lying dead out there right now. Because of what Buchwalter had told him last night, Paight was almost wishing this could be true.

Bishop rode directly to the hotel hitch rail after stopping in front of the Emporium to say something to Kelso and his daughter. He came out of the saddle stiffly, losing nothing of the aloofness that rarely deserted him these days. He waited until he had climbed the steps and stood two paces away before letting his glance inspect the Fencerail men.

"It's a shame you won't have good news to take back to Buchwalter, Paight," he said flatly.

Paight's answer was deliberately taunting. "It's a shame it wasn't our idea. We'd have made it stick."

71

For a moment their open hostility toward each other was deadly, scornful. Then Bishop said: "You won't get the chance again."

"We've got it now if we wanted to take it."

Bishop's face paled under the reminder that Paight spoke the truth, that he would have little chance against these three Dallam men if they chose to make an attempt against his life here and now. He was feeling a sudden let-down, the aftereffects of that first bullet having torn away a piece of cloth from the shoulder of his coat, of knowing how close death had been there on the street, and he was in no frame of mind to bicker with this Dallam rider. He was also, unaccountably, inclined to believe that Paight knew nothing of the rifleman who had shot from the second-story window of the empty building down the street. Because he had lately more and more retired behind the shield of his aloofness, Frank Bishop did that now, stepping past the Fencerail men and as coolly ignoring them as though he hadn't a moment ago been talking to Paight. The muscles along his back tightened as he crossed the verandah to the lobby door and went in, for he knew Dallam's riders to be a tough lot, as proddy and ready for trouble as his own men. He was thinking in that moment that Paight had shown a more level head than Riggs, for instance, would have shown in a like circumstance.

Back on the verandah, Paight felt little satisfaction at having had the last word. Bishop's superior ways galled him deeply, especially since Bill still called himself a friend of the man's daughter. His rancor toward Crescent B's owner came to an abrupt end as one of his men announced: "Here comes Kelso. Let's beat it."

"We'll stay right here," Paight was quick to say. He wanted to speak to Kelso.

He saw Streak first. The big man walked a pace or two ahead of the sheriff, who hobbled along at a faster stride than usual in keeping up with his prisoner. Paight realized that his guess of last night was correct when he saw the gun swinging in Kelso's free hand. The stranger was under arrest. He was hatless and the slashing of gray through the black of his hair was quite noticeable.

As they came abreast the verandah steps, Kelso spotted Paight and called to his prisoner: "Hold on a minute!"

In turning to obey that command, Streak saw Paight and his lean dark face took on a quick grin. "Howdy, scrapper," he said. "He's feeling salty this morning." He nodded at Kelso.

The sheriff ignored the gibe. "Paight," he said, "did you rig this play against Bishop?"

"What good'll it do to say I didn't?" Paight drawled.

"Your word's good enough with me until

73

you're proved a liar, even if you do travel with a mangy outfit. Did you do it?"

"No."

"Did Buchwalter?"

"No."

"You don't know who did?"

"No," Paight said for the third time.

"Then let's go." The lawman motioned his prisoner on up the walk. "Tell Bishop it'll be a good half hour before I can get in there if he needs me."

"You won't be needed," Paight answered.

Kelso's glace narrowed. "Pete's sister ain't sellin'?"

"Not at Bishop's price."

"Then what will she do?"

"You'll have to ask her, Kelso."

Afterward, following Cathy Bishop in through the lobby, Paight was wishing he knew the answer to the lawman's last question. He was worried as he crossed to the small side office the hotel owner had vacated for the meeting between Bishop and Laura Dallam. He was here merely to follow Buchwalter's orders. In doing so, he might be dealing a death blow to Fencerail, to Laura Dallam's future. Had he acted on his personal feelings, he would now be on his way to tell Pete's sister to sell and get out. And Buchwalter's orders were far from that.

They were waiting there in the small room,

Bishop seated at the desk, Laura Dallam standing at the window. She spoke courteously to Catherine Bishop as the other girl entered. Then she saw Bill and her plain face became almost pretty as she welcomed him with a glance.

"We can go ahead now," she told Bishop.

Frank Bishop's look became uneasy when he caught the inference in her words. "Can't we do this by ourselves?" he asked testily.

"No," Laura Dallam told him. "I don't know much about such things. Mister Paight has been kind enough to come here to act for me."

"I won't take long," Paight said. "Is your offer still the same?" he asked Bishop.

"Still the same. Seven thousand."

Paight looked at Laura. "Then we're wasting our time." He nodded at the door.

Catherine Bishop murmured—"Good, I'm glad."—before a glance from her father silenced her.

"You have thirty days before the bank takes over," Bishop said curtly.

"We know that." Paight stepped aside to let Laura through the door first.

She was out of the room and he was turning to follow when Bishop said: "I'll go as high as ten thousand. Not another cent."

Paight didn't even bother to answer.

Chapter Seven

It took Judge Kleefus something under seven minutes to finish the hearing on one Ned Mathiot, the prisoner before the bar, pleading guilty to charges of disturbing the peace. Kleefus was the possessor of a magnified sense of his own importance, of a meticulously trimmed spade beard, of a pair of chilled steel-gray eyes, and some very active stomach ulcers. If Streak had earlier considered the wisdom of taking the judge into his confidence concerning his job here, he ruled it out at his first glimpse of the man's cold exterior. He was even less surprised than Sheriff Kelso when he was sentenced to thirty days in jail and denied the right to pay a fine.

"I prefer to make an example of you, Mathiot . . . if that's your right name," was the judge's searing comment in pronouncing sentence. "Our fair city is not to become the brawling pot of this country."

" 'Boiling pot' is the correct term, Your Honor," Streak said.

Kleefus's gavel smote the block of oak on his desk. "Contempt of court!" he exploded. "We'll make that thirty days sixty!"

"Why be a piker, Judge?" Streak drawled.

Kleefus's face went beet-red. He howled something unintelligible but for the words: "Ninety days!" The hearing ended shortly as Kelso dragged his prisoner from the room and the presence of the apoplectic magistrate.

"I'll probably have you around at election time next year," the lawman sighed as they came out onto the street again. "Why in tarnation did you do it?"

"I'm always this way before breakfast, Sheriff. Sort of light-headed and playful."

"It sure cost you this time. When the judge gets to thinkin' it over, he's liable to make it a year."

"What does it matter how long he makes it?" Streak queried. "I'll be out in a few days."

Sheriff Kelso's glance narrowed. "Brother," he said, "better men than you have tried breakin' out of that jail. It was built to stay together."

Two hours later, a good breakfast under his belt, Streak was inclined to agree with the sheriff. Ledge's jail was more like a fortress than a lockup. The bars at the windows were of two-inch steel, the walls were of rock, at least a foot and a half in thickness, and the roof was of rock slab lying on foot-square beams of solid oak. Yet Streak knew he must get out of here, get out without sacrificing his one small advantage of keeping his identity hidden. On the way back to the jail he had casually mentioned Ed Church's name to the sheriff. Kelso's only response had been: "Never heard of him." The way he said it sounded like the truth.

It looked now as though Ed had never been in the valley, or, if he had been here, had managed to remain so obscure that a sheriff who seemed to know almost everything that went on in the town and the surrounding country hadn't heard of him. Because Ed had dropped so completely from sight, Streak felt it even more urgent that he get out of here and try to trace his friend. But how to do it? It was obviously hopeless to try to break out. He knew no one in Ledge who could help him or would even want to, aside from Bill Paight, and Paight had his own troubles without taking on another man's. Lacking any help, Streak could see no way of leaving Ledge's jail until he had served out the stiff sentence he had brought on himself by goading an irascible judge.

The only answer that finally came to him—and he admitted it was a weak one—was to get outside help. But there again he was stumped. How to do it? He might write Guilford, but that would take too long and might involve too great a risk for Ed Church—if Ed was still alive. So he came back to his primary reasoning, trying to uncover a way of getting outside help without wasting any time. If he could find a way of sending a message to Paight, the Fencerail man might return his favor of last night. Fencerail might even want to hire him, for an outfit in such a precarious position as Dallam's always needed a man who wouldn't back out of a fight.

He was weighing this scant possibility when he remembered Catherine Bishop's words there on the street, her bitter accusation that her father was hiring men to keep the fight alive. Why, then, if Bishop was hiring gunfighters, wouldn't Fencerail? Why wouldn't either side be anxious enough to hire him if he could prove he was worth hiring?

All at once he thought he had it. He was remembering a name and a man, remembering the way Kelso's office down on the street had looked this morning when he and the sheriff had made a brief halt there on the way to court. Had Kelso seen Streak's smile as he reached to the inside pocket of his coat, drawing a letter from it, the lawman wouldn't have been as sure of himself less than an hour later when he dropped in on his prisoner.

The sheriff had barely opened the door and stepped into the end of the short cell corridor when Streak, down on his knees and reaching through the bars of the cell door for an envelope that lay just out of grasp, withdrew his hand and stood hurriedly erect. Kelso frowned, having caught something furtive in his prisoner's hasty move. He saw the envelope and came along the corridor to stoop down and pick it up. As he looked down at it, he said: "This yours?"

Streak shook his head, avoiding the lawman's glance guiltily. "No. I saw it lyin' there and wanted a look at it."

Kelso read the name and address on the envelope. His head jerked up and he eyed Streak narrowly. "I'm damned," he breathed.

Without another word, he pocketed the envelope and left the jail. He hurried down along the alley and was in such a rush to get back to his office that he broke from the co-ordinated swinging hobble that was his usual gait and grimaced in pain as his cane several times missed supporting his game leg.

At his office, Kelso pushed the swivel chair over in front of a deal filing cabinet, sat down, and opened the lowest drawer. It was crammed with Reward notices like those almost completely filling the back wall.

Sheriff Fred Kelso had a good memory. Except for the Reward dodgers of local interest tacked on the wall, he filed the notices in the order of his receiving them. His hand went about a third of the way back in the drawer and began leafing through the sheafed papers. The nineteenth sheet he came to was the one he was looking for. He drew it out and studied it. There was no picture and a somewhat less than complete description of the wanted man. But what there was fit. The name on the dodger was Neale Kincaid, alias Tex Kincaid.

The name on the envelope, the envelope Kelso knew hadn't been there when he left the jail earlier after his prisoner's summary trial, was that of Tex Kincaid. The address was Silver City. And last night Kelso had turned Pete Dallam's roan into the livery corral after taking off a Seitzler, Silver City saddle. This morning his prisoner had asked him to take care of that saddle, claiming ownership of it.

Kelso finished reading the dodger and once again breathed: "I'm damned."

In twelve years of serving as Peñasco County's sheriff, Fred Kelso hadn't once collected a reward. And there, across the top of the dodger with Tex Kincaid's name on it, in bold face print, he read for the second time: *$1000 Reward, Dead or Alive!*

Kelso was usually an undemonstrative man. But now he let out a whoop that made the stovepipe ring.

As the lawman left the office a few minutes later, Harvey Strosnider, owner of the Pride Saloon, hailed him from down the street. "He got clean away, Fred," he announced as he came up on the lawman. "I was on the way in to tell you. Jim's gone out to have another look. He says this jasper was forking a jughead with a splayed left front hoof."

"Who was?" Kelso asked.

Strosnider gave him a peculiar look. "The ranny that tried to cut Bishop down. The one you sent Jim out after."

Kelso remembered now. In his excitement he'd forgotten the hunt for the bushwhacker. He had delegated Jim Burns, the best townsman at following sign, to help.

"I was thinkin' of somethin' else, Harvey," he said. "Where'd they lose him?"

"Four miles above in that *malpais* near Schoonover's place."

"Splay foot, huh?" Kelso mused. "Didn't Snyder down at Agua claim the horse he lost was a splay foot?"

The saloon owner nodded, waited for the sheriff to say something more, and spoke himself when the other didn't. "So it looks like it wasn't Fencerail, after all, Fred. This man may be playing a lone hand here. You better ask Frank Bishop about someone having a personal grudge against him."

Once more Kelso's mind had wandered from the matter at hand. Abruptly he burst out: "Harvey, go across and open up a case of that special bourbon you had freighted in two years ago. I'm buyin' every man in town a drink!"

Strosnider was well acquainted with the sheriff's meager resources and frugal habits. "What's up?" he asked curiously.

Kelso told him.

Within the hour, everyone in town knew that Fred Kelso had stumbled onto a piece of luck and was in the way of becoming a modestly well-off man. Instead of joining the overflow crowd drinking Kelso's whiskey at the Pride, Bill Paight headed straight for Fencerail on learning the news. Shortly after noon he was imparting it—along with a detailed account of the attempted bushwhack—to Tom Buchwalter.

The Fencerail foreman heard him out. Surprisingly enough, he seemed most interested in the bushwhacker. "Who could he have been?" he asked Paight.

"Search me, Tom. They're sayin' it might've been a man workin' off a personal grudge against Bishop."

"That makes sense," Buchwalter agreed, nodding. "Especially since the horse Snyder lost was a splay foot, like this one."

Paight's look grew puzzled. "How does it make sense?"

"Here's how. We go right back to this first stranger, the one that was in Agua the night Pete and Sternes were killed. Supposing, like I said, that he was hired by Bishop. Supposing he came up here to collect his money and got away when Bishop tried to kill him to keep him quiet. He'd hang around, wouldn't he, trying to get even with Bishop?"

Paight breathed an oath. "I never thought of that."

83

"About this Kincaid," Buchwalter said, frowning as he concentrated on some inner thought. "He sounds like a good man. Bill, did you ever know a killer that was worth a damn without his gun?"

"No. They're yellow as hell without an iron to back 'em."

"That's what makes me think we ought to have this Kincaid on our side. You say he put up a good scrap with his fists last night when he . . ."

"A damn' good one," Paight interjected.

"And this reward out for him proves he knows the working end of a Colt. That's a combination hard to beat. In fact, Bill, he may be the very man we need."

"He's in jail," was Bill's caustic reminder.

"That can be remedied." Buchwalter's glance narrowed speculatively. "If he was out, we might be able to swing it."

"Swing what, Tom?"

"Getting those sheep across here, down out of the pass. Bishop has hired some hardcases, but not a man that'll stand up to someone like Kincaid, if I have him pegged right. Bill, I think we're onto something."

"You may be," Paight said dryly. "I'm not."

But presently, when Buchwalter had explained in more detail, Bill understood.

Frank Bishop spent a hectic morning. Too much had happened too fast for him to retain that firm grip on the reins of his thinking that was so typical of him. Outwardly he was his usual well-ordered self. Inwardly he was a bewildered, hurt, and humbled man. Those rifle shots from the second-floor window of that empty building on the street had unnerved him more than he dared admit even to himself. Somehow, it had never occurred to him that men would hate him to the point of wanting to kill him. Then there was the fact of Cathy's scorn, publicly expressed, which hurt far more than the knowledge that a man had been after his life. Bishop hadn't had one pleasant moment with Cathy since her return, since the day of Pete Dallam's death. She hadn't bothered to hide her loathing of him, nor the fact that she placed on him the responsibility for the death of the man she had hoped to marry.

After the meeting with Laura Dallam at the hotel, Bishop had had some affairs to attend to at the bank and was thankful for the comparative peace and restfulness of a private office there. By the time he had finished, he had a better grip on himself.

Out on the street again, during the noon hour, he noticed the traffic in and out the swing doors of the Pride and inquired about it, to learn that Bill Kelso was celebrating, also the reason why. At first he was more impressed by Kelso's luck than by the identity of the prisoner. Then, abruptly, he realized that this Kincaid was an exceptional character to have drifted into an out-of-the-way country like this. He knew two things that gave him a healthy respect for the man. The first of these was the condition of Sid Riggs's face as he had seen it early this morning before leaving the ranch. Sid was a dangerous scrapper, yet his battered and cut face was evidence enough that he had met his equal in last night's brawl. Secondly he had himself witnessed Kincaid's action this morning in carrying Cathy off the street and into the shelter of the Emporium's doorway; he had since learned that Kincaid had grabbed Kelso's gun and shot the handcuffs apart before running out to Cathy. A man with that kind of guts was rare.

A startling and sudden idea sent Bishop's glance along the street. It was all but deserted except for the crowded walk under the saloon awning. Close by, within half a dozen steps, in fact, was the mouth of the alley that led up to the jail.

Bishop was short of breath and his thin face beaded with perspiration as he rounded the down street and shady side of the jail and climbed the gravelly slope to the barred window he knew let into the end cell. His voice bore a harsh, urgent note as he called Kincaid's name softly, stepping up to the opening.

He hadn't hoped for such immediate results. Streak's head and shoulders at once appeared in the window.

"You got my name twisted," Streak drawled. "It's Mathiot. Or are you after someone else?"

Bishop smiled thinly as he paused to get his breath and mop his forehead with a handkerchief. When he felt he could speak without too much effort, he said: "We'll have to make this fast. I don't want to be seen up here."

"Suit yourself," was the prisoner's noncommittal and incurious answer.

"How badly do you want to get out of here?" Bishop had decided to come straight to the point.

Streak's glance narrowed. "It's not a bad hangout," he said. "The food's good and it's clean."

There was something Bishop had to know before he went any further, and this horseplay of words was irritating him. "How does it happen you're in this country?" he queried.

"It's healthier for me than some others I could name," was Streak's reply, seemingly a more direct one. "That is, I thought it was."

"You're on the dodge?"

Streak shrugged and made no answer.

Bishop decided he'd have to make what he could of that first explanation. "Kincaid, I've got a job for you," he said abruptly.

If he had expected Streak to show any surprise, he was disappointed. The prisoner's flat-planed face remained impassive, almost disinterested as he said: "In case you don't know it, Bishop, this is a jail. A mighty tight one."

Bishop lifted a hand in a hasty, disparaging gesture. "Forget how tight it is. If you take my offer, you'll be out tonight."

Now Streak's face did show interest. He even whistled softly in surprise. "That's right tempting. What's the hitch?"

"There isn't any. I'm simply offering you a job at reasonable wages."

"What job?"

"You've heard about the trouble I'm in?"

"All I've heard is that you're a big augur trying to crowd out the two-bit outfits."

"That's not quite the truth. I'm a cattleman. Along with others who think the way I do, I'm trying to keep this country from being overrun by sheep."

"Which makes sense," Streak agreed.

"It'll make more sense when I've had the chance to explain further," Bishop told him. "But right now all I'm interested in is hiring you. I've had to take on some new hands, men I admit I've hired to fight if that becomes necessary. I've made the mistake of picking the wrong man to keep them in line. You know him. You gave him a beating last night."

"Riggs?"

Bishop nodded. "He doesn't have a level head. I think you do."

"You want to break me out of here and have me rod a salty outfit? What's the rest of it?"

"That's all. It won't be generally known that you're working for me unless Fencerail tries to bring in the sheep. When they do, you'll stop them."

"What about your one-legged law? Is he supposed to be sitting around watching? Or have you bought him off?"

Bishop's face colored under the sting of the words. "Kelso will be too busy with other things to bother about you until it's too late. By that time you'll be on your way out of the country. I'll take the consequences for having broken the law."

There was a brief silence in which Streak seemed to be considering the offer. "How much?" he asked finally.

"Name your own price."

"Two hundred a week, a thousand if I can wind it up for good."

"That's a lot of money."

"You're getting a lot for it."

Bishop hesitated a moment. Then, abruptly, he lifted a hand and thrust it through the bars. "It's a deal. Here's my hand on it."

Streak nodded. "It's a deal." He looked down at the rancher's hand and gave a slow shake of the head, accompanied by a meager smile. "I shook a man's hand by mistake once. Got thrown on my back and beat up for trusting him. We'll skip that."

Bishop withdrew his hand, his lips a hard thin line as he took in the insult. "Tonight, then," was all he said before he turned and went down the hill.

Streak watched the rancher until he was out of sight, then stretched out on the cot. He hadn't seen Kelso since the sheriff had left with the envelope, some two hours ago. Consequently, until Bishop's appearance, he'd had no way of knowing whether or not the lawman had swallowed the bait. That Kelso had was now a proven fact.

He lay there, smoking out a cigarette and wondering what the night would bring until shortly after 1:00, when Kelso brought him his midday meal, a thick and tasty beef stew in a lard bucket.

After unlocking the cell door and handing in the bucket, then locking it again, the sheriff leaned against the corridor's rock wall and for a few minutes silently watched his prisoner eat. His face was redder than it had been this morning, the result of more whiskey than he was in the habit of taking at one time.

"You're lucky, Kincaid," he said finally. "You've got at least three days before I get an answer to the wire I'm sendin' out from Agua on tonight's stage. I'll feed you better than they will in that hoosegow in Silver. I know what it's like."

"You're making a mistake, Sheriff. I'm not Kincaid," Streak said between two mouthfuls of the stew he was wolfing. "One of Kincaid's side-

90

kicks gave me that letter to give to Tex if I saw him."

The lawman's glance went a trifle flinty. He ignored Streak's denial. "So you're wanted for lettin' off a shotgun in an express messenger's back? It's funny, but I was beginnin' to sort of take to you before I read that. Right now I can't say I do."

"That sure busts me all up, Sheriff."

Kelso's look turned to disgust at the sarcastic rejoinder. He straightened from the wall and limped to the outside door. On second thought, he wouldn't wait to take the empty bucket back to the restaurant. The Pride still offered its attractions, for Strosnider had thrown in a second case of bourbon free. And talking to Kincaid somehow lacked the exciting quality Kelso had anticipated. The man was nothing but a hard-bitten and cold-blooded killer, regardless of what he had seemed earlier.

In reality, Kelso wanted to leave before the prisoner became his real self, which the lawman imagined might be a disgusting revelation. He didn't admit it, but he was a little hurt to think he had so misjudged a man.

Chapter Eight

The brief dusk hadn't quite given way to total darkness when a whisper of sound, of metal scraping on rock, sent Streak crouching into the cell's back corner. Shortly, when the silence had run on unbroken a few seconds, he stood flattened to the wall and started easing toward the window, wary at remembering that bush-whack through a jail window is no unheard-of thing. At the moment he saw a man's head and shoulders vaguely outlined in the paler darkness of the window, a low whispering voice said: "Be ready to come through fast, Kincaid. When you get out, follow me. Here goes."

The man thrust a heavy iron hook attached to a steel cable through the bars, around four of them, then drew it out again. Streak, reassured, stepped over to get a better look. Although he had expected something like this, a strange amused run of excitement went through him. He was trying to imagine the look on Fred Kelso's face tomorrow morning when the sheriff looked into the cell.

Out there, Streak caught the indistinct shapes of three riders beyond the man afoot. This last, the one who had spoken to him, pulled a short length of the cable through the bars with a sound like the running of a coarse file over rock. Streak saw him kneel and made out that he was fastening the hook to a heavy ring spliced into the cable. Beyond, a big wooden pulley lay on the ground, ropes running through its slots to mark it as the near end of a block and tackle. Barely in sight, some twenty feet from the cable, Streak saw a rope trailing the ground and fixed to the base of one of the stunted but tough cedars that dotted this hill slope.

"Pull, Slim."

Streak barely heard the hoarse whisper of the man afoot that sent one rider out from the rest, the rope end of the block and tackle tied to the horn of his saddle.

All at once the big pulley lifted from the ground under the tension as the rope tightened. It *creaked* an instant, the cable grated and slipped as the two ends of its loop equalized, then Streak saw one of the thick window bars bow outward. Suddenly that one bar broke from its bedding. The others bowed and were taken from the weakened base to be whipped outward into the darkness. Streak put hands on the window's broad and broken sill and vaulted up onto it, belly down. The deafening burst of a gunshot ripped away the night's stillness.

Out there, a man grunted in pain. The instant

explosions of two nearer shots blotted out the sound of his voice. A frightened horse's shod hoofs racketed against bare rock. Just before Streak wriggled out the window and fell, headfirst, to the ground, five feet below, a hand touched his arm and that same hoarse whispering voice snapped: "Quick, feller."

He took up the weight of his fall on one shoulder, rolling to his feet. A gun was thrust into his hand and he wheeled to follow the indistinct shape of his guide as a spasmodic burst of renewed firing cut loose close by.

Streak had a fair idea of the position of the three riders siding the man leading him, who he now followed at a run back up the hill to the jail's rear. When another shape plunged down out of the near darkness from that direction, Streak rocked his gun up, drew wide of the mark, and laid two swift shots past the rider's head. He dodged aside, anticipating the waist-level stab of powder flame of the rider's answering fire. A bullet slapped the jail's rock wall a moment before the gun of the man ahead spoke once. The rider, his horse wheeling sharply away, slumped in the saddle and melted slowly down out of it.

Behind now was utter confusion. Streak's one backward glimpse showed him a riderless and crazed horse pitching in among the riders there. The continuous and unevenly spaced racket of gunfire echoed back from the buildings flanking the street. A man's strident, profane cursing sounded momentarily. The acrid tang of burned cordite tainted the air, and from the left, higher on the hill, new guns sent sharp explosions of sound down the slope.

Streak's guide lunged in behind a big squat juniper and they were abruptly alongside a pair of horses. The man ahead chose the outside animal, leaving Streak the nearest, a scrawny-necked gray gelding. As Streak swung up into saddle, he could catch the labored breathing of his companion. All at once the man's voice lifted in a shrill—"*Yowee-ee!*"—an obvious signal, and he was reining his horse around, raking the animal's flanks with spurs.

Streak followed him closely, the first hundred yards of the gray's slogging run proving his looks exceedingly deceptive. Time and again the animal slipped on loose rock, breaking his stride, but always he would recover, instantly obeying the slightest pressure on the reins. Bending low over the gelding's withers as the air whip of a bullet fanned his face, Streak knew he was sitting a real piece of horseflesh and forgot his lack of spurs. Within two hundred yards they came to an abrupt shoulder of the hill where the going leveled off. There the rider ahead lined out at a dead run. Shortly the sound of the firing on the hill became ragged, sparse, then faded altogether.

They left open ground and zigzagged in

through a thin stand of jack pine, climbing again. The smell of dust kicked up by the horse ahead blended with the clean odor of the pines, reminding Streak once more of the dryness of the country and of the fact that sign would be easy to follow with the top soil baked and crumbling dry. It seemed that Kelso wouldn't have too hard a time telling where his prisoner had gone if he was interested enough to spend some time finding out. But, Streak decided with some amusement, that was Bishop's worry.

The timber gradually thickened and they pounded into the narrow aisle of a little-used trail. After ten minutes of fast traveling along it, the man ahead pulled down out of his run and let Streak close in on him. In this tree-vaulted darkness, Streak could no more than make out the white blur of his face as he turned and called: "We'll ease along and let the others catch up!"

There was something familiar about the voice but Streak couldn't place what it was. "That was close," he said. "Who were your friends throwing the lead at us?"

The rider drew rein, halting close ahead. His reply was preceded by a dry mocking laugh. "Bishop's bunch. We halfway expected 'em."

Tension brought Streak up rigid. Then he relaxed. The laugh told him who the man was. He had heard it once before, last night in the feed barn directly after Kelso's shot on the street as he stood looking down at the battered and beaten Riggs.

"So did I," he drawled. "You're full of surprises, Paight."

"So're you, friend. Last night, for instance. You weren't packing a hogleg. Sort of risky, ain't it, for a man with a price on his head?"

Streak gave the first answer that came to him. "That's the surest way I know of keeping out of trouble."

"Only you didn't . . . Kincaid," Paight reminded him, laying clear emphasis on the name.

Streak's impulse was to tell Paight the truth, that he had used Kincaid's name as a ruse to break jail, but there was something he wanted to know first, something he would like explained in the light of Paight's belief that he was an outlaw.

"What happens now that I'm out?" he queried.

"We've got a job for you."

"Mind letting me in on it?"

"If there's time." Paight stood in stirrups, his attitude one of listening. Streak could hear no sound back along the trail. "Tom Buchwalter, the boss, thinks he can use you," Paight went on. "It'll only be for a day or two. Is that a fair enough trade for busting you out of that lockup?"

"Sounds like it. But what can I do for him?"

"Maybe you've heard our outfit's been trying to bring in sheep? Well, Tom's decided that tomorrow's the day. He's working on the idea that none of Bishop's bunch will care to tackle a tough crew with you leading 'em. You've got a name."

"The fastest man that ever packed a Colt is dead easy game for a bushwhacker," was Streak's drawled reminder.

"That's the chance you're running . . . that Bishop won't go that far."

Out of the downward distance came the muted hoof *thud* of running ponies. Paight's solemn words ended. At once he reined off the trail, drawling: "This just might not be the bunch I'm waiting for."

Streak put the gray over alongside the other's horse, a few feet off the trail, in the deep obscurity of a tall yellow bark pine. He noted that the Fencerail man drew his gun.

Shortly the muffled rhythmic beat of the running horses came abruptly up on them. Shadows raced out of the near darkness and three riders boiled past.

Paight hailed them. One man heard and called to the others and in a moment they had gathered close to Paight and Streak, the winded ponies' labored breathing rising over the sound of straining saddle gear.

One man spoke up immediately. "Art stopped a slug, Bill. He's bleedin' more'n he should, even if it's only a scratch." Streak noticed the man alongside the speaker sitting hunched over in the saddle, holding his right side. "We'd better get him back to the layout fast."

"Go ahead, then," Paight told him. "Kincaid and I are heading for the camp at the needle rock. Remember what you're to do. You'll have a moon in another hour, Slim. Put two men in the house, another in the crew shack, another in the barn loft. Stop anyone you spot riding in across the meadow. Warn 'em once and, if they keep coming, make your lead count. Is it bad, Art?"

"Grazed a rib and slit me open some," the hunched-over rider replied in a voice that was none too steady. "Only I can't get the damn' thing to stop bleedin'."

"Here, let's have a look at it." Paight reined over alongside the man and pulled his shirt aside. "No wonder," he muttered. "You haven't tied it up." With a knife, he cut the tail from the man's shirt and succeeded in binding it around his chest, using his own neckpiece wadded tightly over the ugly-looking wound to stop the bleeding. Finished, he said curtly: "Now shake a leg. Riggs is liable to be on his way up there already."

"We sure as hell give it to 'em," Slim drawled as he swung his pony around and led the others away.

When the sound of their going had faded into the stillness, Paight gave Streak a sideward glance. "Well, are you with us?" he asked. "If you ain't, now's the time to say so. You're free to ride out if you like."

"I'll hear a little more about it."

"That'll take some doing, maybe two hours of hard riding. Buchwalter and the others are waiting for us up above. I'm headed there now."

"Then let's get started."

"We swing off here."

Paight led the way obliquely left from the trail and struck off through the trees. Once again he set a stiff pace, one intended to cover as much distance as possible without wearing out their horses. It was hard going, much of it over bare rocky hill shoulders. This, Streak realized, was Paight's way of confounding anyone who might tomorrow try and follow their sign.

Now, more than ever, Streak realized that this rugged hill valley was a contradiction to any he had known. Instead of the hills smoothing out in the valley's bottom, those they traveled were like the abrupt rises at the very base of high mountains. But within the hour, as the two of them climbed higher, the going became easier and they crossed several park-like meadows breaking the seemingly endless stretches of timber. Once they had the lights of a cabin on their left and Paight took care to keep to the margin of trees that skirted the open ground around it. Another time they struck the line of a three-strand fence and rode what Streak judged to be at least two miles before lining out north again at its corner. From there on they had the light of a waning moon to travel by.

A short time after leaving the back line of the fence they were in a tangle of the roughest hills Streak had ever ridden. A man could easily lose himself in them, but Paight seemed to know where he was going. They rode a cañon that started wide and low-walled at the mouth and soon became narrow and the moonlight shut out by high and precipitous cliffs on either hand. As the cañon's bed narrowed, the continuous roar of a stream was amplified until the sound of rushing water drove out even the rock-slapping hoofs of the two horses. Finally the creek took up the whole width of the narrow defile's uneven rocky floor and they rode within the margin of the foaming water.

The horses had a harder time of it now, unable to see their footing. The gray's energy seemed limitless. Once Paight's horse went down, the rider jumping clear barely in time. He stood knee deep in water. When Streak got down to help him get the horse on its feet again, the man was grinning. It was that same rash grin of last night. Streak decided there and then that, regardless of the ethics of running sheep, Fencerail must have a lot in its favor to attract a man like Paight.

As they started on once more, Streak made a conscious effort to plan his next move. He obviously owed Fencerail whatever help he could give in return for their having risked men in breaking him out of jail. He might be with them a day or two, an interlude during which he would have to forget his main errand here of discovering what had happened to Ed Church. Although this prospective delay galled him, he was a man on whom even the smallest unpaid debt of close friendship weighed heavily. Not to try to repay this debt to Paight, to Fencerail never once entered this mind. What worried him was picking up a line to follow once he finished with this obligation.

The last twenty-four hours had been crowded with tension, suspense, and violence. Streak had bought into a brawl—one of the best he could remember—he had seen a bushwhacker come close to shooting down a woman; he had been arrested and broken out of a jail—and at least one man had come close to losing his life in that break—and now he was running from the law. But what had it all amounted to? Nothing, absolutely nothing as far as helping him accomplish his purpose in coming to this country. In two days he had made but one slight forward step beyond the point Guilford had left him along the pitch-dark trail of Ed Church's mysterious disappearance. That one step had been the discovery that Ed had hired a horse in Agua Verde and completely vanished thereafter to be labeled a horse thief. No one had seen Ed in Ledge; at least Kelso hadn't, and as a peace officer Kelso would theoretically have his finger on the pulse of the town. There was only one thing to do, as Streak saw it. He'd keep on asking questions. He'd ask them of Buchwalter and, later, of Bishop. He thought he knew how he could walk into Bishop's layout and get any answers the man might have to give him.

The tangle of Streak's thinking was interrupted as Paight, close ahead, abruptly put his horse into the middle of the stream and headed for the opposite bank, a good twenty feet away. Streak followed him across, climbed the narrow strip of the far bank, and swung aground, as Paight did. And now that he stood separated by a few feet from the roiled water near at hand, its rushing voice was overridden by a louder one, the thundering roar of a falls. The towering walls magnified the sound and gave it a definite vibration. Streak wasn't sure but what he could feel the solid rock under his boots trembling with the magnitude of the sound.

Paight stepped over to him, cupped a hand at his mouth, and shouted to make himself heard: "There's a big falls right ahead! We go around! Up there's the needle rock!"

His hand lifted high to indicate a vague and high-spired shape ahead darker than the night's almost total blackness. It was only the faint sheen of moonlight on the east face of a slender, nearly vertical rock formation that made it possible for Streak to distinguish it at all.

Paight started up along the streambank. In less than fifty feet it became a narrow ledge choked by a tangle of brush. Paight shouldered into it, stumbling on. Presently Streak could see the gray curtain of the falls dropping a good thirty feet from the higher bed of the stream. A misty vapor dampened his face and made the chill air bite deeper. Gone was the dry dusty smell the air had borne in the foothills below. It was fresh now, smelling of leaf mold and green vegetation.

The ledge tilted abruptly upward, so steeply that Streak had to get behind the gray and force the animal on ahead for fear of being trampled in one of the gelding's lunging upstrides. At one point he had to go to hands and knees. He could have stretched out his hand and had his arm numbed by the force of the falling water. Finally a last reaching step took him to the top of the climb, close alongside the solid oily-looking water where it curled over the lip of its rocky bed before plunging downward.

They mounted again but only to ride as far as the broad base of the formation Streak had made out from below, a high needle rock, now plainly distinguishable through the darkness. Paight swung left, toward the stream, along a sheer granite wall. Within a few yards, Streak picked up a faint rosy tint against the night's cobalt shadows beyond a far turning of the wall. That glow grew stronger as Paight circled.

All at once a fire was in sight, a bright smoke-less blaze burning at the center of a small peninsula that thrust out from the east face of the needle rock and divided the stream at almost its exact center. Streak saw that dividing of the stream into two separate channels and noted it only casually, his glance more interested in the indistinct shapes of several men who stood at the outward limits of the fire's light.

One of these came toward Paight as the Fencerail man rode in on the fire. He was gray-haired, and his sun-darkened face with its white mustache bore a kindly and benign look. Streak guessed correctly that this must be Tom Buchwalter, and again he had the feeling that Fencerail's claims on being in the right in this trouble must have a solid basis of fact. Buchwalter looked like an honest man.

Streak had reined in behind Paight and was lifting his left foot clear of stirrup, about to dismount, when a coarse loud voice called: "You, stranger! Lift 'em!"

Streak's head came around. There, less than ten feet away, close to a thicket of scrub oak, stood a man staring at him over the twin holes of a shotgun's double barrels. The eyes were unwinking and coldly furious in their hard concentration. The face, what little of it Streak could make out as it checked the shotgun's stock, was thin and predatory. Streak settled back into the saddle, slowly lifting his hands.

"Prenn!" Tom Buchwalter spoke crisply, commandingly.

The west-slope rancher ignored him, not taking his eyes from Streak, his weapon held rock-steady and centered on Streak's chest. "You're goin' to do some talkin'," Prenn drawled coldly, "and you'll do it fast. If you're Tex Kincaid, I'm Little Eva. I knew Tex. He cashed in over a year ago. Now come down off there easy and reachin' for the clouds. Bill, take the weight off his belt. Tom, I'll chairman this meetin' from here on for a spell."

Chapter Nine

Tom Buchwalter hadn't been able to peg what was wrong. But something was, definitely. These men, five of them, all small west-slope ranchers, had come here to the needle rock with eagerness and anticipation. Their faces had plainly showed the easing of their long tension. To them, this was to be the end of the long wait. The message Buchwalter's riders had taken to them during the day had been simply that they were to meet at the needle rock at 10:00 that night, that the drive would be made into the valley at dawn of the following morning, and that Buchwalter had found a way of making it without danger. When they had all gathered and he started his talk, Buchwalter had been supremely confident. He had given them much the same story he'd told Bill Paight last night, becoming eloquent as he explained point after point they questioned. Then an insistent and nagging doubt had entered his mind. That doubt was centered on Morgan Prenn. Buchwalter had counted on Prenn to sway the others if they needed swaying. But Prenn had turned strangely silent after his first eagerness. Buchwalter didn't know why.

Prenn had, until now, been the most hot-headed of their number. It was he who had wanted to raid Crescent B the day they all learned of Pete Dallam's death. It was Prenn who had said lustily: "To hell with my outfit, everything! I'll see it burned to the ground and every critter I own layin' dead if I can even things with Frank Bishop!" But tonight, Prenn was silent, his shotgun lying in the crook of his arm as Buchwalter's talk ran on. It almost seemed as though he wasn't listening. So Buchwalter dwelt at length on this stranger his men were breaking out of jail, this Tex Kincaid, the Silver City killer. He pointed out that Bishop didn't have a man in his crew who would dare face Kincaid with guns. All this time he was speaking mainly to Prenn, trying to fan alive that spark of fanatical hatred the man had so far shown toward Bishop.

But the spark somehow died as he talked, for Prenn remained silent. Finally Buchwalter spoke to the man directly, saying: "Morg, what ails you? You haven't said a word."

Prenn shrugged. "Nothin' ails me," he replied. "You've got it all thought out. What's there for me to say?"

"You act like you aren't much interested, now that we've got our chance."

"We'll see how it comes out," was all Prenn would say.

From there on, Buchwalter could see doubt begin to take the others. Snell, for one, had always been a doubtful quantity. He had a family, a wife and two kids. He couldn't afford to lose his slender source of livelihood. Now he kept asking about the stranger. What made Buchwalter so sure that the sight of Kincaid would turn back Bishop and the crews of the other big east-slope outfits and open the way for the sheep?

"Simple enough," Buchwalter replied. "Kincaid's a fighter. Not only with his guns but his hands. If necessary, he'll ride square up to Bishop, throw a gun on him, and . . ." He stopped speaking, his head cocked abruptly to a listening attitude. "I'll let him speak for himself," he said shortly. "This must be him and Bill now."

Prenn was on his feet before Buchwalter had finished, striding cat-like into the shadows beyond the reach of the fire's glow. The others, warned by his strange manner, followed suit. Presently Buchwalter was alone. He walked over toward Paight as his man rode into sight, relieved at seeing a rider he didn't recognize close behind. Then the jail break had been successful. He was almost up to Paight when Morg Prenn called: "You, stranger! Lift 'em!"

The stranger's quick glance toward Prenn didn't escape Buchwalter. As he said sharply—"Prenn!" —he saw the stranger lift his hands. Then Prenn was speaking, his barbed words a final and devastating requiem to Buchwalter's soundly laid idea of what was to take place tonight and tomorrow.

The others closed in slowly around Prenn and the stranger. The look on Bill Paight's face was one of utter bewilderment, almost of hurt. Buchwalter himself could find nothing to say as Prenn's words trailed off and the stillness settled down around them. Even the muted roar of the waterfall seemed hushed, as though waiting for what the stranger had to give as his answer to Prenn's indictment.

Streak, feeling the suspicion that was focused on him, aware that only a slender thread of reason was holding back the unleashing of Morgan Prenn's fury, had a bad moment. Then, slowly, a smile came to his face. He didn't dismount, as Prenn had ordered, but drawled: "Sure, Tex is dead. Last spring I rode a hundred miles to help at his burying. But Tex wouldn't have minded my using his handle to break out of that hoosegow. I had to get out."

Prenn's right eye still stared down the ribbed sighting channel between the shotgun's twin barrels. "Go on," he said tonelessly. "Talk! You ain't got much time!"

"My handle's Mathiot . . . Ned Mathiot," Streak said easily. "I'm from Silver and I came up here looking for somebody. So far all I've collected from a week's ride is a half a beating and a ninety-day jail sentence from a judge with a sour liver. In ninety days the man I'm hunting will have hightailed too far for me to follow. So it was a case of breaking that jail. You'd have done the same."

Now Prenn took the butt plate of his weapon from shoulder, half lowered it to his thigh. "Keep on goin'," he drawled.

"What else do you want to know?"

Prenn jerked his head in Buchwalter's direction. "Tom, here, claims you were askin' questions down in Agua about a stranger that come through a couple weeks ago. That right?"

"Right," Streak replied.

Prenn's gun rocked up to shoulder once again. "Then, brother, you'd better think quick! The gent you're tryin' to find was hired by Frank Bishop to bushwhack Pete Dallam and Mike Sternes. He did a damn' good job. If you're a

110

friend o' his, we're seein' what your guts look like after they've been combed over by a double load o' buckshot! This close, it'll about tear you in two!"

Streak could hardly believe his hearing. Ed Church a killer, a double killer? He glanced at Buchwalter, who said soothingly: "Morg, we've got to hear what he has to say."

"Yeah," Prenn drawled. "Nothin' holdin' him."

In the following brief silence, Streak knew that Prenn's trigger finger was tightening. For a moment he had no notion of what he could do to keep the man from accomplishing his threat. Then all at once he was a man fighting for his life. "Save your lead, Prenn," he said quickly. "Save it if you want to see that bushwhacker stop some. I've been hunting him all over four states for the last six months. When I meet up with him, it's either him or me."

The barrels of the shotgun were no longer as steady as though locked in a vise. "You're huntin' him?" Prenn queried flatly. "What for?"

"To beat half my life's wages out of him. To see him cash in slow, with a hole low enough through his guts so it'll take him a long time. He was my partner, Prenn. Six months ago he left Silver with every dollar I had to my name, left me with a sheriff on my tail. I pulled out of Silver ahead of a posse. I've been hunting that double-crosser ever since."

Prenn slowly lowered the gun, took both barrels off cock, and rested the butt plate on the toe of his boot. "Friend!" he breathed, "that was awful close." He looked at Streak, and now there was no fury in his eyes. Instead, they showed relief and awe.

Streak brought his hands down and rested them on the horn of the saddle. "Now it's my turn to ask a few," he drawled. "You say my partner was hired by Bishop to do a double killing. That's about the sort of work he's good for, providing he can shoot from cover. What's happened to him?"

"No one knows," Buchwalter said, and once again Streak was impressed by the man's mild but firm manner. "He disappeared completely on that splay-foot gelding of Snyder's. Until this morning I thought Frank Bishop had killed him when he came to get his pay for the bushwhack, killed him so that no one would ever know Pete and Sternes weren't killed in a genuine shoot-out. Since this morning I've known he was alive."

"How do you get that?" Streak asked.

"You were on the street. You should know. My men weren't responsible for the try that was made on Bishop. His own men certainly weren't. So there's only one other possibility, as I see it. Your friend did come back up here to collect his pay for his double bushwhack. Bishop did try to kill him and bury the secret. But your partner got away somehow. He was the one forted up behind that second-story window this morning. He tried to kill Bishop, missed, and hightailed. Maybe you heard they ran across his sign and tracked him a ways. That sign was of a splay-foot horse."

Streak took this in with a strong excitement running through him. To conceal his feelings, he swung slowly down out of saddle and ground-haltered the gray. Although Buchwalter's theory couldn't possibly fit Ed Church, Streak knew he was onto something. It was a slender enough clue but it might be a beginning. Ed Church had ridden Hank Snyder's splay-foot gelding out of Agua Verde on the night Pete Dallam and Mike Sternes met their deaths. Today someone had ridden a splay-foot into town, tried to kill Frank Bishop, and ridden the animal out again when he failed. Could it be the same horse? If so, that man, whoever he was, must be found and made to tell what he knew about Ed Church.

Streak had to say something to ease further suspicion of him from these men. So what he told them was: "Then I'm not too late. If he's still around, I stay on. Here's as good a place as any to stay. And if you've got work for me to do, I can maybe pay back the favor Paight did me tonight."

He was looking at Tom Buchwalter as he spoke. Fencerail's foreman gave him a kindly smile, then shook his head gravely. "You could've helped if you'd been this Kincaid. Now you can't. We'll have to give the whole thing up."

113

Streak frowned. "Why? Why not bring your woollies in?"

"Because you're not the man we needed. With someone like Kincaid backing our play, we might've got a few thousand head of sheep through. Now we don't stand a prayer."

"We might as well get on home and sleep it off," Prenn said. "Shucks, I thought we had a chance."

"But they don't know I'm not Kincaid," Streak insisted.

"They damn' well would if it came to a showdown," Prenn growled, disgust in his tone. His rancor wasn't directed particularly at Streak but nicely summed up the fading hopes of the others.

"We ran into Bishop's crew there at the jail, Tom," Paight announced matter-of-factly. "They had the same idea we did, breaking Kincaid out. Art stopped some lead."

"Was he bad hurt?"

"Not bad. He'll be laid up a few days, though."

"Then that's one less man we can count on." Buchwalter shrugged, turned away from Paight, and went over to the fire. He picked up a long stick and started to break the fire up, spreading the coals so that they would be easier to extinguish. "Well, all we can do is pray for another chance."

"Couldn't we think this over?" Streak asked him. "What were you set to do in the morning?"

"Drive a band of a thousand head in over

the east pass above Elbow Lake," Buchwalter told him. "If that had worked, if we'd found we could outbluff Bishop long enough to drive the band across to our side of the valley, we'd have brought in the rest."

"How many altogether?"

"Close to six thousand."

"That's a lot of sheep to get anywhere in a hurry."

"You're tellin' us!" Prenn said ruefully. "We stand to lose everything but our shirts. We can sell back to the outfit we bought 'em from, of course, but we'd take a big loss. If we only had Pete here! He'd have figured out a way. He'd have ridden smack into those east-slope jaspers and talked his way through."

Remembering something Buchwalter had said a moment ago, Streak asked: "You mean you've all along counted on being able to bring a mess of sheep in across that pass over east and drive through Bishop's land?"

Buchwalter nodded. "That was Pete's idea. Like Prenn says, Pete would have made it work somehow. He was going to bring them in a thousand at a time. There's a thousand beyond the pass now. They've been there since a few days before Pete died. Right across here"—he lifted a hand toward the lofty peaks close above, straight northward—"we're holding five thousand more. We've had them there because the feed's better."

"Why don't you bring them in from this way, straight across?" Streak asked. "Then you wouldn't have to cross the valley. You'd drive right down onto your own graze."

"Friend," Prenn said, "you just leave the thinkin' to us. There's only one way into this valley exceptin' from smack across the desert, west and south. That one way is through the east pass. A mule couldn't make it in from the north."

"A mule could," Paight corrected him. He pointed off into the darkness up the creek. "Even a man on a horse could. Pete's done it. He's the one that found the way around the falls. Follow this cañon straight on up and you can make it to the other side without getting above timberline."

"Then why can't sheep come across the same way?" asked Streak.

"The creek divides right here and the two cañons it follows are the only way down," Paight explained patiently. "The fork we came up is impassable for sheep. They'd panic and be drowned getting down around the falls. Below, the water's too deep. The other branch is even worse. No man I know has ever traveled it, even afoot, more than halfway up here. Nope, it won't work, Mathiot."

Streak was looking upstream, up along the gray ribbon of the foaming creek. Although he couldn't be sure, there seemed room enough on the east bank to allow the passage of sheep. He turned and his glance lifted briefly upward, to the high rock pinnacle that rose sheerly overhead. "You say you could drive this far and no farther?" he asked.

Paight nodded, eying him narrowly. He had read something into Streak's words that went deeper than their drawled casualness.

"Let's have this straight," Streak said finally, and now he had the attention of the others. "What's behind this scrap you're having with Bishop?"

"What difference does it make what's behind it?" Prenn muttered.

"I want to know. Buchwalter, what's behind it?"

Fencerail's foreman straightened from raking the coals from the fire. "At first it wasn't sheep," he said. "At first it was a question of water. Two years ago every rancher in the valley belonged to an Association, Pete along with the rest. Over east, right below the pass, is a big meadow leased by the Association from the government. It's big enough to graze twice as many head of cattle as there are in the valley now. But it's good only in summer. It's snowed under every winter, so the outfits don't dare overstock for fear of winterkill. The valley's pretty well shut in below, all but the lower end of the east slope, and the big brands own that."

"Go on, tell him about the Association," Prenn put in bitterly.

"I'm coming to that, Morg," Buchwalter said.

"Mathiot, two years ago the big augurs of the Association got the idea of throwing up a dam below that government lease and catching snow-melt water, storing it over the summer. It was a good idea . . . for them. The east-slope outfits could double their alfalfa yield through the summer with more water. But what about the west-slope outfits, Fencerail, Broken U, Yoke, and the others? We were left out in the cold. Yet, as members of the Association, we were supposed to share the expense of throwing up that dam. You can guess the rest."

"You pulled out of the Association?" Streak asked.

Buchwalter gave a slow nod. "I wasn't here then. I was brought in afterward . . . after Pete and the rest had quit the Association and turned to the idea of raising sheep as the only thing that would save them. I've been a sheepman all my life. That's why I'm here. Now that I am, I'm not much good to anybody. We've been held up by two things. First, by Bishop taking a stand that no sheep were to come in. Second, because the government hasn't yet given us a permit to drive through the lease. We were promised that a federal officer would be in to look things over and decide on the permit. That was over a month ago. He's never showed up. Meantime, Pete and Sternes have been killed. Now we'll never get that permit. The government wouldn't be foolish

118

enough to issue it and start a war. So we've turned to the only thing left us . . . a try at making the drive without a permit. We either bring in sheep or starve. Without the summer feed we've always had up on the lease for our cattle, we won't last another year."

"Then how would you last with sheep?"

"Sheep are different. The profits are bigger. The only danger is in overstocking, overgrazing. I know that danger and can prevent it. If we bring in sheep and use our heads after they're in, we're better off than we ever were with cattle. Bishop says no. He's got his lake up there now and can forget us. He has the guns to back his say. That's where it stands right now."

Streak was building a smoke, seemingly more intent on it than on what Buchwalter was saying. In reality, he had caught and judged every word. He was using this moment to make up his mind, knowing for a certainty now that the thing he had all along suspected was true. Bishop was an autocratic and powerful rancher using a flimsy excuse as his reason for starving out smaller neighbors. What lay behind his tactics, Streak had no way of knowing. Did Bishop want to drive the small ranchers from the west slope and then take it over himself? It seemed a logical guess, particularly in view of Buchwalter's statement that the lower valley in winter was crowded far beyond the capacity of the upper summer range. If

Bishop and the others could get their hands on the small outfits, wouldn't they then be able to make better use of the government lease? Deliberately Streak was arriving at a decision. A few moments ago a startling idea had come to him. Now he was sobered by the thought that he was probably the one man who could make or break these small outfits, assure them of a prosperous future. But were they in the right? After all, wasn't he a cattleman? Weren't they sheepmen? And hadn't his upbringing taught him to hate the sight, the smell, even the sound of sheep? But, somehow, the matter of sheep didn't count now. What did was that poor, hard-working men were being slowly ground to a pulp of poverty under the heel of a range hog. Streak liked these men. He even liked Morg Prenn, under-standing the bitter hate that adversity had bred in the man. Prenn had had good reason to distrust him, to threaten his life.

All at once Streak's mind was made up and his glance came up to travel slowly from one face to the other. Paight he had liked from the first moment of their meeting last night. Buchwalter was no ordinary sheepman; he was level-headed, mild of manner, honesty written in every line of his face. Prenn was hot-headed but sincere. Streak didn't know Snell. The other three hadn't spoken a word, but they had the look of men whose lives had been spent close to the soil, the look of hard and honest men driven to the point of using guns to defend their homes, their futures.

"You can bring your sheep in," he said almost idly. "Not that band you're holding beyond the pass but the main one. By tomorrow night you'll have your sheep inside your fences. Bishop tried to break me out of jail tonight. He still thinks I'm Kincaid. I'll show up at his layout tonight and tell him it took me that long to shake loose from you. I'll tell him I overheard your plans before I high-tailed. In the morning, his crew and all the others on the east slope will be up in the pass ready to stop your drive. You'll send a few men across there and fake that drive while the real one comes down this cañon. How does it sound?"

Prenn's heavy laugh rang out. It lacked all amusement. "Fine, just fine, brother! For all but one thing. There ain't a prayer of bringin' sheep down this cañon. Can't you get that through your thick head?"

"Easy, Morg," Buchwalter said with surprising sharpness. His glance was hard on Streak. "How do we do it?"

Streak told them.

Chapter Ten

The *drumming* of hoofs sounded in along the trail to bring Frank Bishop up out of his deep leather chair and take him to the door. As he opened it and stepped out into the night, he glanced back over his shoulder to the couch where Cathy sat reading, her legs curled under her. Seeing her that way made her father almost wince, so strongly was he reminded of the woman to whom he had so long ago given his name. Ruth Cosgrave Bishop had been in her grave these past four years.

He closed the door softly behind him, a feeling of depression settling over him. The two weeks since Cathy's return had seemed an eternity to him. Nothing he had been able to do or say could stir her from the strange apathy that had taken her since Pete Dallam's death. In her long silence, in the deep hurt he saw in her eyes whenever they couldn't avoid meeting his, he found condemnation, almost bitter hate. He knew, although Cathy had never said so to his face, that she blamed him for Pete Dallam's death. Now, going to the edge of the low wide portal that fronted the big house, Bishop's glance roved the darkness, seeing what lay beyond his vision as though in the light of day. The yard, the tall cottonwoods, the rock-bordered stream fronting the broad square log house made a pleasing picture, a picture of quiet affluence. The working quarters of Crescent B lay down across the stream and out of sight beyond the willow grove. But there, too, the most critical eye could pass inspection on the big barn, the bunkhouse, the orderly array of lesser buildings and corrals, and approve.

All of this Frank Bishop had wrested from the valley wilderness in his own lifetime. He had been the first rancher in this country, the first man to build a home and bring in cattle. Up until two years ago he had taken pride in his accomplishment. Then there had come trouble, nothing much that was definite except his feeling that Cathy had found herself a man who wasn't quite worthy of her. Now that trouble had assumed gigantic proportions and he was no longer proud except outwardly. It seemed that his world was crumbling under him. Tonight he was a bitter, nearly broken old man hiding behind a hard shell of aloofness and austerity he hated as much as others hated it in him. Pete Dallam was responsible for all this, and, realizing what destruction the man had wrought on his own well-being, Frank Bishop hated even the memory of him. Looking back on his own part in the break with Dallam, he saw where he had made his mistakes and, humble now, would have given anything to correct them and bring happiness to Cathy. But because his mistakes hadn't been the chief reason for the way things had turned out, he was hurt more by the turn of circumstance than contrite over any wrongdoing. It was true that he hadn't approved of Pete Dallam, for the man had been too cocky, too reliant on good looks and a nimble wit to meet Bishop's severe standards. Still, he had never mentioned his dislike to Cathy. When Dallam had broken away from the Association and taken his west-slope neighbors with him, Bishop had seen bad trouble in the making. Then, nearly a year ago, when Elbow Lake dam was being built, he had sent Cathy East to visit her Philadelphia relatives, hoping he'd be able to set things right before her return. He had failed miserably. Dallam had never been one to listen to reason, and Bishop's dislike for the man had turned him stubborn and unbending. As a last desperate chance, Bishop had sent for Cathy, hoping that through her he could meet Dallam on something like decent terms. He'd never had that last chance, for Mike Sternes had killed Dallam. He still blamed himself for sending Mike down to meet Cathy instead of going himself. Had he been there with Dallam, the man would be alive today. Perhaps they could have patched things up.

The hoof *rattle* of ponies crossing the creek

bridge at the foot of the yard cut in on Bishop's thoughts, and he came down off the broad step and walked down the slope of the house knoll to meet Riggs and the others.

Riggs was the first to ride in on him, and in the faint first light of the moon that was edging up over the low pass of the eastward hills, the cattleman caught the hard cast of Riggs's face and knew that the man's errand had been futile. Then he saw the limp form slung across the saddle of one of the horses behind Riggs and shock rode through him.

"Fencerail got there before us and busted Kincaid out," Crescent B's new foreman said simply. "Johnson stopped one of their slugs. Cashed in."

Bishop was aware that the house door above had opened a moment before Riggs had spoken, that it must be Cathy and that she had heard what was said. Knowing that this would furnish her one more brick in the wall of condemnation she was building against him, he was at a loss for words.

Riggs thought Bishop hadn't heard and began to repeat himself: "We had trouble, boss. Ran into . . ."

"Take Johnson down to the barn," Bishop cut in, wondering why he had to address the man so curtly. "I'll be along directly."

He watched them turn back down to the bridge and waited until most of them were across it before he could summon the courage to face the house again. As he had suspected, Cathy's slim figure stood outlined in the wash of lamplight in the door. He climbed the knoll and stood before her.

For a long moment, neither of them spoke. Then Bishop said: "Better turn in, Cathy. It's time you were asleep."

Her glance met his and he saw dull anger, something close to loathing in her eyes as he came onto the portal. He felt it necessary to explain. "Kincaid's the man that brought you in off the street this morning. Kelso's been holding him on some trumped-up charge. I thought I could use him and sent the crew in after him. It seems Fencerail had the same idea."

Something in her father's quiet words made Cathy check the embittered outburst that was on her lips. She said finally—"You don't have to tell me these things."—and turned back into the room, crossing it to the door of her bedroom at the far end.

She undressed quickly and got into bed, hoping that sleep would soon blot out the futile turmoil of her thinking. The ambush on the street this morning had frightened her badly, made her uncertain of the stand she was taking against her father. Afterward, she had looked upon the fight Fencerail was making against the Crescent B in a new light, seeing herself as the direct cause of it.

126

Pete Dallam's death had hit her hard, had taken out of her that gaiety and the hope that this trouble would be righted in the end. Since then she had been living a waking nightmare, hardly knowing or caring what turn the feud was taking. But that gun on the street this morning had been real, deadly, and had driven home the seriousness of this thing in her mind until she looked beyond the point of her own personal loss. Out there in the yard a few minutes ago Cathy had had a strange feeling of pity for her father. He hadn't seemed the cool heartless man of the past two weeks but one uncertain and almost humble. It was as though he felt keenly the responsibility for Johnson's death. And this morning she had openly accused him of being a murderer.

She no longer knew her own mind, torn as it was between bitterness over the loss of a man she loved and this stubborn sense of loyalty toward her parent. She was ashamed now of what she had said there on the street in Ledge. Thinking back on it, she fervently hoped that Fred Kelso and this stranger, Kincaid, had been the only ones to hear her. She could trust Kelso to keep the incident strictly to himself. As for Kincaid—well, she couldn't know about him. Several times today she had thought of the stranger with strong curiosity, wondering what sort of man he could be. She could still feel the powerful sweep of his arms as he had lifted and carried her from the street. The deep concern that had been in his blue-gray eyes as they stood there in the store doorway was as clear to her now as when she had first seen it. Those blue-gray eyes had been gentle even in the hardness of anger. Her father had just said that this man, Kincaid, was being held by Kelso on a trumped-up charge. Didn't that mean then that her father had sent the crew in to break him out of jail? Once again anger against her father and his calculatedly superior manner grated against the girl's nerves. She remembered once more that he was, indirectly at least, responsible for Pete Dallam's death, for all this trouble that was now flaring into sustained violence. Then, mercifully, sleep ended the ceaseless whirl of her thoughts.

She wakened to the muted sound of voices coming from the living room. She had no idea of the time, or of how long she had slept, as she lay there drowsily listening. Her father's voice she recognized. The other she didn't, not for several minutes. But when it suddenly came to her that the quiet drawl blending with her father's voice belonged to the stranger, Kincaid, she was instantly and fully awake, and at once she asked herself how he came to be here.

The impulse that took her out of the bed to pull on her robe was at first only one of curiosity to see this man again. She went out into the hall. The door there stood slitted open. She moved it wider, carefully, and could see them standing to one side of the big stone fireplace in the big room, the stranger a full head taller than her father. He stood, tall and straight, his face shadowed in firm lines by the lamplight.

Then, as she was soundlessly closing the door, beginning again to wonder why Kincaid was here, Cathy heard her father say: "Buchwalter knows we've got the pass guarded. How does he think he'll make this stick?"

"They're moving in just as it gets light. He's got better than twenty men to back him. He figures you'll be too late getting enough men there to handle that big a crew or that you'll back down from an open fight. I'm supposed to bluff you if things get too bad."

Cathy tensed, knowing at once that she had overheard something important. The next moment her father was saying: "How did you get across here to tell me this without their knowing? And why?"

"How?" Streak smiled thinly. "Last night when Kelso jailed me, he took away my watch and money. I told Buchwalter and Paight I was riding into town to get my stuff out of the desk in Kelso's office. I'm to show at their camp across the pass an hour before sunup. As to why I'm tipping you off on this, I don't rightly know. Maybe it's because I hate the stink of sheep in a cattle country."

Bishop was silent a long moment, his glance fully on Streak, judging the man, weighing the truth of his story. Then: "I appreciate this, Kincaid. The sheep won't come in. That crew will back down when they see how many men are ready to stop them."

Streak shrugged. "It's your look-out what you do. But you know what's coming now."

Cathy closed the door softly. She hadn't realized until now how rigidly she had been standing, how afraid she had been even to take a good deep breath. So this stranger was an informer! That one fact remained uppermost in her mind as she hastily went back to her room and put on her riding clothes, denims, cotton shirt, and jumper. She had been inclined to like the stranger until a minute ago. Now he became the target of her rebellious anger. She placed him along with her father as the betrayer of Pete Dallam, or better of Laura Dallam, the one who was to gain or lose by this momentous decision of Fencerail to make an attempt at bringing in the sheep. Gone now was her earlier, more tolerant mood. All she could think of was the injustice of her father dictating to a smaller outfit. But for her having overheard the stranger's talk, Fencerail might in the morning have walked into a deadly ambush.

Cathy didn't pull on her boots until she had climbed from her bedroom window and was a good fifty yards from the house. She went on tiptoe down the sloping knoll on which the house sat and across the narrow footbridge leading to the outbuildings and corrals. Her black, white-stockinged mare was in the big corral and came at her whistle. Putting a halter on the mare, she led the horse to the harness shack, where she got her saddle from the pole.

Less than a quarter hour after the closing door had shut out all but the mutter of Kincaid's and her father's voices, Cathy Bishop was in the saddle and riding out the trail that led to the upper valley. And less than a mile out on that trail, where it was flanked on both sides by steep climbing banks, a rider came down out of the near darkness to block her way.

Cathy gasped, so sudden was the rider's appearance. Then, as the mare came to a sudden nervous halt, Streak's even-toned—"We might as well go along together, ma'am."—cut the momentary stillness.

Cathy couldn't believe her hearing. Neither could she summon the strength to put spurs to the mare's flanks, so great had been her fright at the appearance of that shape looming so close ahead.

He put the gray nearer to her, close alongside, and went on: "Next time you listen at a door, keep your face out of the light."

Fury hit her then, a hot blind rage at the man's sureness. She lifted the long trailing ends of her reins and swung them, trying to cut him across

131

the face. His easy laugh sounded as he lifted a hand and caught the leather ribbons. She raked the mare's flanks with her blunt-rowelled spurs. But all that happened was that he pulled the mare down out of her lunge, and then held the animal by the bit chain.

"Why get so riled?" he drawled. "We're both doing the same thing, aren't we, selling out your old man?"

"You're loathsome! You're a . . . !" When she became lost for words, his low laugh sounded again. "Sidewinder, polecat, coyote," he suggested. "Any one of the three would do. Or did you mean to choose a prettier word?"

Calmness took her as abruptly as that first violent emotion. "Let go that bit," she said quietly. "She's got a tender mouth."

"And have you light out on me? Uhn-uh."

"I'll promise not to try to get away."

"That's better." Streak let go the bit chain and reined the gray around so that both animals faced the same way. "I like company on these night rides."

"I'm not going your way," she said, giving the first excuse that came to her. "I'm going over to . . . over to Jensen's. Their baby's been sick."

"You don't say. That's funny. I had it figured you were headed for the sheep camp to tell Buchwalter how I've sold him out." Before she could voice a protest, he went on, his voice more serious now: "You can save yourself the worry, ma'am. I'm with Fencerail, really with 'em. That story I gave your old man will just about wind this up, if he bites on it."

Cathy saw that the levity had gone out of his words. "I don't understand," she said.

"It's a long story. But it amounts to this. About five thousand sheep are coming in over the Arrowheads tomorrow while your father has every man on this side of the valley gathered to stop that small band in the pass. They're only a come-on."

"That can't be! There isn't a way in over the peaks from the north."

"Buchwalter thought the same, until tonight. But there is a way."

"How?"

"It'll keep," he told her. "You're coming along to see the whole thing."

"I am not!" she said hotly.

"But you are, ma'am. We're in too good a spot to have you spoil it. Your father's sent me back to keep an eye on Fencerail."

"I'm with Fencerail, too. Why do I have to go with you?"

"Any girl who will sell out her father is just as liable to sell us out. I'm keeping an eye on you until we've finished this thing."

There was a quiet scorn to his words that stung Cathy worse than the lash of a whip could have. Suddenly she felt shame, a hot tide of emotion that was strong with self-loathing as she realized what this man must think of her. The next instant her pride came back. "Why shouldn't I be on Fencerail's side? You are, yet you blame me for believing in the same things you do."

Streak nodded. "I do. If my father thought otherwise, I'd stick with him."

"You wouldn't if he had killed the man you were to marry, if he'd sent you away for a whole year to keep you from seeing that man."

"It's not my job to judge," Streak said patiently. "The only thing I've got to be sure of is that you don't spoil our chances. So you'll come along with me and stay until we're safe. Am I going to have to put a rope on you?"

"No," she said lifelessly, "I'll do as you say." There was no fight left in her and her pride was touched deeply. It somehow mattered that this man had a shabby opinion of her.

He silently motioned her on, and she put the mare up the trail ahead of him.

About two miles farther on they came to a belt of timber flanking the trail on either side. As they rode into the shadow of the trees, out of the moonlight, he came up even with her and announced: "We'll pull off here a minute and keep our ears open."

With the mare half a dozen paces from the trail,

134

deep in the trees, Cathy stopped, knowing he had called this halt to make sure no one had followed her away from the ranch. He came in alongside and for a brief interval there was no sound but the breathing of their ponies and once the *creak* of a latigo as he shifted his weight in the saddle.

All at once she could stand the silence no longer and said: "Kincaid, you're a hard judge."

"People call me Streak," was his reply. "As for the other, it doesn't matter."

"But it does. I want you to see my side of this . . . this . . ."

The abrupt lifting of his hand checked her words. She listened.

What she heard was the distant muffled sound of a horse trotting fast up the trail.

Chapter Eleven

Fred Kelso had played his hunches tonight and so far they were panning out. He didn't know where they were leading him, for certain things he had seen puzzled him exceedingly. But he was on the way to discovering something. That he knew definitely and without reservation. Because he was a man who tried to see what lay behind the obvious, his curiosity had brought him far tonight. And now he thanked his luck that he hadn't ridden straight in on the Crescent B, but had waited down there by the corrals instead.

The sheriff had followed Kincaid in to the layout. While waiting there, he had seen Cathy Bishop saddle her mare. Now he was following both Cathy and Kincaid away from the layout, wondering where they were going, sensing that he had stumbled onto something important.

Back there in Ledge, he had been one of the first to climb the hill toward the jail after the guns sounded. He had known instantly on hearing the shooting that Kincaid was being broken out of jail. Who could be responsible for the break Kelso had had no way of knowing until he saw Johnson's riderless paint horse trotting off into the darkness around the shoulder of the hill. The paint was easily recognizable. Kelso remembered when the Crescent B man had bought him.

It took something like an hour for the lawman to finish with his explanations and listen to the various conjectures made by his friends on who was responsible for Kincaid's daring escape. Then, knowing that Frank Bishop's crew had been involved in the fight at the jail, suspecting that Fencerail had, also, he turned in for what he hoped would he a good night's sleep. But he was too troubled to rest. Frank Bishop had always been his friend. To think that Frank would take the law into his own hands at a time like this sobered Fred Kelso more than anything had to the seriousness of this feud. The longer he held his eyes shut, trying to force sleep, the more wide awake he became. Finally he struck a match and looked at his watch to see that it was past midnight. It was then that he had his idea, and that idea was backed by an ingrained stubbornness and a righteous anger. Frank Bishop couldn't get away with this!

He pulled on pants, shirt and boots and, getting his cane, hobbled down the sleeping street to the feed barn. He saddled his roan and rode the alley to the upper end of town, heading out the east trail. Kelso didn't know that a rider was ahead of him until he smelled the dust kicked up by the other's pony. Tonight it was his business to be curious about late riders. He cut off the trail and rode hard in a fast circle, approaching the trail again a good four miles beyond the point he had left it. A ten-minute wait brought results. He stood behind a thicket of laurel close to the trail, and presently the moonlight showed him Kincaid mounted on a Fencerail gray riding past. He could have drawn his gun and taken the outlaw easily. Instead, he let Kincaid get well ahead and then followed. For he didn't understand two things: first, the fact that Kincaid was forking a Fencerail pony; second, his heading for the east slope.

Reconsidering the wisdom of trying to follow Kincaid, who he suspected might be doubly wary on his mysterious mission, Kelso played his hunch and again left the trail, this time riding point for the high-timbered hill that backed Bishop's headquarters. He knew the country well, knew that the trail swung a good bit south to serve Bishop's nearest neighbor. So when he tied the roan up in the timber above Crescent B's cook shack and hobbled down the slope with his cane, heading for the big corral, he judged he was in time to witness Kincaid's arrival—if the man was coming here.

Sure enough, Kincaid appeared a few minutes later. Only he took the bridge and rode up the knoll to the house instead of swinging off to the corral. That was proof to Kelso that the outlaw was here to see Frank Bishop. The lawman cursed his luck and wondered what the next move was. With this evidence of Bishop having once violated the law tonight, he knew he would be running a chance in going to the house himself to accuse the rancher of the jail break. Bishop could easily hold him here until he accomplished whatever purpose he'd had in recruiting Kincaid.

The lawman was stumped. First, there was that Fencerail horse Kincaid had been riding. Next, Kelso had all the evidence he needed that Bishop was a lawbreaker. But he was powerless to use it. Typically he loaded his pipe, shielded the match as he got it going, and sat down to think the matter through.

He was sitting there, the pleasing aroma of the tobacco tainting the clean cold air about him, when he saw someone furtively approaching the corral. It didn't take him long to recognize Cathy, nor to read her intentions. He didn't wait any longer but headed for his horse, hurrying for fear of losing her.

Cutting down out of the timber to the forking of the trails at the end of Crescent B's pasture lane, Kelso had to trust his nose to tell him the direction the girl had taken. He rode the town trail for nearly a quarter mile before making sure she hadn't gone that way. There was no dust in the air. He quickly recovered the lost distance and headed up the pass trail. Within two hundred yards the smell of dust told him she was ahead. So as Fred Kelso rode in on the timber that flanked the trail some three miles east of Bishop's layout, he was feeling a certain grim satisfaction in having ferreted out much information in his long night ride. He had proved that Frank Bishop had aided in the escape of a wanted man; this hurt more than he dared admit, for until now Kelso had considered Bishop a close friend and absolutely honest. He had halfway uncovered an intrigue that involved Kincaid in a double-cross of some obscure nature, for the outlaw had been riding a Fencerail pony. He had seen Cathy Bishop setting out on some furtive errand that he didn't doubt was involved in her hatred of her father. All this was adding up to something. What it was he had no way of knowing. But before many more hours had passed he would know a good deal more than he did.

A shape moving toward him out of the trees to his left snapped the thread of Kelso's thinking and flooded him with acute wariness. He had lifted his boots to rowel the roan when Streak rode into full sight. He vaguely made out the gun in Streak's hand and let his boots settle gently to the horse's flanks, spurs clear. For the moment he thought of reaching for his gun. An instant later he knew he didn't have a chance. He tightened the pressure on the reins. It was that simple. No word had been spoken; there had been nothing beyond Streak's sudden appearance, Kelso's careful calculation of his chances, his dismissing them, and his sudden halt.

"Now that's a help," Streak drawled. "I was thinking you'd need some persuading, Sheriff." He rocked his gun back over his right shoulder. "Get over here, Kelso. You've got company."

The roan had taken only three paces off the trail before Kelso saw Cathy Bishop. The shock of his surprise made him breathe his favorite expletive: "I'm damned!"

"So am I," Streak said behind him. "I thought she'd make a getaway while I was after you."

"I thought of it," Cathy said quietly. "But I've

140

decided to go along and see how you're doing it."

"Doin' what?" Kelso asked, more puzzled than angry.

"Fencerail's making their drive into the valley in the morning," Cathy told him dryly. "Kincaid has been kind enough to arrange for me to be there to see them do it. He's evidently going to invite you, too, Fred."

Kelso's head came around. "That's about it," Streak told him. Then, before the sheriff quite knew it had happened, Streak's hand came out and lifted his Colt from holster.

Kelso's anger mounted belatedly at feeling the weight of his weapon lifted from his thigh. "Say, what is this?" he demanded, swinging around fully on Streak.

"Just what she says. We're going on up to watch the woollies come in."

"Not me, brother!"

"Fred," Cathy put in before Streak could speak, "there are a lot of things I don't understand in this. Some you don't, too. Why not go with him and see for ourselves what's happening?"

"Confound it, Cathy, he's a wanted man! And I'm a sheriff, in case you don't remember."

"And in case you don't remember, Fred, there isn't much we can do about it."

Kelso glared at Streak a moment. At length, he shrugged. "Where to?" he said.

Streak's answer was smoothly drawled: "Fence-rail's sheep camp, Sheriff. You'd better lead the way. I'm not sure where it is."

An hour before dawn, three men started climbing the needle rock in the cañon high up in the Arrowheads. Bill Paight was one; with him were Slim Uhler, one of the Fencerail men who had helped him at the jail break, and Fred Sturgis, owner of the Cloverleaf, a small outfit on the valley's west slope. They had brought along ropes, a canteen of water, and a three-foot crowbar.

By the time it was fully light, they were nearly halfway up the spired rock, resting. Paight's shirt clung to his shoulders wetly, even though the air was cold. Ten feet below, Slim and Sturgis sat on a ledge; they were breathing hard and Slim's gaunt face was dirty and streaked with sweat.

"You could've found a better man than me for this, Bill," he complained.

Paight answered a sparse—"Yeah, I could."—and continued his inspection of what lay below.

They had picked themselves a job, or, rather, this Streak Mathiot had picked one for them. Down there, so straight down that Paight could have spit in the water, the knife-edged peninsula beyond the base of the needle rock halved the foaming stream into its separate channels. Upstream for nearly twenty rods the right bank of the creek gave out onto a wide-climbing stretch of talus. Part of that stretch the stream would fill when the right channel was blocked. But there would be room to spare, Paight saw, room enough for the sheep to move down that bank.

Paight's chief worry about this job was the danger of falling rock loosening the foundations of the unclimbable spire towering overhead, of ton upon ton of rock falling to crush him and his men. Streak had said it would be dangerous work and so it looked from here. But Paight gave only scant thought to the risk involved, so intent was he upon making sure of this, the weakest link to the plan Streak and Buchwalter had laid last night at the camp below. About twenty feet above him was a broad shoulder piled with loose rock, the actual base of the high needle rock itself. It was from there that Paight had decided to work. Now, impatient to begin the job, he called down —"Shake a leg, you two!"—and began the rest of the climb.

Another twenty minutes saw them heaving over the first big boulder, a slab of granite two feet thick. They levered it over the edge with the crowbar and stood watching as it whirled downward. It hit a projecting corner with a *boom!* like the blast of giant powder, and struck in midstream of the right channel, geysering water to a height of twenty feet.

Paight said—"Not bad."—and they went to work on the next.

For two hours the cañon echoed with the sharp explosions of falling rock, and below the right branch of the creek became littered with boulders whitening the racing water. One huge rock slab loosed a small avalanche low on the base, dumping it into the stream. Following that, the water foamed through a narrower channel only half its former width.

They heard the bawling of the sheep soon afterward and, looking along the upper cañon, saw the leaders of the band come into sight around a higher bend.

"We're late," Paight said, and tackled the base of the biggest boulder with the crowbar.

When it went over the edge and *boomed* down into the creek, they felt their footing tremble. But now Paight was working too feverishly to notice. Boulder after boulder toppled from the high shoulder, gathering smaller rocks in its plunge toward the creek.

Finally Slim said dryly: "You want to fill up the whole cut, Bill?"

Paight's breathing was coming in huge sobbing gasps; his shirt was torn and his face streaming sweat. He stepped over, and, as he looked down, a broad grin came to his face. "That'll do it," he said, and sat down to build a smoke.

Down there the right channel of the stream was blocked so tightly that only a bare trickle flowed along it. And the sheep were already climbing over the uncertain footing of the makeshift dam, heading down the comparatively dry streambed that would lead them to the west slope of the downward valley. The roar of the falls in the west channel had gained in volume. As far upcañon as a man could see the right bank was a flowing river of sheep.

"I'm so dog-gone tired I couldn't get back down if I had to," Slim declared.

"You don't have to, not now." Paight's look was serene, almost gloating. "We can sit right here and let things take care of themselves. Gents, we've licked Frank Bishop. From now on it's us that'll call the turn, not him."

Chapter Twelve

The saddle of the pass through the eastward hills was graying with the strengthening dawn when Frank Bishop, leading twenty-three east-slope riders, called a halt a mile above Elbow Lake. While his men closed in about him, Bishop let his glance run around the vast reach of the Association's hill lease. It was a sight to warm the heart of any cattleman, a five-by-three-mile span of lush grass country with the dog-leg mirror of Elbow Lake marking its downward limit.

145

Bunches of grazing cattle dotted the gentle incline. There was a chill and a freshness in the air, and the tall grass was silvered with dew. This was something to fight for, Bishop was telling himself, not only this isolated spot but the whole valley. It didn't matter who owned the land, how much or how little, just so long as it remained the cattleman's paradise it was.

Bishop's glance singled out Jensen, his closest neighbor, and he said soberly: "Ed, it isn't too late to pull out of this."

"Hell with that, Frank," Jensen's deep voice grated. "We don't let 'em in."

"Then we split up here. We have the whole saddle to cover. Better work in pairs. When we sight Fencerail, one man's to ride out and give warning. If they don't turn back, the other's to open up. Not to kill, but to warn 'em back. That'll call in the rest. And"—Bishop paused, making sure of their close attention—"pull your sights off Kincaid. He tipped us off on this."

"For how much, Frank?" asked one of the men, somewhat querulously.

"He didn't get a dollar for it," was Bishop's prompt answer. "I don't know why not, but he didn't. The only thing he had to say was that he can't abide the stink of sheep in a cattle country."

There was a murmur of approval at this last. Shortly they went on, fanning out in parts so that by the time they reached the timber below the saddle they had covered better than the width of the pass.

Two miles up from that meadow margin of the trees, Tom Buchwalter rode alongside Streak, their horses at an easy walk. Trailing out behind came the sheep, long, thick, twisting lines of them, flowing in and through the trees. An occasional herder could be seen now and then. Streak and Buchwalter rode idly, the former still wondering at the turn of circumstance that had made him a sheepman for the first and, he hoped, the only time in his life. Last night, at the camp with Buchwalter and Paight, he'd hesitated only briefly in choosing the side he should be on in this war. But now there was a small doubt insistently nagging him. His call on Frank Bishop had given him that. Bishop hadn't been the man of yesterday, the aloof and proud owner of a big brand. Something had happened to him since the ambush on the street. Last night he had been mild-mannered, almost humble.

Streak was half angered by the change in the man, for it raised his own doubts. Bishop had been really pleasant last night. And, contrarily, Streak's temper had been short with Cathy Bishop simply because she was betraying her father. He admitted that she had good reason for doing so. Still, some devilish urge in him had prompted his waylaying her there on the trail after seeing

147

that door letting off Crescent B's living room slit open to reveal her standing there, listening. The same impulse had made him brutally frank with her; he wished now he'd ridden herd on his tongue. At this moment he was heavily conscious of his own part in all this. He, and he alone, was responsible for Fencerail's having found a way of getting sheep onto the west slope without being stopped by the big ranchers. Buchwalter's scheme of bluffing Bishop by bringing this small band in today wouldn't have worked, he knew. So he had himself become the chief instrument for sheep invading an unspoiled and virgin cattle country. Thought of that sobered him.

The more he considered the rights and wrongs claimed by each side, the more confused Streak became. He had instinctively taken to Tom Buchwalter at first sight, regardless of the man being in the sheep business. To Paight, too, without reservation. Prenn and the others were good men. Fencerail had a just grudge to work off against Bishop for, according to their reasoning, Bishop was wholly responsible for the death of Pete Dallam if for nothing else. On the other hand, Streak's talk with Bishop last night had shown him a man far different from the aloof and cool-mannered autocrat he had glimpsed on Ledge's street after the ambush. He decided that the man's earlier manner had been only a shield behind which Bishop hid in fighting for the things he believed right and just. He had made a point of accusing Bishop of hiring the killing of Dallam and Sternes; the genuineness of the rancher's surprise and denial had impressed him. In that moment—all through their talk, in fact—Bishop had seemed sincere to the point of pleading, not proud but harassed and worried over the violence that had been unleashed, terribly hurt by his daughter's loss of faith in him.

Weighing the grievances of both sides, finding that both had rightful claims, Streak's anger was now settling on the one man responsible for all this trouble. Although he had never known Pete Dallam, he knew he would have been galled by the man's rash ways. But for Dallam, the west-slope outfits might have made some sort of a settlement with the big ranchers over the building of the Association dam. Dallam's contrariness had been impulsive, reckless in the extreme. Before this was over, the seeds of hate he had sown would sacrifice more lives. Worst of all were the deep-seated feelings Dallam had aroused in Catherine Bishop, feelings that remained strong enough to have started the breaking up of her family life. The scar of her devotion for Dallam would be with her always, unless something happened to show her how ill-founded they were, and Streak suspected that nothing the future might bring would change her idealistic memory of Dallam.

"Damned if I make head or tail of it!" he muttered, half aloud.

"What's that?" Buchwalter queried.

"Nothing," replied Streak. "I was just wondering what luck we're having."

Hardly had he spoken when Buchwalter reached across and laid a hand on his arm to say gently: "Careful! Something just moved over there." He nodded obliquely off to the left.

Looking that way, downward across a small open swale, Streak was in time to see a thinnish blue puff of powder smoke blossom from a thicket at the instant a rifle sent its sharp explosion ringing through the trees. A bullet ricocheted with a coarse *buzzing* from a boulder face a few feet away, and then a harsh querulous voice called from the thicket: "This is as far as you go, Buchwalter!"

"That'll be Jensen," the Fencerail man breathed. He lifted his voice to call back: "Who says so?"

"Me and enough others to make it stick!"

The voice was strongly hostile and sure. Buchwalter smiled meagerly. "Looks like they bit on it," he drawled to Streak.

"Tell 'em we'll think it over," Streak suggested.

"We've got to argue this some first," was Buchwalter's reply. He called again to Jensen: "We're goin' right on through! It's none of your affair what we do across the valley!"

The rifle spoke again, the bullet slapping the

150

dust so close to one side of Buchwalter's pony that the animal shied nervously, taking a mincing step away from the sound. "There's more where that one come from!" Jensen called. "Only that's the last one we waste!"

"We'll think it over, Jensen!" Buchwalter yelled across to him. He and Streak turned back. A little less than a quarter mile back up the slope, they met the leaders of the band coming through the trees. Behind, the aisles of the timber were filled with sheep kicking up a fog of dust that caught the early morning sunshine and laid sharp planes of light against the elongated shadows under the trees. Buchwalter reined his pony over to the nearest herder and spoke to him in Spanish. The Mexican called a summons that brought two more herders down, and presently the rams in the lead were turned, the band was halted, and the cook's tent pitched part way up a short incline away from the band.

Satisfied with the way his herders had handled the maneuver, Buchwalter came back to Streak. "That's all we have to do," he explained. "They won't warn us back over the pass for another hour or two. I've told Manuel to take his time when they do. By then, it'll be too late. You and I can go across and help with the drive if you feel like it."

"I ought to see Kelso first," Streak said. "Go on ahead. I'll pick up your sign and follow."

He watched as Buchwalter cut off through the trees, marking the direction the Fencerail man was taking. He didn't know this country any too well and the quickest way of getting to the cañon back in the Arrowheads was to follow Buchwalter's tracks. Once the foreman was out of sight, Streak put the gray up the slope toward the pass. Twenty minutes of riding took him across the broad saddle of the pass and down the farther side, into sight of the four tents of the main camp.

He found Fred Kelso and Catherine Bishop sitting beneath a big blue spruce behind the tents. Beyond, a carbine across his knees, the herder Buchwalter had left to guard the two was hunkered down with his back to a low rock outcrop. Kelso was idly whittling on a stick and looked up as Streak approached. His look was bleak and his hawkish face patterned a distasteful grimace when he saw who it was.

"You're beginnin' to carry the same stink as the others," he said flatly.

Strangely enough, Streak saw the same distaste reflected in the look Cathy Bishop gave him. Seeing that, he said: "What's got into you two? You ought to be glad we're doing a real job." He looked at the girl. "I thought this was what you wanted. Dallam's sheep are on their way in."

Cathy's glance refused to meet his. She had no answer for him, but Kelso did. "You've let us in for a hell of a lot of trouble, Kincaid."

"How did you think this could be done without trouble? You've had plenty anyway. This way, someone gets something out of it."

Kelso shrugged. "Forget it," he said. "You wouldn't understand."

Here again was a contradiction, the same sort of contradiction that had all morning been plaguing Streak. It wasn't only the sheriff's attitude that pressed home this fact, but the girl's, too. He had expected to find some animation in her; instead, she held the same unexplained resentment toward him as did the lawman.

"Just where do you stand, miss?" he asked querulously. "For or against us?"

Now Cathy's eyes lifted to meet his. "I don't know," she breathed. "I just wish I had never come back here."

Streak was suddenly impatient to be gone, to be alone and try again to unravel the stubborn knot of his thinking. "Sing out if you want anything," he said tonelessly. "You can ride back down around noon, as soon as it's safe to let you go." He wheeled the gray around, threw in his spurs, and left the camp at a high lope.

Back down the valley slope near the sheep, he purposely cut a wide circle, already feeling a strong distaste for even the sight of the dirty-gray, blatting animals. He picked up Buchwalter's sign without difficulty and began following it, trying now not to think but unable to keep from doing so. For the first time he caught himself wonder-ing if Fencerail was going too far in this move against Bishop. Would the coming of sheep to this valley in the end mean what it had meant on every other range Streak knew where sheep had been allowed to gain a foothold? Would it mean the end of cattle raising in the valley? That was a sobering and awful possibility. And when it happened, wouldn't the name of Mathiot become a hated one? There was only one answer and Streak flinched as he realized it.

He rode warily for better than two miles, not wanting to meet any of the east-slope men. Coming down on the vast hill meadow, Buchwalter's sign swung right and kept to the timber. In the before dawn hours, as he rode the meadow with Kelso and the girl, Streak hadn't quite realized the enormity of this hill graze. Now, scanning it in the full light of day, he breathed a low whistle of surprise. Seldom had he seen such good grass and never so much of it in one spot. Regardless of the drought that was threatening the lower valley, the grass here was green and high and lush. There were countless bunches of sleek fat cattle grazing the downward distance. Below, the crooked mirror of Elbow Lake reflected the brightness of the early morning sun. Far downward, blue-hazed in this beginning of another hot cloudless day, was the long north and south channel of the timbered valley. Beyond that stretched the tawny monotony of Dry Reach, table-flat to the westward horizon.

Streak soberly admitted a real let-down at seeing this picture before him. He felt a disquieting shame at realizing that he alone might be selling out this rich cattle country to sheep. But then, because he had made his decision and intended to stick to it, he closed his mind definitely to this turn of thought and went on along Buchwalter's sign.

Two hours later he was well up a strange cañon far to the north and west, judging it to be several miles east of the one he and Paight had traveled the night before to reach the camp at the needle rock. Buchwalter's sign had led him in a wide arc through the tangle of foothills in the northeast quadrant of the valley. He had distantly glimpsed Ledge, but only twice had he come within sight of a human habitation.

The first of these was a big layout lying downward across a big fenced pasture. Later Streak was to know that this was Jensen's place. The second, at almost the northern limit of the valley proper, was much smaller, an unpainted frame house with a log barn, one small slab shed, and an untidy corral. He was close enough to make out through the trees a legend carved in the key log of the weathered barn's roof: *M.L. Prenn*, A.D. *1884*.

This cañon Streak now traveled had been wide at the mouth and had held its generous span for some three gradually climbing miles. But now, as that other cañon had last night, it was narrowing down to the bare width of a streambed. At that narrowing, Streak abruptly knew where he was, for there was but a feeble trickle of water running along the rocky bottom, and out from the main channel stood pools of water not yet seeped into the ground and the moss that coated the rocks hadn't yet dried. This, then, was the cañon that had been blocked and down which the sheep were being driven.

Streak had long ago lost the sign of Buchwalter's pony over the rocky going and had stopped trying to spot it, knowing there was only one way up the cañon. He wouldn't have noticed the tracks leading out of the drying streambed had it not been for a minor accident. As he was rolling a smoke, reins looped over left arm, the gray slipped on a moss-covered rock and threw him urgently sideways in the saddle. The motion made him lose his hold on the string of the Durham sack and he dropped it. It fell in the black mud of what had only an hour or so ago been the right bank of the stream.

Swearing mildly, Streak swung aground to retrieve the tobacco sack, standing on the narrow grassy bank between the rocky bed of the stream and the steep talus slope that footed the precipitous left wall. As he stooped to retrieve the tobacco, he noticed the fresh imprint of a horse's hoof in the grass. He went to his knees to study it more closely, a sudden constriction of excitement in his chest. The hoof mark was clear and was definitely not that of Buchwalter's horse. The Fencerail animal had been newly shod, but this print showed a worn shoe and, when lined with a second track close by, was definitely splayed.

As he straightened and dropped the gray's reins, Streak was struck by the realization that he hadn't once today given Ed Church a thought. So engrossed had he been in the job at hand that he had momentarily forgotten his real reason for being here. And now he had come across the sign of a splay-foot horse. Ed had ridden Snyder's splay-foot out of Agua Verde better than two weeks ago. Yesterday morning a man on a splay-foot had made an attempt against Frank Bishop's life. Of course there were many horses with toed-out hoofs, but mightn't this track have been made by the horse Ed had ridden? And wasn't it possible that yesterday's bushwhacker had been forking the same animal?

Streak's glance followed the line of the tracks and he saw a break in the sheer wall behind a thicket of white oak. It was nothing but a narrow cleft, a fissure where the wall had split open narrowly, and he barely noticed it. Two paces brought him to another track. He was within a stride of the edge of the thicket now and he scanned the ground to either side of it. More tracks, another set coming from a different direction! Walking over to them, he was further puzzled to find that they had been made by Buchwalter's pony, whose sign he now knew well. There were two sets of these last prints, coming and going out of the thicket. Buchwalter had been here and ridden away.

Momentarily there was a strong wariness in Streak Mathiot. Then that eased; he knew that Buchwalter must have spotted the sign of the splay-foot and been curious enough about it to investigate. That fact alone, the fact of Buchwalter's having been here ahead of him and ridden away, put down Streak's wariness. But his curiosity was still strong and he walked back to the line of the first tracks that pointed toward the thicket. He pushed into the bushes, following it, noticing several broken branches where the horse had pushed through.

Once clear of the thicket at its back margin, he stood only about ten feet from the rock cleft that seemed to go back into the wall to form a narrow box-end pocket. Still, the splay-foot's sign had scarred the loose rocky soil of the talus slope that led up to the narrow slit in the wall. *Now why would anyone be heading in there?* Streak mused.

Regardless of the sign of Buchwalter's pony joining the splay-foot's up the slope, Streak experienced a spine-tingling feeling as he climbed.

It was strong enough to make him brush his low-hung holster with the flat of his hand as he stopped in front of the two-foot-wide crevice. He entered the narrow notch to find it not much wider than his shoulders. It climbed steeply for several strides, then leveled out. Three paces brought him to the point he had thought to be the end of the pocket. But there he came to a right-angle turning, and this deeper fissure seemed to be like the first, dead-ending against the sheer limestone wall a few feet ahead.

He went along it, the sunlight suddenly shut out and the sound of his boots sending up cavernous echoes. The air here was chill and damp, a contrast to the sultry heat Streak had been riding in for the past hours. And now his wariness was keen again, despite the knowledge that Buchwalter had been here before him. He walked with his hand on the butt of the Colt, and, because of the deep echoes announcing his presence, he instinctively tried to move quietly.

Reaching the end of this second leg of the crevice, he came to a second turning, one that swung inward again, following a line almost at right angles to the main wall. Rounding that abrupt bend, pausing there, he saw the narrowed notch stretching on for another twenty feet or so. But beyond that he could glimpse a narrow wedge of sunlit ground. He edged on until, two paces from the notch mouth, he was looking across a grassy pocket to another sheer wall that shut it in. *Good hide-out,* he breathed to himself as he went on, wishing he were to find Tom Buchwalter waiting for him. He came to the end of the slotted passageway and stood there, trying to understand what he saw. The pocket was less than a half acre in area, lushly grassed, greenest at a spot halfway across and to the right where a spring evidently seeped from the ground. On all sides the walls rose sheerly, straight up for a hundred feet or more, as though some giant hand had dug this deep well in the solid bastion of the high cañon shoulder. But Streak's glance took this in only briefly, settling longest on what lay to his left.

Over there a cave mouth holed the wall. It was a little raised from the floor of the pocket. In front of it a smoldering fire sent a blue finger of smoke straight upward into the still air. Beyond the fire a grulla horse stood down-headed, hipshot, grazing. The splay-foot Ed Church had ridden out of Agua Verde had been a grulla. Streak stood a little straighter at sight of the animal, some strong instinct telling him he was on the threshold of an important discovery. Then that inexplicable wariness flooded through him again and made him take a backward step to put himself out of sight of the cave opening. He had to have time to think, to discover why Buchwalter had also seen this and ridden away. Suddenly from behind him came a furtive whisper of sound. Streak threw himself into a headlong turning lunge, lifting the heavy Colt clear of holster. A blow caught him on the back of the head, put a blinding blaze of light before his eyes. He couldn't stiffen his knees to hold up his weight. They all at once buckled and he was falling. Before he hit the ground, unconsciousness had taken him.

Chapter Thirteen

It was a little after 11:00 when two quick-timed shots, then another single one sounded up through the timber below the pass where the east-slope ranchers were waiting.

"That'll be Ralph," said Ed Jensen. Drawing his .45, he answered the signal with one like it.

Four men had been stationed about a quarter mile above to keep a watch on the sheep band. The others, fourteen of them, were waiting with Jensen and Bishop; what they waited for they had no way of knowing, for the halting of the sheep and the lack of any fight from Buchwalter's men still puzzled them and made them undecided what to do next. Shortly they could hear the quick hoof falls of a fast-running horse coming in on them. Then they saw the Jensen rider down through the trees. He was using spurs and rein ends to keep his lathered pony in its tired run. Both man and horse were breathing hard when they came up.

The rider blurted out a frenzied rush of gasped words: "They're comin' in! Thousands of the damned things! Down off . . . off the Arrowheads! All the water's out of the right fork of the Squaw and they're . . ."

"Get your breath and start at the beginning, Ralph," Frank Bishop cut in.

When the Jensen man resumed his talk, he was more coherent. He had been sent in to Ledge before dawn to tell Fred Kelso what was happening at the pass. The sheriff couldn't be found in town. Various guesses were made on where he could be. In the light of last night's jail break, it seemed a good bet that he was either at Crescent B or Fencerail, since the whole town knew by now that it was those two outfits that had fought on the hill by the jail and that one of them had broken Kincaid out. Knowing that Kelso wasn't at Crescent B, Jensen's rider decided to head for Fencerail to try to find him. He'd been warned by a rifle shot to keep his distance as he rode in on Dallam's barn lot. He'd had enough nerve to keep from running and had shouted his queries to the hidden marksman. No, Kelso hadn't been there, and to hell with him, had been the answer. So Ralph had cut straight across the upper valley, riding point for the pass. That had been all of two hours ago.

"It was pretty rough goin' through them hills and I stopped to give my nag time to catch his wind," Ralph went on. "Sittin' there, I thought I heard sheep bawlin'. I thinks . . . 'What the hell, did the boys let 'em over the pass after all?' Then I knew that couldn't be, because the blattin' come from over east, from up toward the peaks. I listened again and couldn't hear nothin'. But it was so late I knew I wouldn't be doin' no good here, so I figured I'd take me a ride, just to see what in blazes was goin' on. I cut over and headed up that right fork of the Squaw just above Prenn's layout. It was dry as a bone! That tipped me off that somethin' was up. I was up six, seven miles when I began hearin' that blasted sound again. It was a lot louder. Then pretty soon I saw 'em above. The bed of that cut was packed wall to wall with sheep. So I hightailed back down before anyone seen me. That's all. Except, dammit, how'd they get there?"

As he finished, not a man had a word to say, so mute were they held by bafflement and rage. Finally it was Jensen's deep voice that boomed out: "Kincaid! It was him! Strung us along with that story he give you, Frank! Tolled us up here out o' the way! The mangy double-crossin' son-of-a-bitch!" With further invective, he added to his indictment of Streak.

"And I could've put a slug in him when him

and Buchwalter come ridin' into that meadow at sunup," Sid Riggs cut in ruefully.

Frank Bishop listened with a feeling of constriction tightening his chest. He had become the leader in this fight against Fencerail. These men had trusted in his judgment, looked to him to furnish the brain work to save their range for cattle. Now, with stunning swiftness and cunning, Fencerail had in one brief morning accomplished something these men had supposed could never happen. Sheep were on the west slope, "thousands of the damned things" as Jensen's rider had put it. And here, helpless and their strength bunched, were the men who had sworn to defend the last square foot of the valley with their lives, if need be, to keep sheep out.

All at once the tension drained out of Bishop and he was calm, almost offhand as he said: "We'd better go on home. When we find Kelso, we'll see what we can do."

"Home, hell!" his foreman exploded. "We can go across there and put the torch to every layout on the slope, burn 'em out, cut their fences, set fire to their feed stacks!"

"No, Riggs," Bishop said before anyone else could approve the suggestion. "We've stayed with the law in this so far. We stick with it now."

"What law?" growled Jensen. "Where is it?"

"Maybe we ought to be thinking of exactly that," Bishop said. "I have the feeling that Fred

Kelso may be in trouble." He saw several of the men frown, led away from the main subject by his suggestion. He went on with it, hoping in this way to sway the rest from violence: "He wasn't at Fencerail. He wasn't in town. We know he hasn't been near any of our places. Then where is he?"

"If I ain't mistaken, we're about to find out."

Everyone looked at Jensen, wondering at his strange words. They saw him looking up the slope through the trees. Following his glance, they took in Kelso, his cane slung from a thong on the saddle cantle, riding down toward them. Close behind him came Cathy Bishop on her white-stockinged black.

Frank Bishop was the least surprised of them all at his daughter being here. The past two weeks since her return had hardened him to the unexpected where she was concerned. But as the others stood wordlessly in their amazement at the appearance of the sheriff, Bishop had his moment of deep regret, of near humiliation at knowing how far apart he and Cathy had drifted.

Kelso drew rein close by. After a moment in which no one spoke, he growled: "Well, ain't any of you goin' to ask where we been?"

It was Riggs who finally said: "I hope it ain't like it looks. You weren't in on this double-cross, too, were you, Sheriff?"

Kelso gave the man a withering look before his glance settled on Bishop. "You're licked, Frank," he intoned. "Licked good and proper. There's enough sheep comin' down the Squaw to take over the whole west slope. Furthermore, they've done it legally. You can't go to court with it. The only slip-up they made was corrallin' me and Cathy and holdin' us up here while they did it. Kincaid's the man responsible for that. So Fencerail's in the clear." As he spoke, he had been filling his pipe. Now he scratched a match on the seat of his denims and, having got the pipe going, flicked the match away.

"Why are you telling me all this?" Bishop asked.

"Just so you'll know how you stand," was Kelso's level rejoinder. "Mind, I ain't sayin' I like the way it's turned out. But I'm danged good and fed up over the hell that's busted loose here! ¿*Sabe?* From now on things quiet down or I fill me out some warrants and get to work. It won't be so good if one of them warrants has your name on . . ."

Sid Riggs let out a yell and ran in toward the sheriff. Kelso at first misunderstood his move and started to reach for his gun. Then he saw Riggs swing aside and begin tramping on the bed of pine needles close to where his horse stood. A blue pencil of smoke was lifting from the spot, and Kelso saw that his match, carelessly thrown away, had ignited the tinder-dry matting that blanketed the ground under the nearest tree.

Having stomped out the fire, Riggs scowled up at the lawman. "This is all we need to wind things up," he drawled. "A good blaze. The whole valley'd be gone then instead of just the west half."

"I forgot how dry it was," Kelso said simply. He glanced again at Bishop. "Just to keep things straight, I'll tell you right now that I'm splittin' the reward on Kincaid with any man who brings him in. You ain't goin' to say later I played any favors."

Bishop gave a slow nod, seeming scarcely to have heard the lawman in the intentness of the regard he put on his daughter. "And you, Cathy?" he queried. "Where have you been?"

"With me," Kelso was quick to put in, trying to save the girl. "Now don't ask how she got there. This ain't any time to bring up family squabbles. The whole lot of you better get on home and thank your lucky stars you didn't lose eight or ten men by hellin' across there to the Squaw to stop that drive."

"Who says we still ain't goin' over there?" Riggs bridled.

"I do!" exploded Kelso. "I wasn't just talkin' through my hat about fillin' in some warrants! The first east-slope man that sets foot on the other side of the valley will be liable to arrest for trespassin'. And the lockup's big enough to hold a lot of you."

It was strange and awesome for these men to see the turn things were taking. Fred Kelso was a cattleman, turned sheriff because of a leg lost in a fall from a horse. It had never occurred to the cattle owners that he would one day be siding against them. Most of them thought he was doing exactly that now. The truth, however, was that Kelso was using the only means that occurred to him of preventing further bloodshed. Bishop could see that. So could Jensen, and this ordinarily hard-headed man was sobered now by the realization that things had reached a deadly serious stage when Kelso would risk losing this many friends to keep the peace.

"I reckon we needed this, Fred," Jensen admitted quietly. "Thanks for haulin' us up short before we stuck our necks out too far." He caught Kelso's grateful glance, then let his own run the circle of faces, singling out his men. "We go back down," he told them. "As soon as we cool off a little, we can begin figurin' what we're to do."

Riggs, however, could see only what lay on the surface, Kelso's seeming betrayal. "To the devil with that," he said. "The least we can do is . . ."

"Riggs," Bishop said sharply, "Jensen's right. We go back down." He nodded to his daughter. "Coming?" he asked.

In that moment, Cathy Bishop felt the stir of an old, near-dead feeling. Forgotten now was the bitter animosity that had been in her of late. She knew that her father would ask no questions, make no condemnation of her. All at once she wanted to go to him, to explain everything, to ask his help and in turn try to help him in this ordeal. Now that the thing she had hoped for had been accomplished, now that her father was humbled and could no longer dictate the affairs of this range, she felt sorry for him, wanting a return of that lost companionship and love. Somehow she felt she wasn't worthy of his love any more. Only time would heal the wound of their differences, if anything could. But from now on she was going to try to make up for the things she had taken from him. She said—"Yes, Dad, I'm coming."—and rode across to him with a smile that put mute wonder and gratitude in his eyes. Her heart was almost too full to take in the welcome he gave her.

Chapter Fourteen

Sid Riggs slammed the door as he left Crescent B's living room. Clamping on his Stetson with a vicious pull, he came off the portal's one step and started down across the yard to the bridge, his stride choppy and quick. Clouds banking the sky obscured even a hint of starlight, and twice he stumbled as the unevenness of the ground tricked him. Both times he cursed savagely; the last half hour with Frank Bishop had been a strain on his unstable temper and Riggs was mad clear through.

He crossed the bridge and swung left, toward the bunkhouse light. Suddenly the nervous stomp of a standing horse struck against the stillness. Immediately wary, Riggs halted and turned to face the sound. Hardly was he set when a gun's rosy flame stab patterned the darkness a bare thirty feet away. The explosion racketed back from the nearby outbuildings in a double thunderclap. Riggs clawed at his gun as a gray blob of shadow came at him out of the obscurity. It was a horse, and, as the *thud* of the animal's quick-striking hoofs warned him to step aside, he made out the sound of another pony heading out of the trail at a hard run. The gray came so close to running him down that Riggs reached out defensively and caught a hold on one of the animal's horn-looped reins. Gun in hand, he jerked the animal's head around until he was at a stand. Then he saw the low, shadowed bulk in the saddle. Reaching out, he felt gingerly there, identifying a man's shoulders, arms, and head. Down the trail, the fleeing rider had gone nearly out of sound reach.

Riggs lit a match, concealing its flare in his cupped hand, and permitted himself a very brief inspection of the body roped to the horse's saddle. Immediately he recognized who it was from the band of gray hair streaking the man's dark head, and breathed: "Kincaid!" A moment later he sensed that the house door had opened, and looked off there as Frank Bishop called down: "Riggs! What was that?"

A streak of deviltry was in Riggs tonight, that and the hard words just passed between him and his employer made him answer quickly: "Thought I spotted a coyote prowlin' around the chicken pen down here. Missed him."

He didn't take a full breath until the door had closed on Bishop. Then, excitement strong in him, he started for the bunkhouse, leading the gray. He smiled tightly when he saw that the light there had been put out. The shot was responsible for that.

As he came in on the well cupola, between bunkhouse and cook shack, a curt voice called from behind it: "Sing out, you!"

It was Luke Black who called. Well knowing the man's impulsiveness and his skill with a gun, Riggs replied hastily: "It's me, Luke. Give me a hand here, will you?"

The cowpuncher came over. "Who fogged out the road there a minute ago?" he demanded. Then, close enough to see the gray's burden, he let out an explosive imprecation.

"You bring him in, Luke," Riggs ordered. "Give me a little time to get things set. Who's here?"

Black, who was one of Crescent B's most recent

recruits, knew immediately what was in Riggs's mind. "Baker and Matt hit for town while you were at the house," he answered. "Phil's here. So's Shorty." Thus briefly, he informed Riggs of the whereabouts of the only four old hands who had approved of Bishop's action today in backing out of the fight.

Riggs approached the bunkhouse. "Shorty! Phil!" he called. "Shake a leg. Don't show a light."

Shortly half a dozen men stood grouped around him before the darkened bunkhouse doorway. They had come up out of the shadows from all directions. Riggs's glance singled out the two questionable hands and he told them: "I spooked a jasper hidin' in the willows over there below the bridge. He beat it when I called to him. Phil, saddle up and make a swing out around the pasture. Shorty, work out the trail a ways and keep your eyes open. Stay out there till I send word for you to come in."

"What good'll that do on a night like this?" Phil Harris said querulously. "It's black as the inside of my hat out there."

"You want to stick here and have 'em pick us off like a bunch of sittin' birds?" Riggs asked curtly. "Suppose they're set to make a try at us tonight?"

"They got enough to do without botherin' about us," Harris grumbled.

"Then who was that hidin' down there by the bridge?"

This reminder evidently carried its intended weight, for Harris and Shorty walked off toward the big corral beyond the barn.

As soon as they were out of hearing, Riggs said, low-voiced, to one of the others: "Sam, get over and help Luke. The rest of you inside." The way he spoke made them move quickly.

In less than a minute, they were all in the bunk-house, and Riggs was closing the door. Luke and Sam had stretched Streak out on one of the bunks lining the end wall. As he bolted the door, Riggs asked: "Is he alive?"

"He's breathin'," Sam answered.

"Good. A couple of you hang blankets over the windows before we strike a light."

As the sound of men moving around the pitch-dark room began, someone asked: "What's comin' off here, Sid?"

"Plenty," Riggs told him. "You'll hear it as soon as we have a light."

When the wall-hung lamp finally shed its orange glow over the big room, Riggs was standing with his back to the door. He blinked against the glare a moment, then glanced to the bunk in which Streak lay. The rest looked over there, one or two going bug-eyed in wonder as they saw who it was.

"We've got Kincaid and he's alive," Riggs told them. "That gives us a chance. I'll tell you about it in a minute. First, see what you think about this.

We're through here, through tonight. Me along with the rest of you. Bishop laid down his law and I wouldn't take it." He drew a piece of paper from his pocket. "Here's a note to Adams at the bank. He's to pay us off tonight. I told Bishop we didn't want any more of his grub or his lousy beds. He said we could stay on if we got the chips off our shoulders and let Fencerail alone. Anyone with a hankerin' for that better speak out now." He paused.

"Hell with that," Black said. "I get me my pay and leave this blasted country."

"Me, too," said another.

"Same here."

When the comment had subsided, Riggs went on: "Someone was waitin' there by the bridge with Kincaid. He was the one that threw the shot, just to make sure Kincaid's horse was spotted. Which means Buchwalter's finished with Kincaid and is throwin' him to the wolves. He likely thought we could save him some trouble by puttin' a bullet through this owlhooter ourselves. Instead, we're goin' to use Kincaid."

"How?" Black asked.

"First, Kelso said he'd split the reward with anyone that brought Kincaid in, didn't he? So there's five hundred we divide among us. But that ain't what I'm gettin' at. How bad do you boys want to tie into Fencerail before we hightail?"

Charley Riling, who seldom spoke unless

spoken to, drawled: "So bad I can taste it, Sid. It wasn't Paight's fault he didn't bust my jaw the other night."

Riggs thought of something. "Luke, run on up to the house and get Pinto down here. He hated Dallam like poison. He'd never forgive us if he wasn't in on this."

When Black had gone after Pinto Sanders, the cook, Riggs went on: "We ride to town, turn Kincaid in, and get our pay. Then we head for the west slope to see if we can stir up some trouble."

"Them sheep buzzards'll be lookin' for a play like that tonight," Sam reminded.

Riggs nodded. "They will. Only we'll go around 'em. They can't be everywhere at once. And we're goin' to make Kincaid tell us what trails they're watchin'." He started toward the bunk where Streak lay, adding: "Get a bucket of water, somebody."

By the time Black came in with Pinto Sanders, they had emptied a bucket of water into Streak's face with no noticeable result and were about to try and force some whiskey down his throat. Riggs, putting the bottle to Streak's mouth, stepped away from the bunk as the door slammed, and looked at Pinto.

"Did you tell him, Luke?" he queried.

Black shook his head.

"Pinto, this is that gent Kincaid we were tellin' you about . . . the one who sold out the boss today."

The change that came over the cook would have startled anyone not acquainted with a certain item of local interest that had happened some four years ago. Pinto, a stranger to the valley, had sat in on a friendly game of draw poker his first night in Ledge. Gambling and drink had always been his weaknesses, and that night both had conspired to empty his pockets of a sizable stake he had intended using to buy a small brand that was being auctioned off by the bank next day. He'd taken too much whiskey and crowded his luck too far with a man toward whom he'd taken an instant dislike. That man had been Pete Dallam. In the final hand of the game, Pinto had turned reckless. Until then he had been a small winner in the game. But, his brain fogged with alcohol and his confidence supreme, he had tossed every dollar of his money to the table's center and challenged Dallam to match the amount and make the deal. Dallam had won fairly. Everyone but Pinto knew that. Pinto had never been sure that he wasn't tricked. Too broke the next day even to buy whiskey enough to help him through a bad hangover, he had taken the first job that came along, the cook's job at Crescent B. Since that day he had never tasted whiskey. And since that night of seeing his meager savings go into another man's pocket he had become a silent, taciturn man. Only one subject could prod him to anything but the mildest response. That one subject was Pete Dallam. Since Dallam's death all the vitriolic intensity of his hate had been directed at anything bearing any relation to Fencerail. Now, at Riggs's words, his narrow and ordinarily mild-looking face took on a look that was ugly, vicious. He said nothing, but looked down suddenly at Streak with a stare that was bright with hate.

"We're tryin' to bring him to, make him talk," Riggs added, and turned back to the bunk.

He forced some whiskey into Streak's mouth. Suddenly Pinto stepped in and struck Streak a hard blow across the face. The blow was so hard that it rocked the unconscious man's head around.

Streak's eyes came open and he stared at them dully. Pinto stepped away. For a moment no one spoke. In that brief interval Streak tried to steady his reeling senses and get ready for what he knew was coming. He had been pretending these last minutes, for he had regained consciousness as he was roughly pulled from the saddle of the gray out in the yard. At first he had been groggy, nauseated, and so weak that he doubted he could move under the terrific throbbing pain that seemed about to burst his skull apart with each motion of his body as he was carried in here. He hadn't known where he was. But as Riggs spoke in the darkened room, he gradually arrived at the truth. There was nothing Streak could remember of those long day hours but a brief return to consciousness there in the grassy cañon pocket by the cave. He had been too weak to move then and had seen only the shadow of his captor as the man knelt behind him and hit him again to knock him unconscious for the second time. He supposed that a gun had delivered both blows; it had been, at any rate, a hard and weighty object, for he could still remember that bone-crushing sensation so like a time, long ago, when he had had a bottle broken over his head. Now, looking up into the line of faces beside the bunk, he was trying to think of a way out of this. The bucket of icy well water dumped in his face a minute ago had sent a shock clear through his body. He had stood it without flinching, without betraying his return to consciousness. It had helped him think, cleared his head a little more. He had refused to swallow the raw liquor Riggs forced between his lips. But for Pinto's quick reading of the truth, that he was shamming, he might have gained more time. But the cook's blow had come too suddenly, with too much shock, for him to pretend any longer.

Riggs ended the momentary silence by saying: "Nice goin', Pinto. So he was playin' 'possum, eh?" Staring down at Streak, his glance held a mute warning. Suddenly Riggs reached out and, taking a hold on Streak's sodden shirt front, hauled him to a sitting position. "So they used you all they could and tossed you to the wolves," he drawled. "Now you'll do your stuff for us. Just take your time rememberin'. We want to know what trails Buchwalter's crew is watchin' tonight. We're goin' across to pay that bunch a little visit."

Streak momentarily hung his head, hoping that the dizziness hitting him would pass. It did, shortly, and he looked up again at Riggs. "I haven't known a thing since around noon. If Buchwalter's closed the trails, I . . ."

This time it was Riggs who hit viciously hard, his hand fisted. The blow caught Streak fully on the mouth and knocked him back so that his head *thumped* against the board wall. Then, catching Streak by the shirt again, Riggs hauled him to his feet. With his free hand he cuffed him twice across his bleeding lips. Again his drawl came smoothly, tauntingly: "In case you're interested, friend," he said, "Kelso ain't particular on whether you're brought in dead or alive. We got all night for this."

Streak shook his head to clear it, wiping at his bloody lips with the back of his hand. Without Riggs's tight hold on his vest and shirt, he couldn't have stood alone. He knew that Riggs meant to do exactly as he said, either beat the wanted information out of him or kill him trying to. Glancing beyond the man at the others, Streak caught the same cold viciousness written on all their faces. These were the men Bishop had hired to make his fight for him; they were men who

179

knew death, whose guns had probably dealt it on occasion, and this small matter of making a man talk would be child's play to them.

He would have to make up a story to give them. But he needed time to think one out. "I'll take some of that whiskey now," he said. "Sure I know where Buchwalter's got his guards." He put a whine in his voice, knowing that it would fit with their opinion of him. "But how about a drink first?"

Riggs loosed his hold and Streak sat down on the bunk's wet blankets. It was Pinto who proffered the half empty pint bottle, whose glance clung to him longest and with no pity. Streak knew that he would have to give them a story that sounded logical, that he didn't dare elaborate on it too much, for the cook's questioning eyes bored into him as though ready to detect the slightest untruth in what he was about to say.

The shock of the whiskey hitting his stomach revived him, wiped out the dizziness, even dulled the ache in his head and eased the puffed, swollen feeling of his lips. He took a second long pull at the bottle and handed it back to Pinto. Only then did he tell them: "They're holding the sheep in that big meadow below Prenn's tonight until they've worked 'em all down the cañon." This much was the truth, at least so far as Streak knew. But from here on he would have to make up a story. "Buchwalter's using most of his men to cover the east trail out of Prenn's. He said something about putting the rest on one that went south."

Riggs nodded. "That's the town road."

"He's got men there," Streak went on. "A few are helping his *Mejicanos* push the sheep down the cañon. That's about all I know except that Buchwalter told his bunch to shoot for keeps if they burned any powder."

Sid Riggs looked at Sanders. "Anything more you want out of him, Pinto?" he asked.

"What about the upper meadow, north and west?" Pinto asked Streak. "Is that open?"

"As far as I know."

Pinto was evidently satisfied. His glance left Streak for the first time and he turned away. "Let's ride," he said tonelessly.

"Any ideas?" Riggs spoke to the cook's back.

They all waited for Pinto's reply. Because of his known hatred for Fencerail, he had now become their temporary leader, with even Riggs relinquishing authority to him.

"A few," Pinto said. "I'll think 'em over on the way in. Luke said you're all quittin'. That means it don't matter how far you go in this, don't it?"

"Not one damn' whit," Riggs said flatly. "All we want is time enough to turn this noose bait over to Kelso and collect our pay. From then on, anything goes."

Chapter Fifteen

Fred Kelso went to bed at dusk, weary to the bone from having been up all last night and from today's long ride down from the pass. His brain was feeling that same deep fatigue, for he had never in his life known the torment of such confusing indecision as the day had brought. Last night, knowing that Bishop had been involved in the jail break, Kelso would have gloried in seeing the man take a licking such as the day had brought. He should have been relieved at Buchwalter's having found a way of bringing his sheep into the country without violating any law or endangering more lives, for it meant a secure future for Laura Dallam, and Kelso sincerely liked the girl. Still, before sleep brought its welcome relief, he was constantly nagged by the feeling that a great injustice had been done that day, that this country would never again be the same.

The pounding of a heavy fist on the front door of his small slab house some four hours after he had hit the blankets brought Kelso slowly awake to that same bewildering torment.

"Hold your horses!" he bawled as the knocking came again, and took his time about pulling on pants and shirt. He was still half asleep as he limped to the door and opened it on Sid Riggs, but what Riggs had to say jerked him fully awake.

"Kincaid . . . ," he echoed. "You mean you got him?"

"Right out here." Riggs nodded to the group of riders who made a blob of dark shadow against the faint glow of the store lights farther down street.

By the time Kelso was at the jail, unlocking the cell adjoining the one with the damaged window and seeing his prisoner of yesterday once again behind the bars, he knew that something ominous lay beneath the surface of Riggs's casualness. The man's story was too blithe, too cocksure. Kincaid, so Riggs said, had showed up at Crescent B about two hours ago. The outlaw had been bleeding about the head and face and was unconscious, roped onto his horse. Someone had brought him as far as the bridge, fired a shot to spook his horse on in to the layout, and ridden away again before he could be seen. The rider had been a Fencerail man, of course.

"But why didn't Buchwalter bring him in to me if he was through with him?" Kelso asked. "He could use that reward the same as you."

Riggs merely shrugged the question aside. "No tellin'," he said. "Buchwalter's thinkin' ain't always as straight as it ought to be." He held out his hand. "Where's the money?"

"What money?" Kelso bridled. "I got to collect that reward before I split with you, don't I?"

In his hurry to finish this part of tonight's job, Riggs hadn't considered this. At first he was angry, but then caution overrode the other emotion and he gave an easy laugh. "Never once thought about that, Sheriff," he admitted. "But when you collect, send my half along . . . general delivery, Las Cruces."

Kelso's brows lifted. "Cruces? You leavin'?"

Riggs nodded. "Tonight. Bishop's got his tail tucked too far to suit us."

Kelso's look was one of outright relief. "I'd be a liar if I said I was sorry to see you go, Riggs."

"What you think ain't likely to start us bawlin'," was Riggs's tart rejoinder. "But remember. Half that reward is mine. I'll be back after it if the *dinero* don't turn up."

"You'll get it."

Knowing the sheriff for a man of his word, Riggs was satisfied with that promise. Without further ceremony, he left the jail and for a few moments Kelso was listening to the sound of horses going down the alley toward the street. Only then did he remember his prisoner and go over to the cell, holding his lantern high so that he could look in at the man. He gave a long sigh. "You've sure dished out a lot of hell since you hit here, brother," he said. "Now someone's dished it out to you. Looks like they run a horse herd over you before they turned you loose."

"Maybe that's what they did." Streak had been sitting on the cot and now stood up, wincing as his head renewed its dull throb. He came to the cell door. "Got any tobacco, Sheriff?" he asked. "I lost mine. We might as well smoke while we talk."

"Who's goin' to talk?" Kelso pulled a sack of tobacco from his coat pocket and handed it across, scowling belligerently. "I'm goin' home to get some shut-eye."

"You might be interested in hearing a certain story," Streak said.

"Not even a bedtime story," was Kelso's answer. He lowered the lantern, about to turn to the outside door.

Streak lifted his right boot from the floor and thrust it through the bars. "Pull this off, will you, Sheriff?" he said. "My head's liable to bust if I lean over."

Kelso looked at the boot, making no move to reach down to it. A thin smile came to his face. "And have you kick my teeth in?" he drawled. "Unh-uh. You busted out of here once. You don't get another chance."

"Suit yourself. But stick around. There's something you ought to see." Streak went to his knees, his face twisted as the bending over set up the ache in his head. He pulled the boot off and tossed it out through the bars onto the corridor floor. "See if you can pry the heel off, Sheriff."

"Why should I?"

"Because there's something under it you might like to look at."

Curious now, yet hesitating as he tried to read some trick into Streak's strange request, Fred Kelso looked down at the boot. At last he stepped over and warily moved it farther from Streak's reach by pushing it a few feet across the floor with his cane. Only then did he set the lantern down and pick up the boot. He tried to pull the heel loose. When it didn't come, Streak said: "Use your knife."

"What is this?" the lawman asked. "You tryin' to make a fool of me?"

"No. Go ahead."

Kelso took out his knife, opened the big blade, and forced the point in between the sole and the built-up high heel of the boot. In another moment he had pried the heel loose. Something he saw glinting against the lantern light between the two layers of thick leather made him hurry. All at once the nails came loose, and the heel fell to the floor. Along with it dropped a shiny metal object that rang when it struck the rock. Staring down at a deputy U.S. marshal's shield, Kelso was wordless.

"If I hadn't lost my coat, you could tear out the shoulder lining and have a look at my papers," Streak said. "Since it's lost, you'll have to take my word for it that Jim Guilford swore me in over in Johnsville five days ago."

Kelso's glance lifted abruptly from the badge to focus on Streak. "How'd you get this badge, Kincaid?" he asked. "Did you kill the man that wore it?"

"Jim Guilford sent me in here to find out what had happened to one of his deputies, a friend of mine," explained Streak. "This deputy's handle was Ed Church, and he was on his way to settle that matter of issuing a permit to Fencerail. You remember my asking about him that first night? Ed was the horse thief you say stole Snyder's splay-foot the night Dallam and Sternes were killed. But he wasn't a horse thief, Sheriff. He was a federal officer."

The lawman's seamed face had gradually taken on a frown as Streak spoke. Now he said: "The splay-foot's gone. So your friend . . . if you're not makin' this all up . . . is still a horse thief."

"He isn't. Yesterday, the man who made that try at Bishop here on the street was forking a splay-foot. You ran across his horse's sign. Today I was riding that blocked-up fork of the Squaw when I happened onto a pocket in the east wall of the narrows, a mighty fine hide-out. What started me up there was seeing the track of a splay-foot pointed toward it. Whoever rode him up there got in behind me and belted me across the back of the head with an iron. I was out cold all day. Tonight that same ranny turned me loose at Crescent B. Whoever he is, he knew Bishop's crew would be out after my hide. He didn't count on them bringing me in here alive." Kelso heard his prisoner out without interruption. He had nothing to say when Streak had finished, so the latter added: "I used Tex Kincaid's name to get either Fencerail or Bishop enough interested in me to bust me out of here. Right then, I didn't know where you stood, so I wasn't trusting you to see that." He nodded down to the badge. "Now I know you aren't for either side. If you'll check with Buchwalter or any other Fencerail man, he'll tell you that Morg Prenn came awful close to shooting me last night because I claimed to be Tex Kincaid. You see, Prenn knew that Kincaid had cashed in about a year ago."

Suddenly the sheriff's frown eased. "Maybe you're who you say you are. Then again, maybe you're runnin' another sandy."

"Would I half tear my head open to back a made-up story?" Streak asked. "Kelso, I'm a federal officer, here to find out what's happened to the first man Guilford sent in. I'm almost sure Ed Church is dead. As an officer of the law, you're bound to help get the answer."

"*If* you're who you say you are." The lawman put undue emphasis on his first word. The past two days had implanted in his mind too strong a suspicion of Streak to be rooted out at once. "Supposin' this gent Church came in as you say. Supposin' you met up with him, found out who he was, and decided it might come in handy for you to have this badge. Don't forget that envelope I found layin' here on the floor, friend."

Streak's patience was running out. He was beginning to feel better physically, for the weakness of the past two hours was wearing off and his head did not ache so much. But having had an inkling of what Riggs and his men were planning for the night, it seemed absurd to have to stand here locked in a cell trying to argue a stubborn sheriff into believing him to be what he claimed to be. He said levelly: "That envelope was addressed to me, Ned Mathiot, and I rubbed out the name and wrote Kincaid's instead. I've already told you why. If there was time, you could ride out to Prenn's and have Buchwalter prove what I say."

"If there was time?" Kelso queried. "Why ain't there?"

"Riggs and his hardcases are headed for that meadow below Prenn's to do a little butchering before they leave the country. Tonight. Right now."

Kelso took the cane from his arm and leaned on it, his glance narrowing in proof that he believed at least this much of Streak's story. "Then I'd better get goin'," he said, reaching for his lantern.

"You won't have time."

"But I will. On the way down the street, I spotted someone duckin' into that alley alongside the Emporium. Unless I'm wrong, it was Bill Paight. I might happen to find him at the hotel callin' on Laura Dallam. He's gone sort of sweet on her."

"Better hurry!" was the urgent word Streak sent after him as Kelso went out the corridor door.

Bill Paight wheeled back into the friendly darkness of the passageway alongside the Emporium, for a moment tense under the threat of having been seen by the Bishop riders on the street. But as they filed past, not looking his way, he relaxed and his homely face was slashed by a cocksure grin. He was wondering, idly, just what Sid Riggs would do if he knew what the darkness of this alleyway held concealed from him. Suddenly Paight's grin vanished. He saw the gray horse and the man on it, his wrists bound to the horn of the saddle and his boots roped to the cinch. At first he couldn't believe his eyes. When he was sure it was Streak, Paight's first involuntary impulse was to reach for his gun. But then his fingers slowly relaxed on the handle of the .45 as he saw Kelso. He might have had his try at freeing Streak but for the presence of the sheriff.

He knew what he would do. Tom Buchwalter was in town, at the hotel seeing Laura Dallam. It looked as though Streak was headed for jail again. Bill and Buchwalter could do something about that.

Turning up the walk and keeping to the deep shadows under the awnings, Paight headed for the hotel. Once the shock of having seen Streak a prisoner to Riggs and the sheriff left him, his mind went back to the insistent worry that had brought him on the long ride in here from Prenn's meadow. Three hours ago, as Fencerail's crew ate a hasty meal by their supper fire in the meadow where the sheep were being held, Paight had gone up to Buchwalter and asked about Streak. The foreman's answer had been: "Bill, he's gone. Nothing else can explain it. I left him up at the pass this morning. He was to follow me down here. That's the last I've seen of him."

Bill hadn't exactly worried about Mathiot. But he had been a little hurt to think that the man would simply drift without letting anyone know he was going or without the thanks they all owed him. And his regret was keen on another score. Momentarily forgetting his one reason for staying in this country, that reason being Laura Dallam, Bill realized that he'd halfway been planning to pack his possibles and side Streak Mathiot whenever Streak left the valley. Fencerail's trouble was about over and the life of a glorified sheepherder had no appeal for him. He had been unconsciously drawn to this lean tall stranger and the prospect of siding him for a time appealed strongly.

Then the thought of Laura Dallam jerked to an

abrupt halt this trend in his thinking. For the first time in these few days since meeting the girl, Bill asked himself straightforwardly just what his intentions toward her amounted to. In the end, over his second steaming cup of coffee there by the fire in Prenn's meadow, he reached the sobering realization that he was in love for keeps and that his footloose days might be over. This, of course, providing Laura would have him. And from that moment on he forgot about Streak and thought only of the next time he'd see Laura. He hoped it would be tonight but then knew it wouldn't be; every man was needed at the camp.

He was therefore pleasantly surprised when a little while later Buchwalter came over to him and said: "Bill, we're hitting out for town. Miss Dallam ought to know how things are going."

So they had saddled fresh horses and come in here, Bill unusually talkative and light-hearted with the prospect of seeing Laura. Then, as they rode into the upper end of the street, Buchwalter had abruptly jolted him by saying: "I'll go on alone and see her. You prowl around and keep an eye open for any west-slope men that drift in. We don't want to buy into any trouble. If any of 'em show, come up to Miss Dallam's room and tell me."

Paight would have argued with anyone else, for he had so far been in on most of the dealings with Pete Dallam's sister. However, Buchwalter's mild and gentle way bore no disputing. As foreman, it was probably Buchwalter's place to carry such important news as this they were bringing tonight. Bill, after all, was nothing but a top hand and could expect no favors. So he kept his mouth shut, glumly taking his post to keep an eye on the street after they'd tied their horses in the alley, and he had watched Buchwalter enter the hotel by the back door.

Now he had a legitimate reason for going to the hotel. Yet the prospect of seeing Laura was somehow less exciting than it would have been a minute or two ago, for the sight of Streak had sobered him, wiped out the lighter side of his thoughts. He hurried on, the empty street reassuring as he took the verandah steps and went in the lobby door.

The big downstairs room was deserted. He went up the stairs two steps at a time, the carpeting deadening the sound of his quick footfalls. Because he didn't want to be seen or heard, he slowed at the top landing and went down along the upper hallway as quietly as he could. Laura's room was Number 21. He stopped before her door and lifted his hand to knock.

As his fist was falling, he heard Buchwalter's voice through the thin panel: "You'll leave at five in the morning. I'll have a rig hired to take you down. You'll be able to make the morning stage."

"But why shouldn't I stay over one more day?"

came Laura's answer, as Bill's clenched fist froze motionlessly a bare half inch short of knocking.

"I don't want you to see Paight." Buchwalter's voice had lost its gentle note and was sharp-edged, authoritative. "That was the agreement. You were to follow my orders. Now you have them. You're also being well paid. A thousand is big money."

Bill felt his face go hot in a blend of sudden shame and anger. What agreement was Buchwalter talking about? What was he buying from Laura that would be worth $1,000? How could he be in a position to order her around? He had little time to get his answers, for Laura's voice sounded again, saying coolly: "I wish now I had never come here, never let you talk me into this."

"You wouldn't like it if I told Paight who you really are, would you?" Buchwalter said smoothly. "Do as I say and he'll never be any the wiser. After all, Laura, you aren't the marrying kind. Not with your . . ."

The sound of heavy uneven steps on the stairs, close below the landing, came to Bill then. As he swung away from the door and made quickly for the dark stairwell at the rear of the long hallway, he realized that he had been so engrossed in hearing what Buchwalter was saying that he had almost failed to hear that other sound announcing the approach of a man up out of the lobby. His thoughts seethed in a bewildered torment as he made the back stairs barely in time to keep from being seen. He stood there listening to the man coming down the hallway, knowing by the broken stride and the tapping of the cane that it was Fred Kelso.

The sheriff knocked on a door and shortly Bill heard the *squeak* of hinges as the knock was answered. Then Kelso was saying: " 'Evenin', Buchwalter. I didn't expect to find you. Saw Bill Paight down on the street and figured he was on his way here."

"No. Miss Dallam and I had some private matters to discuss," came Buchwalter's smooth reply. "I'm saying a temporary good bye to her. She's decided she must take a short trip back East, now that we've accomplished something for her. She won't even wait to say good bye to her friends but insists she has to take the morning stage out of Agua. Wish you'd help me try and talk her out of leaving in such a hurry."

"Now that's a shame," Kelso said. "We'll be sorry to see you go, ma'am, and glad to have you back again. Buchwalter, there's something I want to ask you. Riggs just rode in and brought Kincaid with him. Don't ask me how they picked him up. Kincaid's story don't make much sense, unless you explain something. He's claimin' now that he isn't Kincaid and that you know it. Something about Kincaid bein' dead and Morg Prenn havin' caught him in a lie last night. Is he tellin' the truth?"

"This is the first I've heard of it, Sheriff," was Buchwalter's immediate reply. "Of course he may not be Kincaid, as he says. But if he isn't, I don't know it."

"Then he's makin' up that story about Morg knowin' he was usin' a fake handle?"

Buchwalter's gentle laugh sounded down the hallway. "Sheriff, don't you know by this time that Kincaid's about as smooth an article as you'll ever come across? He's got a brain as sharp as a razor. He's the one who thought up the way to get the sheep in. But as for his story of Prenn having caught him up last night, there's nothing to it. I was with Prenn all night. To my knowledge, he and Kincaid didn't have a word to say to each other."

"It sure beats hell how he had me believin' him," Kelso said. "Well, I won't take up any more of your time. Oh, somethin' else, Buchwalter. He's also claimin' he's a federal officer. He had a deputy marshal's badge hid in the heel of his boot. Says he's in here lookin' for a partner of his, another federal man that disappeared a couple weeks ago."

"Did you ask him how he got the badge?"

"I did. And I think I know now. Well, don't worry about it. 'Evenin', ma'am. Sorry you're leavin'."

"So am I, Sheriff. Good bye," Laura Dallam said.

Kelso had taken a few strides back along the

hallway when Buchwalter called after him: "Sheriff! It might be a good thing to keep anyone from seeing Kincaid, now that he's in jail again. He might get outside help again."

"Not this time," came Kelso's emphatic words. "No one sees him, no one but me. He's in there to stay."

Chapter Sixteen

Fred Kelso walked the jail alley haltingly, feeling his tiredness again and leaning heavily on the cane as he favored his game leg. Tonight he felt like an old man and this had him worried; there was nothing he dreaded more than growing old. He wondered why he was bothering to come back up here to call Kincaid a liar. He would get little satisfaction out of it, for he had never been a man to take pleasure in recrimination. The truth was that, having suffered several severe setbacks in his first favorable judgment of Kincaid, he was now beginning to look on the man as a curiosity and was interested in finding out what his prisoner would try next. This had become an absorbing battle of wits to the sheriff; he had won this last round and it would bolster his shaken belief in his own judgment to win again.

He unlocked the door, stepped inside, and groped for the lantern he'd left hanging from a spike in the wall.

"I should've had sense enough to save myself that walk," he said tartly. "Saw Buchwalter. He made you out a pretty sizable liar, fella."

He squinted as he lit a match and touched it to the lantern's wick, waiting for a reply from Kincaid that didn't come. As soon as he had the wick adjusted properly, he hobbled on down and stood opposite the door of his prisoner's cell. He caught the reflection of light from the marshal's badge that still lay on the floor. It put a smile on his hawkish face.

"You damn' near sold me your bill of goods," he growled. "It's a wonder I didn't turn you loose."

Only then did Streak step into the light, coming to the front of the cell. He leaned against the barred door indolently, left shoulder to the grating, and blew the ash from the cigarette he was smoking. The fragrance of the tobacco had driven out the dry, musty taint of the air. Streak took a long drag on his smoke, exhaled slowly, and pointed with the cigarette to the head of the corridor the lawman had just left. "Company, Sheriff," he drawled.

Kelso's head came around. He gave a visible start, then lifted his right hand clear of his side when he saw Bill Paight standing, spraddle-legged, his back to the wall on the hinge side of

198

the jail entrance. Paight's thumbs were hooked in his belt. His long-barreled .45 hung limply from his right hand. The stony expression of his homely face didn't change as his glance met the sheriff's.

"Bill's got a different story," Streak went on. "You probably don't believe it. But be polite and listen anyway. Go ahead, Bill."

As Paight began his venomous and bitter indictment of Buchwalter, Streak kept his glance chiefly on the Fencerail man. He and Bill had had only a few words before the lawman's prompt arrival. But in that brief interval Streak had sensed a shocking change in Bill, a bitterness that he had never suspected could be in the man's make-up. Now, hearing Bill elaborate on what had happened there in the upper hotel hallway, he knew that the man was deeply hurt and ashamed. Aware for the first time of Bill's feelings for the girl who had posed as Laura Dallam, Streak saw at once that she was responsible for this sudden change in the man.

At one point, when Bill spoke of the girl as "that woman," Streak cut in with a sharp: "Pull in a little, Bill. You may've got Buchwalter pegged right. Gents like him can fool you because they act and talk like they'd fit behind a pulpit. But don't damn the girl just yet. Wait till you have the chance to talk to her yourself. Buchwalter may be holding something over her head and making her do this."

"Who said anything about her?" Bill bridled. But when he went on, Streak noticed that he didn't mention Laura again. The effort of talking seemed to affect Bill as much as violent physical exertion. His face shone with perspiration, although the chill of the night was beginning to be felt in here. He was short of breath when he finished.

That intensity of his, more than anything else, convinced Fred Kelso. His eyes were wide in bewildered conviction as he looked at Streak. "Maybe I'm gettin' too old for my job. But danged if I've known who to trust." He let out a long sigh, lifted his shoulders as though shrugging away the fog of unenlightenment just lifted from his thinking, and reached for his keys.

When the cell door stood open and Streak stepped out to pick up the marshal's badge, Kelso asked: "What comes next, Mathiot?"

Streak ran his hand over his cut and swollen lips, considering an answer. Before he could speak, Bill rasped harshly: "You two do what you want. I'm going back there to the hotel."

Streak said—"Sure, Bill."—knowing that nothing would satisfy Paight until he faced Buchwalter. But, as the Fencerail man turned to the door, he added: "Before you nail up his hide, though, hadn't we ought to think this out?"

"Think what out?" Bill asked tonelessly, his hand already on the door's locking bar.

"First, Buchwalter's working with someone in this."

"Sure. With the girl."

"No, someone else. He couldn't have been the one who made that try at Bishop yesterday on the street, the man on the splay-foot. He wasn't up in that hide-out today when I got belted over the head. If he had been, I'd have seen his horse. So, whatever he's after here, he's got help. Have you stopped to think who it could be, Bill?"

"No. What does it matter? We know Buchwalter's the big augur in this . . ."

"In what?" Streak cut in. "You know two things. First, he's hired a nice girl to come in here and pose as Pete Dallam's sister. Next, he's got a reason for wanting me out of the way or he wouldn't have lied about what Prenn said last night. But as to why he's done these things, we're as far from the answer as we were before we found him out."

"He might be after Fencerail," Kelso pointed out.

"If he was, wouldn't he keep that girl here until she could sign over an option or a deed to him? No, that doesn't hold water. She's leaving in the morning, leaving for good. So we've got to look further for what we're after. And how can we do that if you go up and measure Buchwalter for a coffin, Bill?"

Paight's look was undecided now. Streak's

words had told, for shortly Bill let his hand drop from the lock bar. "What am I supposed to do," he drawled flatly, "let him walk out of this with a pat on the back?"

"No. Whatever play he's making, he's only begun it," Streak told him. "He wanted those sheep in here so bad he could taste it. Now that he's got this far, let's see what he does with 'em. For all he knows, I'm in jail, out of his way. He doesn't like that much, but it'll have to do . . . since either his plan or that of the jasper he's working with went sour when Bishop's crew didn't finish me off. All right, Bill, let's give him the rope to tie his own noose with. You're supposed to be waiting down there on the street for him. Get back there and let on like nothing's happened. Ask him questions about the girl. Even let on that you'd like to go up a minute and see her. He won't let you, of course. Ride back out to Prenn's with him. Meantime, Kelso and I can get up there and maybe throw a surprise into Riggs's bunch when they ride in . . . if we're not already too late."

Kelso nodded immediate agreement. But Bill seemed hesitant. He said: "There's one or two things about this I no *sabe*."

"There's a whole lot I don't," Streak said gravely. "I come in here looking for a friend. I forget him and tie up to a sheep outfit because I think they're being tromped on by a range hog.

Now it turns on they're crooked as a gang of card sharks and this so-called range hog is nothing but a nice gent protecting his rights. I'm no closer to finding out what happened to my partner than I was before I headed in here. I should've been looking for Ed the last couple days. Instead, I've been figuring ways for sheep to take over a cattle range. Talk about no *sabe*, I really don't."

"What about your sidekick, Mathiot?" Kelso asked. "Any ideas?"

Streak shook his head. "Ed had a pretty good think tank. It's a cinch he isn't our man on the splay-foot. He wouldn't choose Bishop without reason and wouldn't try to bushwhack him if he did. He wouldn't be the one that slugged me over the head, either. So I get only one answer."

"He's dead?" Kelso said quietly.

Streak nodded. The look on his face softened that on Paight's, who was quick to say: "What I've got to settle with Buchwalter can wait." He pulled back the lock bar and opened the door. "See you gents later. In case you want to find me tonight or in the morning, I'll be at the needle rock up the Squaw. The main branch is over its banks and Buchwalter wants to blow the rock out of the other channel as soon as he can. He's sending me up there with a case of dynamite right after we get back to Prenn's camp."

"Remember, Bill," Streak cautioned, "you still

think Tom Buchwalter's about the finest, whitest, kindest old gent that ever lived."

"Sure. He's got a halo bigger'n a wagon wheel hanging over his head. And what looks like shoulder bones sticking out under his coat is wings sprouting." Bill's answer eased Streak's worry. The rash grin that slashed the man's broad, freckled face as he went out was even better.

As the door closed on him, Kelso turned to Streak and eyed him closely. "You don't look like you're in such good shape to ride very far tonight," he said. "Better let me get some help and go by myself."

"You don't think I'd miss this, do you?" Streak managed a smile. He wasn't feeling any too good, but, in comparison to the skull-bursting throb that had been in his head at Crescent B, the dull ache there now was a keen relief. He added: "You'll have to hunt me up a cutter and some shells somewhere. Our friend on the splay-foot must've taken a liking to mine."

"You can take your pick down at the office," was Kelso's answer. He limped to the door. There he hesitated, turning to Streak again. "It won't do much good to say I'm sorry about this, Mathiot," he muttered. "But I sure as hell am. I misfired on you from the beginnin'."

"And if I hadn't thought you were a Bishop man, you'd have known about me that first night." Streak's swollen lips made his smile a little crooked. "We both made wrong guesses. But that's over with. From now on out, it'll be different."

Fred Kelso was no longer tired and depressed. He knew that the night might bring added violence. Still, he wasn't uncertain any more. He'd seen this Streak Mathiot operate and he couldn't put down the hunch that things were due to make a turn for the better.

Laura listened at the door of her room till the sound of Tom Buchwalter's deliberate tread faded down the stairway. Then she reached for her coat that hung over the back of a chair, threw it about her shoulders, and went out into the hallway and down into the lobby. She was taking a chance, she knew, for she had had a taste of Buchwalter's explosive anger tonight and wouldn't soon forget it. Still, it was worth running the risk of that anger again if she could catch only so much as a glimpse of Bill Paight. She hadn't known Bill was in town until Kelso mentioned having seen him down on the street. Knowing he had come in with Buchwalter and would probably be leaving with him now, Laura cast aside all caution and went out onto the verandah.

As the minutes passed without sight of the man she loved, a feeling of hopelessness and depression settled over her. Finally she caught the sound of ponies going out the alley in back of the hotel, and with the fading of that sound, her heart seemed to stop beating, for she knew that those distance-muted echoes might be the last link between her and Bill Paight. Buchwalter would naturally have entered the town furtively after the day's happenings and it was reasonable to suppose that he and Bill would leave the same way.

She drew the coat more tightly about her shoulders and took a chair at the shadowed end of the verandah, despair strong in her. Tomorrow's dawn would see her gone forever from this country. She could never hope to come back to it, for sooner or later the treachery of her being here and posing as Pete Dallam's sister would be discovered. To think that Bill would one day perhaps hate and loathe the memory of her was the hardest of all to take. That thought lay behind her not having touched the ten crisp $100 bills Tom Buchwalter had so casually tossed onto her bed up there in her room. She needed the money badly. Yet the thought of taking it seemed dishonorable. For it had come to represent the betrayal of the one man she had ever deeply cared for.

Her disappointment at not having caught a farewell glimpse of Bill eased. Wasn't it better to remember him as she had last seen him, before this shadow of her treachery loomed between them? Then, she had been able to answer his smiles and his warm glance with a genuine emotion that was unspoiled with such bitterness as she had felt tonight. Even yesterday she had put off facing the final reckoning, never dreaming that it loomed so close. And now, so suddenly that it still brought up a constriction in her throat, she had come to the realization that she was in love, deeply and sincerely, that the price she was paying for having earned Buchwalter's money was too high.

She became so engrossed in trying to discover a way to avert her personal tragedy that she wasn't aware of the two men coming up the walk until they had stopped below her beyond the verandah rail. Only when Streak touched the brim of the battered Stetson the sheriff had loaned him and said—" 'Evenin', Miss Dallam."—was she prodded from her deep and miserable absorption.

She didn't know Streak. But she did know Kelso. His being here brought up a strong fear in her; what she was afraid of she couldn't have explained, yet she definitely was just that.

Streak didn't wait for her to answer but went on: "We hear you're leaving in the morning, ma'am."

Now she remembered that Buchwalter had told Kelso she was going. She replied—"Yes, I am."—not knowing what else to say.

"You're catching the morning stage out of Agua?" Streak asked.

She nodded. "I'm sorry to be going. But something urgent has come up back East where I've been living. I must go back there for a few weeks." She managed this explanation with effort, at the last moment remembering what Buchwalter had told her to say.

"Now that's a shame," Streak drawled. "Bill Paight will be plenty put out that you didn't wait to say good bye to him."

Laura felt her face go hot. "I wanted to see Bill before I left," she said truthfully. "But it wasn't possible. Tell him I'll be back soon."

"If you could only stay over a day in Agua, maybe we could fix it so you could see Bill," Streak said. "I'm seeing him, sometime tomorrow. If he knew you'd be down there, he'd likely kill a horse getting to see you. He might not turn up until late at night, but he'd make it some way."

"Would you . . . would you tell him I'll be waiting?"

She had spoken impulsively, before she quite realized what she was saying. She was about to correct herself, to tell this pleasant-spoken stranger that there was a reason why she had to leave at once, when he said heartily: "Would I? Be glad to. That'll please Bill. Good night, ma'am."

And before Laura could summon the courage to tell him that she had spoken too hastily, that she could never see Bill again, and that she had lied about coming back, Streak and Kelso were going on up the walk. She wanted to call out after them. Still, she didn't. And in another moment they were out of sight as they turned into the big maw of the livery barn's runway door above.

"Wonder if we did right?" Kelso asked, as he and Streak took down the lantern hanging by the door of the empty office and started back toward the stalls.

"She's running from something. That's sure. Whatever it is, it's better that she and Bill have the chance to talk it out face to face than her leaving and his hating himself for ever liking her. Say, we better get a move on."

Streak's Fencerail gray had disappeared with Riggs and his men. Kelso found another horse in a back stall, a close-coupled bay with a white star on its forehead. He also pointed out Streak's own saddle hanging horn-roped with several others in the narrow aisle by the lot door, drawling: "Plenty's happened since you forked that hull comin' here. Maybe things'll come a little straighter when you're settin' it again."

Once out of the corral lot behind the barn, Kelso astride his own horse, they quickly put the lights of the town behind, the sheriff striking at once into the northward hills, riding point for Prenn's meadow. Even with his game leg, Kelso showed himself to be quite expert in the saddle. Only once, as they stopped to breathe their horses halfway up the rocky and timbered shoulder of a steep ridge, did they take time out for talk.

It was the sheriff who said worriedly: "I'd sure

like more to go on in this mess. This jasper with the splay-foot, for one thing. What's he gettin' out of this? And who is he?"

"I've got a notion," was Streak's reply. He was building a smoke and didn't look at Kelso as he spoke. "But I'll keep it to myself until I know for sure."

The lawman frowned, trying to study Streak's expression in the darkness and unable to see much. "You really mean that?" he asked. "You know who he is?"

"There's only one answer, if I've got it figured right," was all Streak would say.

When they went on, Streak was thankful that the lawman had checked his curiosity. There were things he would have liked to ask Kelso and any further urging might have broken down his resolve to keep his suspicions to himself. But he would have to do exactly that, for only a day perhaps, or maybe for much longer. If he could but get another look at the cañon hide-out, have an uninterrupted quarter hour in which to examine it, he would be sure. Until he made his careful inspection of it, there was no point in airing his theories and throwing another complication in the way of the men who were fighting to bring peace to this country. Paight had enough troubles of his own, Frank Bishop had his, and Kelso would need proof before he could act. The proof, Streak felt, was there at the hide-out if he could only spot it.

But, before he could look for it, there was other work to be done.

Kelso was traveling fast, probably realizing what a long start he had given Riggs and his men. In something under an hour after they started, the thin light of a moon relieved the total obscurity of the night. Much of their going was through timber that was heavy with undergrowth. From the way they rode, never swinging far wide of the direction Streak had taken from the start as they left town, invariably coming on the few fences near their corners, the lawman showed flawless judgment and an intimate acquaintance with the country. Streak doubted that Riggs's bunch had traveled nearly as fast, and, as the miles dropped behind, he began feeling easier about the Crescent B foreman's threat made back there at Bishop's bunkhouse.

"We're close now," Kelso announced finally as he trotted his pony onto a trail marked by an occasional blaze on a tree.

"What happens when we get there?"

"We can at least put 'em on their guard. They can throw some men over west and north and . . ."

Abruptly he stopped speaking. The sound of his voice was taken up by the distance-thinned pound of guns, fast-timed, angry. It held on insistently instead of breaking off and Kelso listened for a good half minute before lifting his heels and spurring his pony to a full run along the trail.

Streak followed and over the pound of the gelding's hoofs caught the continuing echoes of gun thunder.

Suddenly the trees thinned and they were at the lower edge of a wide-climbing meadow. Streak pulled alongside the sheriff as the latter lifted an arm and pointed northward. "There's the camp!" Kelso called. Looking off there, Streak caught the pinpointed light of a fire. Then he saw what looked like a cloud shadow dropping down off the far western edge of the meadow. He couldn't understand it, for a quick glance above showed him that the sky had cleared in the past hour; it was cloudless and star-sprinkled. All at once a muted low rumble came across to them and with that sound Kelso reined his horse to an abrupt halt. Streak listened beside him as the sound swelled in the still air, broken only occasionally now by the sound of a single shot.

"I don't get it," Kelso said tonelessly.

"It's a stampede."

"Sheep wouldn't run that way. Come on! Let's get across there."

"You go. I stay here. Remember, I'm supposed to be in jail. We'd better let 'em keep on thinking I am."

"Where'll I meet you?" Kelso asked quickly.

"Up the cañon. I'll swing off there and wait. Bring Paight along if you can."

The sound of Kelso's going was drowned out

by that growing thunder from up the meadow. It was an eerie sound, one Streak couldn't define. As he sat waiting, that shadow in the moonlit distance of the upper meadow began slowly moving, growing in outline. There was no reason for its being there that Streak could see. It and the indefinable sound that came from up there gave him a feeling of strange awe, almost fear, so that he wanted to turn and ride into the shelter of the nearby trees.

Chapter Seventeen

Riggs signaled a halt as he reached the margin of the timber high along the western border of Morgan Prenn's big meadow. Letting the others come up on him, the ex-Bishop foreman carefully inspected what lay ahead. The waning moon laid a feeble and ghostly light across the broad open reach of grass that tilted gradually downward to the bed of the now dry fork of the Squaw and climbed gently beyond to give the meadow a deep saucer-like formation. The far-off and constant blatting of sheep was a noise that grated on Riggs's hearing and screwed his face into an expression of deep disgust.

He looked longest at the distant pinpoint of rosy

light that marked the campfire of the west-slope crews. That fire was close to the creek at almost the exact center of the meadow. To this side of it and beyond, splotched patterns of massed gray shapes showed against the darker shadow of the grass. Riggs judged that most of the sheep were down out of the main cañon.

Pinto Sanders, coming up on him, said sparsely and acidly: "Good thing there's a wind at our backs."

Riggs faced the cook. "Ever hear of stampedin' sheep, Pinto?"

"No. They're too dumb to run much."

"Think we can shoot enough to make much of a dent in 'em?" The question was barbed. Pinto had so far kept silent on whatever idea he had, and Riggs now faced the prospect of their having made this ride for practically nothing.

"No, I wasn't thinkin' of wastin' much lead," was Pinto's calm rejoinder. He appeared to be looking north, up the meadow toward the timber there.

Luke Black spoke from behind, his sarcasm biting: "Just take your time lettin' us in on this, Pinto. We got all night."

Pinto ignored the jibe, lifting an arm and indicating the direction in which he'd been looking. "We ought to find 'em off there somewheres."

"Find who?" Riggs said, his patience worn thin.

"Prenn's cattle."

"What about 'em?"

"He ain't had time to move 'em far," Pinto told him. "And we do know they'll stampede."

"What good'll that do? It'll cost Prenn only a few extra days' work roundin' 'em up."

"You come along," Pinto said, reining on ahead. "It's goin' to cost him a damn' sight more'n that!"

They had to be satisfied with this cryptic statement as they lined out behind Pinto through the trees. Had he been anyone else, they would have let him go on alone.

It was better than a mile to the head of the meadow and in covering that distance Pinto didn't once leave the trees. The rest caught his wariness and were careful to ride silently, skirting windfalls and brush. When he made the second halt at the edge of the timber high on a hill shoulder, looking down across a westward slanting pocket that cut back into the trees from the head of the meadow, they had before their eyes evidence of the shrewdness of Pinto's guess. Down there, dotting the open ground, was Prenn's herd of cattle. Riggs privately estimated their number to be close to a hundred and fifty. Still, he couldn't see where this was leading them.

"All this chasin' ain't savin' our horses much," he said bluntly.

Once again, the intensity of Pinto's concentration on his own private revenge made him overlook this barbed comment. He said quietly: "I didn't want to tell you till I got you here. Thought you might not go in on it. But here's what we can do. There's likely a man down there somewhere ridin' the mouth of this pocket, keepin' them critters penned in. We can forget him. All but two of us can get up at the far end and open up at the proper time with our irons. The two we leave down here ride out into the grass a ways and steer the herd when it busts out of here. From there on, things ought to take care of themselves."

For a brief moment, these men were silent under the surprise of seeing how simply but completely Pinto Sanders had planned wholesale destruction of the sheep band. It was Luke Black who finally breathed: "Holy smokes, Pinto, this is more'n we bargained on. I thought we was goin' to shoot up their camp and cut down a few woollies, but this . . ."

"If you've turned chicken, beat it, Black," Pinto said flatly.

Black started to protest, but Riggs cut him off with a sharp: "Lay off, you two! Who cares how much hell we bust loose here tonight? We'll be on our way out in another half hour. Luke, you and Belden get out there in the meadow. When these critters bust out, swing 'em straight across at that fire. Stay with 'em all the way. We'll meet right here afterward and light out for Agua. Snyder'll rent us some horses and we'll get fresh relays at the stage corrals crossin' the desert. We'll catch a train out of Johnsville before they can get any word out. If we do this right, they'll remember us as long as they live."

"One thing more," Pinto said. "They'll know who did this. Don't lay your sights on a man. They're better off alive and fumin' over this than they are dead and puttin' a price on our heads."

Riggs heard the cook out, then reined aside and started down into the pocket. Black and Belden swung back through the trees, the former telling the nearest rider as he left: "Give us time to get set."

Pinto didn't go along with the others but put his pony several paces out from the tree border and sat, looking down at the indistinct shapes of the bunched cattle, his face set bleakly yet triumphantly. It occurred to him that this was a shabby revenge, but it was next best to the impossible that, for him, would have been that often-imagined meeting with Pete Dallam, a gun in his hand.

The minutes dragged for Pinto. He became restless, halfway suspecting that Riggs at the last moment was backing out. Finally he made up his mind to ride down and see what was the matter. Suddenly the guns cut loose, their thunder rolling in sharp echoes up the slope, their powder flashes winking in the downward darkness. With the explosions came a blend of sharp, yipping yells. The cattle started moving, slowly at first, then faster. All at once they were running away from the noise, away from the pound of hoofs coming from the head of the pocket. They were no longer bunched but spread out in frantic flight, each animal for itself. Then came a thin but solid line, gathering breadth, as the half-wild steers that had begun the stampede raced for the big meadow. Other tardy animals fell in with them and the thickness of the line grew until it was a formless and seething wave flowing toward the mouth of the pocket.

From the meadow, a lone shot rang out. A man down there gave a shout that was all but swallowed by the thunder of the stampeding herd. That man, Pinto surmised, must be the rider who had been standing guard at the mouth of the pocket. Pinto now spurred his horse out into the open, lazily riding the flank of the herd. The moon's light was strong enough so that he saw the main body of steers when they broke out of the pocket. Only then did Luke and Belden lend the terror of their guns to the panic already pushing the herd. Instead of spreading farther, as they had first threatened to do, the swing animals crowded back into the main body, trying in their headlong flight to get as far as possible from the thundering concussion of the guns flashing against the sideward darkness.

From the high promontory of the slope flanking the pocket mouth, Pinto Sanders watched a grudging dream take shape in reality. He could see the dark mass of the cattle herd flowing relentlessly down the long gentle incline toward the main band of sheep, between the pocket and the fire by the creek. And now a shot or two came from off near the fire, explosions that sounded feeble and inadequate against the roar of six hundred hoofs pounding the turf.

The massed sheep to this side of the creek broke rank at the last, feebly, then milled frantically as the crazed steers plunged down on them. To Pinto, it was like watching a blunted axe head descend lazily on a gray and aged round of cottonwood. But the axe, which was the herd, didn't stop once it had buried itself in the wood. It went on through, as though some giant hand of tremendous power was pushing it, through and beyond the band, straight for the creek and the fire beside it.

The details were blurred now by distance. Pinto couldn't make out much but the scattering of the last remaining fragments of the broken band of sheep and of the relentless onward surging of the cattle, beginning to spread now. The main stem of the herd reached the creek and crossed it. The fire suddenly went out. There came ragged gunfire from the direction of the camp. Then the herd was climbing the far slope, the stampede slowing, yet just as relentlessly overrunning the smaller bunch of sheep across there.

Pinto looked away, breathing a long, deep sigh. "That's from me to you, Dallam," he drawled beneath his breath.

Chapter Eighteen

Dawn's first feeble light filtered through the ground haze that lay over the meadow to reveal the shambles that had come during the dark hours. Westward from the creek, in line with the pocket mouth, lay a broad and grayish-red swath of sheep carcasses. Eastward and almost centering that slope were others, fewer, but their number awesome to the weary red-eyed men who circled and rode down to what had two hours ago been a pleasant camp.

There they found utter destruction. The charred remnants of the fire lay scattered over a rough circle some thirty feet across. What had last night been Morg Prenn's new buckboard, serving as chuck wagon, was now a mass of splintered wood and twisted iron. All but one wheel had disintegrated, and that single wheel leaned crazily on a two-foot length of broken hickory axle, its iron tire twisted and pointing to the sky like a gnarled oak branch. Vari-colored fragments of blankets lay beaten into the ground, a saddle with a broken tree and a torn skirt sat astraddle the cook's overturned Dutch oven. Nearby the bean and beef breakfast stew that had been cooking on the fire made a muddy hoof-churned puddle.

The cook had miraculously salvaged a few edibles from the ruins. At a new fire well away from the old camp, he was brewing coffee in a dented two-gallon pot and spooning pan bread into a smoking fry pan that had come through unscarred. Below his fire, legs up over the creek-bank, lay a horse carcass while nearby a soiled tarp covered what had yesterday been a big and hearty Fencerail rider. Jim Brewster had been a heavy sleeper, the hardest man in the bunkhouse to wake of a morning; this morning he wouldn't have to be awakened.

Tom Buchwalter and Fred Kelso stared at the stricken camp, then up along the carcass-dotted western half of the meadow down which they had just ridden from the timber at its edge.

"Morg!" Buchwalter called.

Prenn and three others were digging a grave for the dead Fencerail man. At Buchwalter's hail, Prenn straightened, running a hand over his sore back; he had wrenched it during the stampede last night in being thrown from his crazed pony but had miraculously escaped further injury by firing into the herd and swinging it away from him. He now thrust his spade into the mounded fresh earth beside the grave and strode over, weariness deeply lining his dark face.

"I didn't want the others to hear," Buchwalter said as Prenn came up. His expression was grave, worried. "Morg, it looks bad. We've lost over a thousand head. Nearly a third."

Prenn's brows lifted. "That all?" he said ironically. "I thought it'd be more. Well, what do we do about it?"

Buchwalter glanced at the sheriff and lifted his shoulders in a shrug. "Fred says nothing."

"Nothing!" Prenn exploded. "Why, damn it, I'll go after Bishop myself and . . ."

"Hold on, Morg!" Kelso cut in. "We know who did this. It was Riggs and his sidekicks. I know for a fact that Frank Bishop fired the lot of 'em last night . . . even gave Riggs an order to Adams on drawin' their pay while the bank was closed. They were in town and I saw Riggs. He bragged he was comin' up here. I tried to beat him but wasn't soon enough. So Bishop didn't do this. Fact is, he showed he was through with this fight when he let Riggs go."

Prenn's look was one of sullen impotent anger.

"Of course, Riggs is on his way out," Buchwalter said. "We could never catch him."

"What the hell are we supposed to do, take this lyin' down?" Prenn blazed. "We lose a third of what we got in this in one night. If it can happen once, it can happen again. Bishop may have been through with the fight yesterday. But when he hears how easy it was to do this harm, he'll damn' well be back in it up to his whiskers again."

"I'll see that he isn't," Kelso said easily. "You haven't broken a single law gettin' these sheep in. Bishop can't make a move against you without breakin' one. If he does, I lock him up."

Prenn gave a dry laugh that had its unspoken meaning, implying that he would like to see Kelso have to make good his brag.

"I'll lock him up, sure as hell's hot!" the lawman repeated. With a last stony glance at Prenn, he reined his pony away and over toward the cook's fire.

When Kelso was out of hearing, Buchwalter's face shed its benign look and he said quickly: "Two can sit in on this game, Morg. Just wait."

His tone, clipped and hard, surprised Prenn even more than the inference of his words. "Don't go makin' it any worse, Tom," Prenn said quickly, suddenly about-facing in his attitude. "We can't stand any more losses. It'll be a month before we can gather in that herd again. I'm taking a big loss there, too. They run a lot of weight off last night in that stampede."

"Never mind your loss," was Buchwalter's cryptic answer. "I've got an idea. This may be settled before you know it."

"That ain't sayin' which way it'll be settled,"

Prenn stated grimly. Because he had never before seen this side of Buchwalter, because he didn't understand how such a mild-natured man could assume the cloak of hardness the Fencerail man now wore, he went on: "Tom, I'm worried. Let's don't do anything for a day or so until we can cool down and think things over."

"We'll see, Morg," was all Buchwalter would say on that score. "I'm on my way up the cañon. Got to see Paight about getting that rock blasted out of the channel. He left with the dynamite when I told him to, didn't he?"

"Been gone about two hours," Prenn answered. He nodded across to the grave that was nearly finished. "What about Jim here? Hadn't you ought to read a service over him before you go?"

"How long before you're finished?"

"Oughtn't to be much more than another hour."

"Then it'll have to wait till I get back."

Prenn frowned. "When'll that be?"

"No telling. Maybe the middle of the afternoon. Maybe later."

Prenn's look was one of shock. "Jim ain't in any shape to stay long above ground, Tom. It gets powerful hot here in the middle of the day."

"We'll bury him this afternoon," Buchwalter said decisively, and turned away, starting up along the line of the creek.

Prenn gave his friend's departing back a long and puzzled inspection. Buchwalter obviously wasn't himself this morning. Final proof of that lay in his callous attitude toward the burying of his crew man. He'd lost his gentleness, his milkiness of manner, the moment Kelso's back was turned. That in itself amazed Prenn. He had never suspected Buchwalter of being capable of such cold brutality. He had the disturbing thought that he'd hate to cross the Fencerail foreman when he was in a mood like this. And, because he had never thought of Tom Buchwalter in this way, he was much impressed and unaccountably disturbed. It was he himself who usually needed to be hauled up short of an impulsive action; now, contradictorily, he had been trying to stop Buchwalter from some unexplained violence. Worst of all, now that Buchwalter had shown this little-known side of his nature, Prenn felt lost and uncertain. Buchwalter had always been a cool-headed leader, sure of himself. He was no longer that. Prenn didn't like this new Tom Buchwalter he had just glimpsed.

Because of his uncertainty, Prenn acted on a queer, inexplicable impulse. He went across to the cook's fire where Kelso was wolfing a big slab of pan bread and drinking steaming hot coffee from a bent tin cup.

"Fred," Prenn began abruptly, "you'd better hurry that and go along with Buchwalter."

Kelso's glance was puzzled. "Why should I?"

Prenn was caught short in his impulse. For a

moment his loyalty toward Buchwalter and his suspicion of Kelso as being a Bishop man kept him silent. But in the end his worry over the change in Buchwalter outweighed his reticence. "He's actin' a little off his feed," he said finally. "Talkin' about getting even with Bishop. Whatever he's up to is important enough so that he's holdin' up the buryin' until late afternoon. Says he's goin' up the cañon to see Paight about blowin' the channel clear. Maybe he is, maybe he ain't."

The sheriff's glance swung up along the line of the creek to where Buchwalter was disappearing beyond the crest of a low knoll halfway to the mouth of the cañon. "I'll just tag along after him," he said.

"Don't let on like I told you anything," Prenn cautioned.

The lawman nodded, limped across to his horse, and climbed into the saddle. Yet he didn't immediately follow the Fencerail man, going instead up toward the eastern edge of the meadow where several riders were working to round up the thin remnants of Prenn's cattle herd. Only when he'd given Buchwalter a good ten-minute start did Kelso follow.

He had at first been more irritated than surprised at Prenn's strange request and might have acted on it less promptly had it not fitted in with his plan for meeting Streak up the cañon. The tempers of these men were worn thin with the ruin the night had brought and his first notion was that Prenn was imagining something. But then he'd had a thought that startled him, and it was this idea that had made him delay following Buchwalter until the man was well ahead of him. Wasn't it possible, he had asked himself, that Buchwalter and the man who rode Snyder's splay-foot were known to each other, that they might even be working together in this still obscure purpose that had involved paying a woman to pose as Pete Dallam's sister? Yes, he decided, it was possible. He wondered why he hadn't thought of this before. Furthermore, hadn't Streak already guessed that connection between the two in naming a meeting place?

Entering the wide mouth of the cañon, riding past the last large bunch of sheep being driven toward the meadow by three Mexican herders, Kelso had added reason to respect the abilities of the man he had discovered wasn't an outlaw but a federal officer. And because he had proof of the directness with which this Mathiot acted, he now hurried a little, afraid that in letting his quarry get so sizable a start he might lose sight of both him and Streak if the hide-out was in reality Buchwalter's goal.

Three miles of going put Kelso in unfamiliar country, with the cañon narrowing from its generous width to little more than the scant breadth of the dry streambed. He had often fished the lower cañon of the Squaw, but had never explored these narrows where the walls shut out the sunlight and the slender margins of the stream were a tangle of chokeberry, alder, and scrub oak. Once the deep shadows of the towering walls pressed in on him, he was uneasy with an insistent feeling of danger being close ahead.

When Bill Paight stepped out from behind a dense oak thicket close ahead, when he saw the grave and dogged set of the Fencerail man's face, that feeling became even stronger.

And Bill's first words didn't ease his worry. "Better get in here out of sight," came the Fencerail man's clipped, low-spoken drawl as he turned and stepped out of sight into the brush.

Kelso was quick to follow. Behind the thicket, in a shallow indentation in the wall, stood the bay gelding Streak had ridden out of Ledge last night. Alongside was a brown with a Fencerail brand. The cinches of the two saddles hung loose and the horses stood hipshot, reins knotted to the lone dead branch of a lightning-blasted pine stump. Beyond, against the foot of the sheer climbing limestone, were the two cases of dynamite Kelso had seen Bill pack away from Prenn's wrecked camp in the darkness two hours ago.

"Where's Mathiot?" was the lawman's first query as he dismounted.

"Following Buchwalter. Wouldn't let me side

228

him. He was sure you'd be along." Bill spoke softly, as though afraid of his voice carrying too far.

"Well, now I'm here. Let's get on after him." The sheriff lifted a boot to stirrup, about to mount again.

But Bill shook his head. "Streak said to stay set. That hide-out entrance is only a few rods above. He seemed to think Buchwalter was headed in there, 'cause he set out after him afoot. You think he's right, Kelso?"

"About what?"

"Buchwalter being in with this jasper on the splay-foot."

Kelso nodded. "I thought of it. But what does Mathiot think he can do alone? There's two of them. He isn't in any shape to handle much trouble."

"He's better'n he was when you saw him last. I made him get some shut-eye while I watched the hide-out. He was more like himself when I woke him a few minutes ago."

The lawman went over to tie his horse with the other two. "You and me are goin' to walk up there after him," he said.

"I wouldn't. So far Streak's guesses have panned out. He told us to wait here. I'm waiting."

Kelso reluctantly accepted this verdict, reached his cane down off its saddle thong, and hobbled over to join Bill in hunkering down with his back to the wall close to the horses.

Presently Bill asked querulously: "What's this adding up to? Buchwalter ain't what he lets on to be, the girl sure fooled us, and now Streak's got it in his craw that Buchwalter's working with this stranger on Snyder's grulla. Not a bit of it makes sense."

"Not yet, but it will. We're onto something this morning. I wish Mathiot would get back."

"He said he wouldn't be long."

Half an hour dragged by, Kelso occasionally shaking his watch to be sure it hadn't stopped. They could hear the whisper of a freshening breeze whipping across the top of the walls high overhead. At the end of forty minutes the sheriff abruptly came erect.

"To hell with this," he growled. "You can sit here if you want. I'm goin' to see what's wrong."

"Give him a few more minutes."

But at the end of an hour even Bill's patience was ended. He agreed that they should go at least as far as the hide-out entrance.

There, standing at the foot of the narrow wall crevice, Kelso looked in along its shallow length, turning finally to give Bill a quizzical glance. Bill had his gun in his hand and motioned the lawman on ahead with it. They went through the same wary pantomime at the notch's second turning. Edging into sight of the third narrow passageway, Kelso abruptly stiffened. He didn't wait for Bill but limped quickly on ahead. Only when he knelt down beside a man's shape lying huddled at the pocket entrance did Bill see what had made him hurry.

Tom Buchwalter lay face down, his head pillowed on one bent arm as though he had purposely stretched out there to catch a brief nap. But the swelling over his exposed ear belied this intent. His Stetson lay a few feet away, a dent at the side of its flat crown evidence of the severity of the blow that had struck him down.

"At least it ain't Streak," Bill whispered finally.

Kelso's glance swiftly ran around the pocket. It was empty. Buchwalter's horse wasn't in sight. Neither was the grulla. A sudden panic welled up in Kelso and he called loudly: "Streak!"

The echo of his voice came back at him and struck more faintly against the pocket's far wall in a prolonged and eerie fading.

"Streak!" he called again, more loudly.

And again the echoes were his only answer.

Chapter Nineteen

Streak had known that his guess was right the instant Buchwalter reined in and sent that furtive backward look down along the narrow corridor of the cañon. From that moment on, he stalked his

231

quarry as warily and patiently as an Apache.

It was a full quarter hour before he stepped around the final turning of the hide-out entrance and brought the grassy sunlit pocket into view. That pleasing vista broadened before him as he cat-footed the length of the passageway. Shortly he could see the two horses, Buchwalter's and the grulla. And finally he could see the two men. He experienced a momentary and numbing shock at sight of the man leaning against the high and narrow cave opening talking to Buchwalter. It was Ed Church!

Excitement held him rigid, unbreathing, refusing to believe what he saw, yet having the proof before his eyes. He was unmistakably seeing Ed's high shape that didn't appear as tall as it was because of a barrel chest and thick arms. He would have known the rawhide conch-buttoned vest anywhere. Familiar, too, was the horn-handled gun, the lazy pushed-back set of the tan narrow-brimmed Stetson. And the sunlight shone fully on dark auburn hair exposed by the back-tilted hat. Suddenly Streak let his breath out in a gusty exhalation, his glance holding to the tied-down holster low along the man's thigh. The position of that holster told him a lot. Into his consciousness sounded clearly remembered words he had years ago heard Ed lazily drawl: *Pack your iron below the knee if you want, friend,* Ed had said as he and Streak argued the best position in which to wear a gun. *As for me, I belt mine tight and high. I never was hell on wheels for a fast draw. It's what you do after you unlimber your iron that counts.* Ed Church had never worn a holster the way the man across there with Buchwalter was wearing his. Rather, Ed's was always belted awkwardly high, at waist level. So this wasn't Ed Church.

In that moment the feebly glowing spark of hope that Ed still lived died within Streak. Across there stood a man who looked enough like Ed Church from a distance to be his twin. He wore Ed's outfit, probably down to the boots. Ed himself would be wearing those clothes if he weren't in his grave. And now Streak had again the thought that had been plaguing him all night. He had dreamed of it in that brief and fitful two-hour sleep while Bill stood guard at the hide-out entrance before dawn. It came in a single word, and that word was a name, the name of the man across there he was sure now had killed his friend. A cool and furious anger welled up in him. His hand lifted toward his holster. He felt his palm cool and moist, and deliberately wiped it along his thigh before lifting the .45 clear of leather. He drew back the Colt hammer slowly, easing the catching of the sear with a steady pressure of the thumb. He lifted the weapon and rocked the sights into line with the broad chest of Buchwalter's companion. The range was long for a gun he had never before used. But in his anger Streak's thinking wasn't rational. His finger laid pressure on the trigger.

All at once his quarry straightened from that indolent stance against the rock wall and lazily turned and strode out across the grass toward the grulla. Lowering the gun, Streak heard the man speak gently to the animal, the even drawl of his voice drifting clearly across: "Steady, boy, steady." Then the animal was being led back toward the slitted cave entrance.

Time and again during the next few minutes, Streak tried to lay his sights surely on the man, but each time, as he made ready to shoot, his target would move, busying himself in saddling the splay-foot. Finally the man who looked so much like Ed Church led the animal up to the cave entrance, into it, and out of sight. Streak heard Buchwalter say: "Make sure of it. This is our big chance."

Buchwalter's turning and leading his horse toward the pocket entrance nearly caught Streak unawares. Had he not a few moments before stepped well back into the narrow channel to rest the .45 against a narrow rock shelf and steady his aim, Buchwalter would easily have seen him. As it was, he had time to draw back out of the other's sight.

In the following brief seconds, he wondered what he should do. Then he knew. He wasn't going to leave this place until his gun had brought down the man he was sure had killed his friend.

About four feet short of its abrupt outer opening, the left wall of the narrow corridor in which Streak stood was indented deeply enough to conceal him from anyone looking along the passageway. He eased back into the shallow hollow and waited, the slur of Buchwalter's boots against the tall grass clearly audible now as the man approached.

Then Buchwalter's boots grated against the rock as he entered the passageway. All at once the Fencerail man was within reach. Streak lifted his gun and laid a sharp, nicely placed blow alongside the older man's head. For one instant there was amazed and fearful recognition in Buchwalter's eyes. Then his spare frame went loose, he tottered forward, and his brief expression of mute astonishment was wiped out as his eyes rolled up in the vacant stare of unconsciousness.

Streak caught him as he fell, eased him to the ground, and snatched the horse's reins from his hand before the animal could jerk loose and shy back into the hide-out. He spoke soothingly to the animal a moment, edged out past him, and dropped the reins.

He knew that the momentary advantage he had gained might end at any moment. At first puzzled by Buchwalter's companion having led the grulla into the cave, he was now even more intrigued by the mystery of the man's failure to reappear. But, so long as he remained out of sight, Streak still had the chance to surprise him.

Quickly Streak began circling the pocket, knowing his quarry wouldn't be overly curious if he heard someone moving about. About ten feet from the narrow high entrance to the cave he paused, a beady perspiration cooling his high forehead. He took the time to thumb open the loading gate of the .45 and spin the cylinder. All but one chamber was loaded. He let the hammer down on that empty chamber and edged nearer the cave mouth, not stopping until his shoulder was close to the break in the wall.

Breathing shallowly, standing motionless as he listened, he was shortly rewarded for his wariness when from the cave came the muffled hollow ring of a horse's shod hoof striking against rock. The sound seemed to come from a distance, as though sounding up out of a deep well. It puzzled Streak but at the same time was faintly reassuring. He steeled himself to make the move he knew might mean instant death. Then, in a sudden wheel, he spun in through the cave mouth and slammed hard against the right-angling inside wall, gun arcing up to elbow level.

The explosion of a gunshot he had expected as a certainty didn't come. He took three quick strides that put him well inside the entrance and into deep shadow. Pausing there, letting his eyes gradually focus to the semidarkness, his stomach muscles knotted at the still expected threat of a bullet coming out of the darkness at him.

All at once the tension eased out of him, for again he caught the sound of a few moments ago; only this time it was but a faint far-off echo, muted by distance, barely audible, coming from deep in the cave, and on the heel of that sound came another equally as faint, the querulous clipped tone of a man's voice raised in anger.

There was a moment in which Streak felt a relief so acute that it left him weak. He had made his bold entrance firm in the conviction that he faced a shoot-out. Instinct had told him that the element of surprise might spoil the aim of Ed's murderer, gave him the hope that he could get in a telling shot before he was cut down. Now came that far-off echo of a voice telling him that he was momentarily safe, and the let-down was severe. He was still alive and the man he was hunting didn't know he was here.

The cave was obviously deep, probably roomier farther back than here near the entrance. That alone could explain the disappearance of the grulla and its rider, the echoes that came from such a distance. But why the man he hunted had led the grulla in here still remained a mystery. Considering his next step, the old wariness in him again and his momentary uncertainty forgotten, Streak's glance roved the faintly lit corridor directly ahead. He saw rumpled blankets lying at the base of the opposite wall. Beyond that crude bed was piled a disorderly array of unopened cans, tomatoes, beans, a half-empty flour sack, a salt jar; half a side of bacon hung from a cord tied to a rock finger that stuck out near the top of the head-high and insloping limestone wall. A lard pail, Dutch oven, frying pan, and coffee pot completed the furnishings of the cave. Streak knew that someone, probably Buchwalter, had brought these provisions and utensils here. There were plenty of signs—empty cans, the half-used bacon—that this was not a new camp.

Now that he had made certain of his advantage over Ed's killer, Streak felt nothing but a wish to get what was coming over with. He had never before planned the killing of a man but now he set about it meticulously, cold-bloodedly. Kneeling, he took off his boots and tossed them into the space between the blankets and the wall. For a moment he tried to think of a way to avoid outlining himself against the light coming from the cave mouth, but in the end he knew he would have to risk this.

As he started back deeper into the cave, reaching out with his left hand to guide himself by the feel of that wall's contour, every instinct in him was sharpened by the threat of the danger that lay in wait. Somewhere ahead was a man who would kill him as quickly and mercilessly as he himself would kill. He owed it to the memory of Ed Church to outwit this man. Within a dozen steps, the line of the cave tunnel angled abruptly and he was in total darkness, no longer endangered by the light at his back. Twice he stumbled over the rocky floor's unevenness. The rock was damp and felt cold and slippery against his socked feet. He had to go on slowly. But this didn't worry him; there was plenty of time, for the killer couldn't get past him and away.

The farther he went the more Streak wondered at the absence of all sound. There was the whisper of his hand palming the wall and the faint slur of his feet sliding over the floor. But, aside from that, nothing interrupted the utter stillness of this cavern. Gone were those telltale sounds of a minute ago. The stillness was ominous. For all Streak knew, he would stumble on the man he stalked at any moment. Perhaps the killer had come as far as the turning, seen him, and retreated to lie in wait at a spot of his own choosing. Thinking that, Streak drew the Colt again and lined it into the pitch-blackness ahead.

His reaching hand felt the wall angle sharply. He stopped, listened. Still no sound. He advanced a sideward step, groping with his hand to determine whether the rock was only indented or turning down another corridor. That step brought him into sight of dim light down another angling aisle of the tunnel. At first he thought he might be seeing the light of the lantern the man ahead had most surely brought back here to light his way. But the radiance was too pale and colorless for lantern light. He started on toward it, warily, soundlessly, gun cocked now. And the light strengthened as he advanced.

When he could make out the break in the rock along the top of the tunnel, he stopped, understanding that it was daylight that shone through and onto the tunnel walls. He didn't go on until he had studied every shadow, every outline, every break in the wall. Finally he was sure that a man couldn't be waiting concealed up there.

He stood at the lower mouth of a broadly climbing chimney and looked obliquely upward a hundred feet and out into a patch of dazzling blue sky where a hawk wheeled lazily in the heavens. It was hard to believe what he saw, harder for his disappointment. The long-climbing alley of the chimney, a fault that had doubtless been washed clear by centuries of rain and erosion, offered a second entrance, or exit, to the cave. He realized that the sounds he had heard back there near the pocket entrance must have been made by the grulla in climbing the steep angle along the fault, that the man's voice must have sounded in an irritable oath as the grulla balked at a particularly steep part of the climb.

Forgotten now was the wariness of the past few minutes as he started up the chimney. His shirt was plastered to his sweating back as he pulled himself up the final ten feet on hands and knees. Suddenly the broad view of a flat piñon-studded mesa lay before him. Westward, the line of the cañon showed plainly, more closely a deep and twisting cut in the surface of the mesa. Beyond, the flats stretched out for perhaps a quarter of a mile, finally giving way to a tangled and barren maze of sharply rising hills. To the north, the mesa continued on for a lesser distance before butting a series of stepped hills that were timbered in their higher reaches.

Up there Streak could make out the high pinnacle of the needle rock along the line of the cañon. The spired peaks formed the upward horizon, patterned sharply against the deep blue of the morning sky. To the south, the mesa soon gave into a torn and rocky maze of thinly timbered hills; he could remember the look of those craggy slopes as he had yesterday seen them from the lower end of Prenn's pasture, forbidding, seeming too tangled and rocky for even a horse to travel.

It was eastward that Streak found what he was looking for. Momentarily outlined at that limit of the flat, fading from sight in a dark belt of pine that blanketed the first abrupt hill, he made out the moving shape of a rider. He glimpsed this for an instant only, at first not sure that he had seen it. But when he was sure that he had seen the man he was hunting, hope flowed strongly in him again.

He turned quickly and started back down the chimney into the cave.

A quarter hour later Streak was leading Buchwalter's pony up out of the chimney. The horse was breathing hard, shoulders glistening from the effort the climb had cost him. Streak sat down a moment to catch his breath. His lean face was lined with sweat, his shirt clung to his broad, rope-muscled shoulders, and, when he took off his Stetson to mop his brow, the line of the hatband was imprinted damply in his waving black hair; never had the pattern of the pure gray hair been so pronounced against the black as now. Streak was tired, weary to the bone, and his head was aching once more, but his sharp-planed face bore a smile; it wasn't a pleasant expression but cold and deadly as he looked eastward and marked the spot he was to ride for.

Knowing that a long and hard ride might lie ahead, he spent a few minutes letting down the stirrups on Buchwalter's saddle and readjusting the blanket under it before he tightened the cinch. He wanted everything to be right when the moment came to face Ed's murderer. A short stirrup or a loose cinch might mean the difference between a poor shot and a good one. He wasted more precious seconds emptying his borrowed gun and several times testing the trigger pull. When it came to needing the weapon, he wanted to know the feel of it.

One regret rode with him as he swung into the saddle and started out across the mesa. He hadn't taken the time to go back into the cañon and tell Bill where he was headed. Down there he had felt strongly the urgency to get back here and set out after the killer; there hadn't seemed time to go back into the cañon. Now he was wishing he had, for eventually Bill, and perhaps Kelso, would tire of waiting for him and come to investigate. Unless they could make Buchwalter talk—and Streak supposed that the man would have a glib story— they wouldn't know where he had gone. They might just possibly explore the cave and find the chimney climbing to the mesa, but Streak doubted that. They would be too interested in forcing Buchwalter to tell the truth, and that, Streak guessed, the Fencerail foreman would never do.

This regret was keen as he put the strange animal to a high lope across the half mile distance that separated him from the timber where he'd last seen the man on the grulla. Pulling down out of his run as he neared the trees, he began casting for sign. Presently he found it clearly marked in the sandy clay, the track he knew so well, that of a right forehoof widely splayed.

The sign led him into the jack pine and dense clumps of second-growth aspen, which here was floored with white-oak bush and barberry. Still, the tracks were fresh and plain enough so that he could easily follow them along the narrow aisles the grulla had traveled. Within three hundred yards the smooth contours of the ground broke off to a rocky ravine slashed with series of steep hummocks that formed the shoulder of the first long hill.

Now Streak could understand Bill's claim that only a few men knew this vast northeastward lip of the valley. There was nothing to bring a man up here, no grass, no trails, no goal beyond that hitherto impossible one of finding a pass across the Arrowheads. Without a thorough knowledge of the country, a rider could easily become lost in this thickly wooded hill tangle. It would be hard to get a glimpse of the valley proper from here, for there was always a maze of hills in the foreground to confuse, to make a man doubt his sense of direction. He found himself already doubting his and for that reason tried to imagine the exact spot he was traveling.

Prenn's meadow, he knew, lay somewhere downward and to his right. East of Prenn's, angling slightly southward out of the direction he'd traveled yesterday in coming down from the pass, was more timber that stretched all the way south to the creek that wound down from the dam at Elbow Lake, past Bishop's, and finally past town. To the south of that creek were the big outfits whose unfenced sections took up the many miles to the valley's southward limit. Then from this point in three directions, except to the west, lay an enormous expanse of waste and virgin timberland, uninhabited, untraveled, covering the whole vast sweep of the valley's northeastward segment all the way up to the meeting of the two lines of mountains.

Streak had no way of knowing what errand had taken the man on the splay-foot away from the cave. He was puzzled at the direction in which the sign was now leading him, for he judged the direction to be almost due east. No definite purpose that he could think of could bring a man up here. The farther the devious line of the sign led him, the more Streak began to wonder why the man he was hunting had ridden this way.

The breeze that had sprung up so abruptly at dawn had now strengthened, still coming out of the northeast. If it held this way, Streak supposed that it would bring the overdue rain the valley ranchers had longingly awaited. It was a gusty wind, bending the tops of the aspens in fitful sweeps. It moaned softly through the tops of the taller trees, the Douglas firs and the blue spruce. Except for that sound and the muffled footfalls of his pony, the forest seemed strangely silent. Every sense in Streak was acute to a high-strung caution. Ordinarily he could have depended on the scream of a jay or the scolding of a squirrel to warn him of his drawing up on the grulla's rider, but as the miles fell behind, his pony settling down out of its first nervousness to the steady going, he felt the lack of these sounds. Only once did the voice of the forest break its silence, as faintly, in the distance, Streak caught the shrill whistle of a camp robber.

He came suddenly upon a small park-like glade clear of trees. It lifted with the gentle slope of a hill, grassy, open for a scant hundred yards except for the shadow cast by a giant fir growing at nearly its exact center. A covey of dusky gray grouse whirred out of the grass and drummed across into the shadowed obscurity of the timber off to his left. He didn't know why he stopped at the tree margin, but he did, that deep instinct of wariness strangely halting him.

Streak saw the blue gunsmoke blossom from the tree border across the glade even before the hard pound of the shot sounded. He felt the searing burn of the bullet along his left upper arm even as he rolled from the saddle. His hands took up the shock of his fall and he threw his body in a tight roll toward the thick bole of an uprooted tree close by. A geyser of black earth mold whipped his face, marking the striking of the second bullet. Then he was safe, the gnarled roots of the tree with its pressed earth shielding him from the gun over there.

A brief silence held on, during which he reached for his gun and laid it on the dry matting of pine needles ahead of him. He felt a cool wetness along his left arm and shifted position a little, looking at the crimson stain on the sleeve of his shirt. Through the tear in the cloth he could see the shallow bullet crease in the flesh. A meager smile touched his face and a rash devilment was all at once in him. He pushed up onto elbow and called: "You'll have to do better than that, Dallam!"

A mocking yet pleasant-sounding laugh was his first answer. Then Pete Dallam's deep bass voice warned: "Just keep your distance, friend. That's all I ask." There was a brief pause, in which the stillness, with even the wind momentarily gone, pressed in on Streak. Then: "Who are you? Mathiot?"

"Good guess," Streak replied. "Come out and show yourself."

"No, thanks!"

Streak could think of nothing further to say. He began to look around and finally saw how, without exposing himself, he could worm his way under the dead tree's horizontal trunk and across to the thick trunk of a nearby fir. He had crawled under the tree when abruptly the sound of a pony's hurrying run sounded across to him. He lay still, listening, as the animal went away. Pete Dallam hadn't stayed to fight.

As he was coming to his knees, Streak all at once went rigid. From across the glade where Dallam had been came a *crackling* sound. He stood up, looked across the expanse. A sheet of orange flame was jumping from the bottom branches of a pine over there. Before Streak could move, it had consumed the crown of the tree in an explosive puff, whirling sparks aloft. Dallam had set the forest afire!

Chapter Twenty

Cathy Bishop had left her room early that morning, glancing in at her father's door across the hallway to see that he was already up. Crossing the living room, she found the table at its far end strangely lacking the breakfast furnishings. Only then did she realize that she had heard no sounds from the kitchen since she had wakened.

The kitchen was deserted. There wasn't even a fire in the big iron range. Cathy went to the outside door and glanced out across the yard to see her father climbing the knoll from the creek bridge.

The look on his face as he came up gave her a twinge. He shrugged and held his hands outspread. "Looks like we have the place to ourselves, Cathy," he said in a lifeless voice. "Even Pinto's gone."

Cathy was suddenly and strangely happy with a deep, new feeling toward her parent. Last night she had wanted to go to him, to talk to him, to try to heal the open wound of their relations, but he had been busy with Riggs until very late, so late that she gave up hope of seeing him. His statement that they had the place to themselves this morning put a new light on the outcome of that talk with Riggs. But Cathy wasn't thinking of getting an explanation for the absence of the crew, for Pinto's abandoned kitchen. She was thinking of the father she had once known, that sure, calm-spirited man of a year or so ago. Frank Bishop was no longer himself. Now, by the look on his face, she could see that he didn't know where he stood with her. He was humble, appearing almost apologetic for having spoken. The crew had obviously deserted, and he seemed to expect that his daughter, too, was on the point of leaving. An impulse she wouldn't have resisted could she have checked it sent Cathy down out of the doorway and to him, reaching up to lay her hands on his shoulders. Her eyes became tear-filled as she looked into his face and saw its wonderment and uncertainty. Abruptly the emotion that was in her welled over and she murmured: "Dad, it doesn't matter. We're together, you and I. Dad, I . . . I'm glad it's just us."

The amazement, the stunned elation that crossed Frank Bishop's face was good to see. All at once his arms came out and swept her to him. He pressed her head gently to his shoulder. Then, tenderly, he kissed her on the forehead, saying thickly, low-voiced: "Cathy, girl, you mean it. Can an old man say he's made some mistakes?"

"If you'll let me say the same, Dad. My mistakes have been the worst."

That morning was to be long remembered, both for this beginning and its final ending. Cathy cooked breakfast, and for the first time in many months the big main room of the house rang to her laughter. The change that gradually came over Frank Bishop wiped years from the look of his face and ended once and for all that aloofness and severity behind which he had retired these last weeks. He seemed almost young again.

The only serious talk they had was of the crew's desertion. "Riggs combed me over last night for not making a fight of it," Bishop explained. "I gave him his time, along with half a dozen others he brought in. They evidently decided not to stay the night, because Riggs wanted an order to Adams to get their pay. But Pinto . . . I can't understand his not being here."

"Where are the others, Shorty and Phil and the rest?"

"In town," Bishop said. "I told 'em at supper last night that they needed a night off. George wanted to get a letter off home. Two of the boys stayed on after Riggs had gone. I sent them in later to keep an eye on him. But I don't know about Pinto."

"What's going to happen from now on, Dad?" Cathy asked.

He shrugged. "I don't know. I haven't made up my mind to anything. I'm going across to see Jensen this morning and talk it over with him."

"Can we get along with sheep across the valley?"

"We'll have to. I'll have to make my peace with Buchwalter. I could even go in and have a talk with Laura Dallam."

"Would you let me do it . . . see Buchwalter and Laura?" Cathy asked on impulse.

Her father gave her a surprised glance. "Why, of course, Cathy. But that's my chore."

"No, it's mine. In a way, all this has happened because I loved the . . . wrong man." She got those three words out with difficulty but meant them. The old hurt was gone. "It's up to me to make the peace. I'll find Buchwalter and tell him how we feel. Laura likes me. I can make her understand that we're sincere."

"Go ahead. Only I'd just as soon do it."

"But I want to. You can go on over to Jensen's."

He helped her saddle the black at the big corral and watched her ride out the trail. It was like old times, like those early mornings when she had been a gangly girl and he had invariably come down to the corral to see her off to school. This morning, Cathy realized, was a momentous one in her life. She had made peace with her father. Never had she felt quite so deeply thankful for anything. The growing realization that she no longer cared for Pete, that she wouldn't even if he were alive, was so contradictory that she wondered at herself. But the feeling was genuine. Trouble and worry had pushed her to the breaking point; now, in this rearrangement of her thoughts and hopes, Pete Dallam became nothing more than the cause of the most unpleasant and heartbreaking period of her life.

As she came abreast the lane to Schoonover's place some miles below the ranch, Cathy was assailed by memories of Pete that were too strong to put down. This had been the place she many times had secretly met Pete in the days when her father wouldn't allow him to come to the house to see her. Off this side lane branched a little-used trail that ended on a small section of abandoned farmland topping a rim some three miles to the north. Cathy had often ridden to the rim with Pete. The memories of those days were alive and fresh and a little galling.

On sudden impulse, she turned into the lane and was presently headed up the rim trail. Some small inner doubt needed satisfying. If she could but stand there on the rim and come to grips with her sharpest memories of Pete, suffering no regrets, she felt that she finally and absolutely would know that his memory meant nothing to her any longer.

Once, when the timber flanking the trail thinned, she happened to glance behind and notice the sky to the south. A hazy cloudbank was building over the far desert. It might mean that rain was on the way, or it could mean nothing, for late summer weather in this country was unpredictable. Cathy was only later aware of this thought; at the time it was an almost unconscious one.

The rim was as she remembered it, the bare ground weed-grown and badly eroded. She got down out of the saddle and ground-haltered the mare while she walked over to sit on a low outcrop very near the edge of the drop-off. The cliff fell sheerly and it had always made her uneasy to look down that hundred feet. Pete, she remembered, had been scornful of the height and would stand at the very edge with his back to the void.

Sitting there, her memories of past visits to this place very dear, Cathy could feel no sense of loss or sadness over Pete's death. *It's gone, forever,* she thought, and was suddenly glad to be alive and free, to be here without Pete at her side.

For the first time her glance went into the distance rather than to things close at hand, out across the vast tree-mantled sweep of hills lying between this rim and the upward Arrowheads. She saw something she couldn't understand. It made her catch her breath and abruptly come to her feet. At first she didn't believe what she was seeing. But there it was, a stark reality. Miles to the north and higher than this rim, a pale grayish pall of smoke lay over the forest. For a moment it looked like a low-hanging cloud. Then she knew it was the smoke of a fire. Even as she watched, it fanned out before the wind, growing in density.

Through the years, Cathy had come to a growing awareness of the danger threatening the east slope by the occasional late summer droughts. Once she had seen a small timber fire and it had terrified her, even though it had come in a comparatively wet season and consumed only a small acreage of trees. Now, to see the awful possibilities of what that distant blaze would do to dry timber on this windy day, she stood rigidly in cold terror.

She ran across to her horse, her first impulse to ride to Schoonover's and give the warning. In the saddle, she reined the black over closer to the rim, looking northward again, trying to pick out some landmark she could name to locate the fire. Now she saw a second blob of smoke, much nearer than the first. Her panic mounted. She lifted the reins to turn away from the cliff's edge.

Suddenly a sharp echo from below the rim shuttled up to her. Its rock-on-rock explosion startled her as it did the mare. It came again, more plainly. She looked downward and saw nothing. Dismounting again, she walked closer to the drop-off.

A hundred feet below, straight downward, the

rotten talus of the rim's footing sloped out to the rocky dry channel of a wash. Beyond the arroyo a wider strip of ground strewn with broken boulders climbed to the margin of a belt of jack pine blanketing a near hill spur that paralleled the rim. Riding that slope was a man who kept looking back over his shoulder toward the trees. There was, even from this acutely upward angle, something familiar about the firmly erect way he sat his grulla pony.

Once he stopped, half turning his horse so that he could get a better look behind. Then Cathy knew what it was about him that seemed so familiar. He rode the way Pete had ridden, standing in stirrups, free hand gripping the swell to keep erect, rein arm held close to chest. It was the way nine out of ten men rode a trot. Still, the exact stance was so strikingly like Pete's that it gave her a start.

She laughed nervously, and was turning away when the sharp explosion of a gunshot racketed up to her. She looked downward again. The grulla's rider was out of the saddle, behind his pony, a gun in his hand. Suddenly he came erect and emptied the weapon in a burst of sound upward toward the trees. Out of the trees plunged a rider on a sorrel horse. The sorrel took three strides before it all at once lost footing and pitched forward in a broken roll. The rider was too late in kicking his left boot from stirrup. Cathy choked back a cry as the animal rolled on its rider's leg. The man's upper body was wrenched back sickeningly, knocking his hat off. At the instant Cathy recognized the man she knew as Kincaid from the slashing of gray on his head, his long frame went limp and he lay back loosely, the horse rolling clear.

Cathy knelt transfixed with horror as the grulla's rider calmly walked up the slope, the gun still in hand. He stood over Kincaid, lazily pushing back the curl-brimmed Stetson. He took it off and ran his hand across his dark sorrel head. And by that gesture, Cathy knew that she was seeing Pete Dallam. It was the way he did it, his gesture so soundly remembered, so distinctive of Pete. Had Cathy doubted the move itself, there was the color of the hair to label him. Her whole body trembled, a dappled wave of white light danced before her eyes, and she grew faint. Still, she couldn't move, couldn't take her eyes from the pair below.

Pete presently leaned down, took Kincaid roughly by an arm, and heaved him up onto his back. He staggered under the load as he went up the slope and disappeared into the trees. Cathy felt hysteria begin to work in her. She checked it with a force of will she hadn't known she could command. Pete Dallam was alive!

Knowing that, the peace of mind she had found this morning crumbled like a rotting, spineless thing, crumbled and lay in ruins. Pete not only was alive; he had killed a man. Or he had watched a man die as coolly and as heartlessly as he would have watched the painful branding of a yearling. Pete was alive! Her thinking became an intolerable torment. What did this mean? What furtive errand had brought Pete to this out-of-the-way spot? Why had he fought Kincaid and what was he doing with him now?

Even though every instinct warned her to leave this spot and be gone, Cathy had to see the end of this. She waited, straightening her arms to keep them from trembling, trying to regain control of herself. The thing that finally quieted her was sight of a blue curling finger of smoke mounting above the crests of the pines across from her to flatten to the wind. Hardly had she seen that telltale mark of a fire when Pete reappeared. He sauntered down to the grulla and built a cigarette. In the saddle, he stared a moment in the direction of the smoke. Then, with a lazy touching of hand to hat brim in a mocking salute, he put the grulla on down the wash. In less than half a minute he was lost to sight around a lower turning of the rim, the grulla at a run.

With the last sight of him, the dread deep within Cathy at the knowledge that Pete Dallam lived died slowly. Yes, he was alive. But she had seen him kill a man; she had seen him carry the body of that man into the trees and set fire to the forest, probably to destroy the evidence of his act. It was

Pete, then, who had started those other fires!

At that point of stunning insight, Cathy became utterly confused. Couldn't it have been Pete, then, who had made the attempt at ambushing her father the other morning in Ledge? If he was alive, then who was the man in the grave marked with his name in the cemetery down at Agua Verde? Did it mean that Pete had committed two other murders to arrange the sham of his own death? Yes, she was sure of it. But why? Why these murders and now the final staging of this fire that would so completely ruin all the east-slope ranchers?

Then the picture lay clear. Pete Dallam, balked by her father's stubbornness, by his own inability to make himself one of this country's biggest men by fair means, had seen the chance to do it another way. Ambition had always driven him relentlessly, although Cathy had never realized until now how strong a part of his make-up that ambition was. By disappearing, by shamming his death, he had relaxed the vigilance of the men who held rein on him. By bringing in his sister, deceiving even her, he had roused sympathy for his cause. But for a poor turn of luck, he would have killed Frank Bishop and gone unpunished. With a better turn of luck, coming in the form of Kincaid's brilliant maneuver of bringing in the sheep, he had accomplished what might otherwise have taken him months, even years. And today, his sheep safely in the valley, Pete Dallam was surely and decisively putting an end to all opposition by starting a forest fire that would gut the entire east slope and ruin the men who fought him.

A blend of loathing, disgust, and fear was in Cathy. The loathing and disgust came when she realized that she had once, even yesterday, loved this power-mad killer with her entire being, even to the point of not stopping at the betrayal of her father. The fear was for the awful picture of what this valley would become before the day was over. With this wind, there was nothing to stop the ruin promised by those three smoky marks so palely patterned against the dark blanket of the forest.

A gusty shifting of the wind brought the acrid smell of smoke to her. She looked downward, faintly hearing the *crackling* of flames as they gained headway in the tinder-dry undergrowth of the jack pine across from her. Knowing she should at once start for home and give the warning of what was coming, she still hesitated. She was thinking of the man who had, before yesterday's dawn, forced her to accompany him to the sheep camp above the pass. A subtle attraction she had found toward Kincaid still lingered. Perhaps it was backed by her now conscious comparison of him to Pete and the knowledge that he had been a far better man than the one she had loved. There had been no arrogance in him, only a sureness tempered with a genuine kindliness. He had been so courteous and soft-spoken. A genuine sadness was in her. Of all the indictments so suddenly and staggeringly shaped against Pete Dallam, this killing of Kincaid was the worst in her mind. She felt an unaccountable sense of deep loss and realized now that Kincaid had been very much in her thoughts since that morning he had carried her in off the street in Ledge. She knew, too, that his seeming poor opinion of her had been the first thing to open her eyes to the injustice of her attitude toward her father. One of the sharpest regrets she had ever experienced came at the moment she realized she could never now tell Kincaid that he had been wrong about her, that she hadn't betrayed her father. For Kincaid was dead, struck down by a man she had once loved. She wanted to cry. Yet the tears wouldn't come. It was as though the shock of the past minutes had numbed her to the point where she could only dully feel any emotion.

With a last deliberate glance downward at the fire—she could see tongues of flame licking the crowns of two of the trees now—she turned and started walking over to the mare. Suddenly she stopped, a horrible thought gripping her. *Suppose Kincaid wasn't dead? Suppose Pete had left him there, unconscious, to burn to death?*

She ran to the edge of the drop-off again. Some two hundred yards down along it there was a break in its perpendicular line. A section of the rock had rotted and fallen, leaving a steep incline down which it might be possible to pick her way. The footing would be dangerous, for there were places that dropped sheerly still, but she was going to go down there.

Chapter Twenty-One

An insistent note of warning gradually penetrated the pleasing shroud of drowsiness that cloaked Streak's consciousness. It kept nagging at him like a persistent little devil with a pronged fork, prodding him out of his utter serenity. He did his best to ignore it. Then he came fully awake, and retched and choked as the suffocating bite of smoke bit deeply into his lungs.

When he opened his eyes, he saw what was the matter. A short glowing length of a branch lay near his face. The smoke was coming from the scorching the glowing coal was giving the matting of dry needles underneath it. Only now did Streak associate that subdued roar with anything tangible. He pushed up onto one elbow, winced as a stab of pain cut across the middle of his back, and looked above. Flames were engulfing the crest of a nearby tree. Suddenly he remembered.

He had followed Dallam's sign for miles after their first encounter, after he saw he didn't have a chance of battling that first fire. He came on the second blaze to find that it had already gained more headway than the first. Only then did he realize that the original fire had been no accident. Dallam was firing the east slope.

Streak had caught up with Ed's killer there below the rim, nearly had him. Then some sixth sense had warned Dallam and he had thrown that lucky shot toward the trees, sensing his danger. Streak's pony had been skin-burned by the bullet and lunged out of cover. Dallam's second bullet brought the horse down. Streak could still feel the sharp torture of the rock corner biting into his spine as the falling horse half rolled onto him.

Now he understood why he lay here. Dallam had expected he would never recover consciousness. If anything was left of his body after the fire, there would be no bullet wound to point to murder. Dallam had taken a chance and not a very long one at that, Streak decided, staring up at the bank of flames off to his left.

It was when he struggled to sit up that he found he couldn't use his legs. A paralysis deadened all feeling in his lower body. After a moment he fought down the panic and stopped wasting his strength. Lying there, he tried to think coherently. The smoke ahead thinned momentarily and he saw the gray face of the rim through the trees, not far away. He should be able to crawl that far, he decided. He started pulling himself along with his arms, dragging his useless legs.

He wormed his way toward the tree margin for about thirty feet, then another twenty, feeling the hot breath of the mounting flames gather in intensity. When his strength began going, he rested more often. Time and again he had to roll onto his back or lie on his face to reach around and knock off burning branch ends that fell on him. His face was runneled with sweat and the air had become fouler and the coughing hurt more, but he was getting there.

Suddenly a dull explosion sounded over the roar of the flames. Ahead, a foot-thick tree lazily fell directly across his path, its trunk and branches solid sheets of flame. At first he couldn't believe it. His mind couldn't take in the fact that he was hopelessly blocked, that he was to die here. So overwhelming was this defeat that a half-mad laugh welled up out of his parched throat. The tree's trunk, held by branches only two feet off the ground directly ahead, was a good sixty feet long. To the left, alongside its earth-torn bole, two other bigger trees were solid sheets of sky-leaping flame. Off to the right, the blazing crown of the fallen pine had already ignited the drought-dried tangle of an oak thicket. Between these two impassable barriers, the length of the tree was one long line of flame. To go around either end was as impossible as crawling under the tree.

Streak had always thought of death in a fatalistic

way, seldom letting his mind dwell for long on where or how he might meet it. It would come when his number was up; nothing he could do would ward off his ultimate end. Once, facing a pepperbox Derringer in the trembling hand of a crooked monte dealer, he had imagined he felt the touch of death's hand on his shoulder. He had brushed the weight aside in a gesture that was meaningless to everyone who saw it but himself, and thereby distracted the gambler's attention for the split second necessary to knock the Derringer aside. But now he knew that death was near, standing more certainly beside him than that other time. He felt strangely calm. But he felt cheated, too. For, able to use his legs, he could have walked scornfully out of the inferno that was gradually closing in on him for the kill.

Once more Streak pushed his upper body from the ground. This time he tried to rock backward onto his knees. He shut out the roar and whine of the flames in his concentration on making his body bend to his will. Finally he was on hands and knees. His useless legs were half supporting him. Now if he could but crawl up to that blazing tree stem ahead, only that far, he knew he would live. He could stand the heat he knew would sear the flesh about his waist if he could only get close enough to the pine to throw himself belly down across it and fall to the other side. He took his weight from his right knee, trying to crawl.

Suddenly he went too far off balance. He fell on his side and lay there doubled up, gasping to breathe.

He tried again. He rolled onto his stomach, then back to his knees. Now he could move his left leg a little. He lifted the weight from his left knee and moved it forward almost a foot. He shifted his weight off the other knee—and fell sideward again. It took him some time to pull in enough air to end the spasm of retching that racked him. But now he couldn't push up onto his hands. He was too weak.

Finally he just lay there, waiting idly, watching the vertical sheets of flame devouring the timber about him. A fire was a beautiful and an awesome thing. Streak didn't even mind the scorching heat now. With a force of will, he forgot the pain in his starving lungs.

As he felt consciousness slowly leaving him, he straightened and looked ahead once more to see the symbol of his death, the flaming tree that had blocked his escape. Through the bluish fog of smoke he could see the cool gray face of the rim, the last tree at the forest's edge hardly ten good paces away. Something moved out there, a hurrying upright shape that was but a shadow through the smoke. Some stricken fear-crazed animal running from the fire, he thought. All at once that shape took on substance, became a man running in toward him. He cried out hoarsely, but then his cry died against the angry crescendo of the fire's roar. It would be Dallam, of course, come back to make sure of his demoniac act of violence.

Streak's first thought was of his gun—that he didn't have one. The Colt Kelso had loaned him lay somewhere out there near his horse. If only he had the gun, he could take Dallam with . . . He saw the wealth of long dark hair topping the figure out there and instantly forgot Dallam, recognizing Cathy Bishop. He called again, his shout nothing but a hoarse croaking. By some miracle, the girl seemed to hear him. She stopped, looked his way, and then ran in past that outermost tree and toward the downed blazing pine.

She was close, barely the length of a rope away from him, when she lifted an arm to shield her face from the heat and stopped. He could catch the agony written on her face as she once more took a forward step, then quickly backed out of range of the searing heat. Then he heard her call faintly: "Kincaid! Kincaid, where are you?"

He shouted again and this time she did hear him and looked directly at him. He could see her decide to come closer to that burning tree between them and he called hoarsely: "Get back! No use!"

Desperation made her ignore his command. Again she came on toward the tree, this time three steps. Abruptly she tripped and fell to her knees and until she had crawled back once more he had an agonizing moment of fear that his call had brought her to her death. That torturous moment strangely calmed the seething torment of his mind, and now his whole being, his every thought was concentrated on saving this girl. He forgot himself in face of a sudden understanding that it meant a great deal to him that Cathy should live. He had that moment of insight before his mind shuttled back to a thought he'd had a moment ago when he saw how close, yet how infinitely out of reach, Cathy stood from him. He knew then how he could get her to leave this spot, at least for a few moments, and perhaps, if he could get her to leave now, it would be impossible for her to return—for the blaze was spreading faster, whipped by the wind.

"Rope!" he shouted, hardly sure that she could catch his voice over the pulsating booming of the fire. "Get the rope off that downed horse!"

Cathy's face lit with sudden gladness and she turned away, running out from the trees. That picture of her, beautiful, radiant in her thankfulness as she left him, was the last picture he would have of her, Streak supposed. He had that one deep pang of regret that made him forget the others, the knowledge that he would never again see this girl who was risking her life to save his. Then he closed his eyes, wanting to keep that image of her fresh in his mind. He didn't mind what was coming now.

"Kincaid!"

He thought he was remembering her first cry of a minute ago. Then her voice came again: "Kincaid, you've got to try! Here! Look at me."

She stood four or five paces beyond the tree, her arm again shielding her face. When he saw how much closer the flames had leaped to each side of her, he called frantically, incoherently a warning that was lost in the inferno of sound. She smiled as she shook loose the first two loops in the coil of the rope she had taken from the saddle of Buchwalter's dead pony. He watched her make the first cast, expertly, and the next moment saw that what she was trying was impossible. She was trying to throw under the horizontal trunk of the tree, through the tangle of blazing branches there.

He managed to shout—"Over it!"—before a spasm of coughing doubled him up and made him gag for breath. He clutched at his throat to ease the constriction of the muscles there and could smell the singed hair on the back of his hand.

Cathy coiled the rope again, swung the small loop she had shaken through the hondo, and made her second throw almost blindly, for a billowing cloud of smoke abruptly fogged the tree from her sight. But the loop arced true over the blazing log and fell on Streak's legs. The next moment he was gripping the hard-woven manila. He knew at once that Cathy didn't have the strength to pull him. Also, that the rope, lying across the blazing tree trunk, would burn through almost at once. Those two facts, coupled with the knowledge of what he had let himself in for—he would somehow have to pull himself up and over the glowing flame-stippled stem of the pine—told him that Cathy was needlessly risking her life, that the faint hope of getting out of here alive was a forlorn one. Still, he owed it to Cathy to make the attempt. When he had shown her how hopeless his situation was, he could make her think of her own safety. She was pulling at the rope, trying to move him. He shook his head, hoping she would understand, and started pulling himself hand over hand toward the downed tree. She did understand, for she took a sideward step and wound the rope around the wrist-thick stem of an aspen sapling as he lay face down and gasping for breath after his first effort.

Streak found his arms stronger than he had thought them. Soon he was bowing his head before the furnace-like heat that radiated from the blazing pine. He would look up now and then in his efforts, seeing the smoking line of the rope lying across the blazing wood. Why didn't it burn through?

He dragged a deep, gagging breath into his lungs and pulled himself up to the tree. Catching a hold with one hand on the rope where it lined up and over the flaming wood, he reached with the other for a higher handhold, steeling himself against the bone-deep burn he knew was coming. He turned his face from side to side, unable for long to stand the intense heat on one portion of it. His free hand was almost touching the glowing wood when suddenly the rope let go and he fell in and almost under the tree. The glowing coal of a branch end burned deeply into his shoulder and he gave a spasmodic lurch away from it. Lying there, lifting his head to catch a final glimpse of Cathy, he saw her turn and stagger back out of the trees and go to her knees at the edge of open ground.

At last she had been forced to think of herself. He lay wondering how much longer he could hold that final precious lungful of air. When he no longer could, the end would come quickly. He saw the sagging rope on the tree's far side sag even farther. Abruptly its burned-through end fell to the ground. The red glowing tip scorched his fingers. He clutched it, hope suddenly alive in him. For the far end was still fastened to the sapling!

He dragged his half-paralyzed body a foot farther under the flaming pine, another, two more, clawing aside the burning and smoking branches that lay in his path. His lungs cried for air. Still, he wouldn't take another breath, knowing that to do so was to die almost instantly and in agony. Along his back he felt the searing heat of the red-hot wood pressing down on him. Then the heat was strongest along his legs, at the back of his calves. In those final seconds, as the patch of ground before his eyes danced in misty, wavering indistinctness, he wriggled forward as far as one fresh handhold would take him. He had an instant of realization that he had been able to bend his left leg and push with it, that the paralysis there had gone. Then the air left his lungs in a final heaving gasp. He drew in another breath. The heat of it parched his throat, made him cough convulsively. He couldn't breathe this air but had to. Mercifully consciousness left him and his long frame relaxed against the smoking earth.

Chapter Twenty-Two

"Bill, I'm scared," Fred Kelso told his companion, and his voice carried a strong note of apprehension.

"Who isn't?" Paight said. "But we're going on. He's somewhere ahead. He's got to be."

Kelso had a moment ago insisted that they should ride straight for Bishop's place to give warning of the two fires that were raging on the east slope. Bill had argued that they should stick on the sign they'd been following for better than the past hour. That sign was two sets of blended tracks, one of them a splay-foot's.

"They've seen the smoke by now," Bill argued. "And maybe Streak needs help."

Kelso nodded. "Then let's get goin'," he said, and followed Bill's lead.

The sheriff had no more doubt than Bill did that there was a good chance of Streak being in trouble. It was a certainty that whoever Streak was following had started the two fires, and a man who would do that wouldn't hesitate to kill anyone watching him if he got the chance. Kelso couldn't make so much as a guess as to who was riding the splay-foot.

They had been lucky back there at the hide-out. Letting Buchwalter lie where they found him, they had gone into the cave. They had found the chimney and run onto the sign near the mesa opening. They had gone back for their horses and come straight on, sticking to the sign. Just now they followed the sign down an abrupt slope and were soon out of the timber, with a high limestone rim close on their right.

Bill suddenly drew rein. "Which way?" he asked, studying the ground close ahead. "The splay-foot headed down there in the open. There goes Streak's sign off toward the trees. Which one do we take?"

Kelso had been looking down the line of the rim. He answered flatly: "Neither. There's someone down there. And there's more smoke."

Bill saw a figure coming out of the tree margin on down the line of the wash. He could see what looked like a down horse beyond the figure. Above, a billowing cloud of smoke fanned out and rode the wind. He touched spur to his pony and raced down the rocky draw at a hard run. For an instant he had a wild hope that the man down there was Streak, then he knew it wasn't, for Streak was taller than this man. He heard Kelso coming along behind, falling back gradually because his horse didn't have much of a run.

About fifty yards away he recognized Cathy. A moment later he saw her stumble and go to her knees, looking behind her. The only recognizable thing about the girl was her raven-black hair that she wearily brushed back from her face as Bill rode up. Her face was smudged and reddened, her right sleeve torn at the shoulder. A curl of smoke lined out from a hole low on the leg of her denims.

She didn't know Bill was there until he had vaulted from the saddle and beat out the still smoldering cloth at her leg. Even then she looked up at him with a dull, lifeless stare.

He put his back to the pressing heat coming out of the trees, took her by the shoulders, shook her. "Cathy, what's happened?"

"He's in there." She nodded toward the spot where he had first seen her as she staggered into the open. "I think he's dead." Abruptly her voice grew louder, touched with hysteria. "Bill, get him out!" She tried to struggle to her feet.

"Get who out?" he asked curtly.

"Kincaid!"

Sudden fear struck through Bill. He wheeled and ran in on the trees, ignoring the wave of heat that seemed as tangible as a solid wall, ignoring, too, Kelso's shout behind him. When he was four paces in past the first tree, he saw the rope wound around the sapling. He dragged in a deep breath that smarted his lungs, ran to the rope, and pulled on it. Ahead, it disappeared into a gray wall of smoke. So close to right and left that it scorched his shirt, solid sheets of flame were devouring the drought-dried timber.

For a moment, as he pulled on the rope, Bill could feel a weight on its far end. Then that weight suddenly let go and the empty end of the rope snaked out of the smoke fog ahead. Just as suddenly Bill realized that Streak must have had a hold on that rope. Shielding his face from the heat by an upthrust arm, he staggered into the smoke. Within two steps he caught the pinkish glow of the tree ahead, felt its added fiery breath without understanding what it was. For a moment the heat was so intense that it drove him backward a lurching stride. But Streak was in there somewhere and that thought finally drove him on again.

He stumbled over something soft and yielding and looked down to see a huddled shape lying at his feet. His lungs crowded for air, he lifted Streak's loose weight and turned to stagger back toward the tree margin. But for Kelso coming to help, he wouldn't have stayed on his feet.

Cathy was farther out toward the foot of the rim now, holding the two frightened horses. Together, the sheriff and Bill carried Streak there and stretched him out in the flat, narrow bed of the wash. Kelso took the horses while Cathy came to kneel beside Bill.

They looked at Streak in awe. His face was blackened, mostly by grime, his high forehead blistered in patches and the shirt along his back burned to tatters. Beneath the remnants of his shirt the skin was splotched redly with livid welts. At the left side of his head the hair was burned away in two places.

Kelso said urgently in a loud voice to carry over the roar of the fire: "We've got to get out of here . . ." He broke off abruptly as he came up and looked down at Streak. His mouth fell open. "Is he dead?" he breathed.

Bill put his hand on Streak's chest to feel for a heartbeat. His glance went savagely toward the flame-streaked margin of the trees, as though by that grim look he could silence the pulsating air and deaden the sound that made it hard for him to tell whether or not the wide chest under his hand was moving, whether or not he could feel that faint beat of the heart there.

Cathy and the sheriff watched him with fear-patterned faces. His look gradually became bleak, unpleasant. He took his hand away and put his ear to Streak's chest in a sudden despairing gesture that had its eloquent meaning. For a moment Cathy and Kelso could see that he wasn't sure, for the beginning of a light of hope came to his eyes. Then that died out and he straightened slowly and even more slowly shook his head.

All at once Cathy reached out and struck him sharply across the face. Her eyes were ablaze with a wild and hysterical anger. When she tried to strike again, he caught her wrist, calling sharply: "Cathy! Don't! Get a grip on yourself!"

She seemed not to hear him, for her voice was shrill as she cried: "You were his friend! Why weren't you with him?" Then, as abruptly as that violent emotion had struck, it left and her shoulders sagged. She said lifelessly: "I'm sorry, Bill. But I tried so hard."

"We all did," Bill said tonelessly. His look went up to the trees and down along the line of the timber, seeing that the fire was now racing to enclose the lower end of this long pocket footing the rim. All at once he took Streak by the arm, half lifted him, and managed to throw his limp weight over his shoulder. "We've got to get out of here."

Kelso held his shying, frightened pony while Bill lifted Streak and laid him across the animal's withers. Then, handing Bill the reins of the second horse, the lawman swung up into saddle. Cathy seemed apathetic, staring at Streak's head listlessly hanging down, seeming unaware of their danger. Not until Bill caught her by the arm and pushed her toward his horse did she seem to realize what they were doing. Then with a last glance toward the flame-sheeted trees where she had fought to reach Streak and failed, she let Bill help her into the saddle. He mounted behind her.

Two hundred yards below the point where they started, they had to turn and ride back a few rods, for a sudden gust of wind whipped streamers of live flame out of the trees and barred their narrowing path. Bill's horse started pitching and Bill vaulted aground to hold the fear-crazed animal, Cathy still in the saddle.

It was during their brief halt here that Cathy's glance lifted to the rim. "My mare!" she called to Bill. "She's up there! We can't just leave her!"

Bill's glance followed hers. Here the rim had lost some of its height and its line wasn't so sheer. In abrupt decision, he handed her the reins and shouted to Kelso: "Meet you on the trail above!" Before the sheriff understood, he was climbing the talus that footed the bare rimrock.

Cathy watched him until Kelso reined in alongside. "We'll make a run for it," he told her. "You're first." He struck the Fencerail animal hard across the rump with reins.

For a few moments as her pony ran wildly down

along the last narrow open finger of the wash, the orange line of burning trees terribly close, Cathy could feel the dry and blistering hot breath of the flames. A cloud of acrid smoke engulfed her for an instant. Then she was in the clear, the untouched timber close ahead, and the air was fresh and good to breathe. She caught the echoed pound of Kelso's running pony close behind.

The sheriff rode around her as they entered the trees, evidently having guessed Bill's errand, for he swung right and up the timbered slope of the rim's lower line in the direction of the trail Cathy had ridden in. Within five minutes he cut sharply left through a clump of pine seedlings and found the faint line of the trail. It seemed only a minute or so as they sat there wordlessly, listening to the now muted roar of the downward fire and the labored breathing of their winded ponies before they caught the sound of a fast-running horse. Shortly Bill came toward them along the narrow aisle of the trail, astride Cathy's black.

As he drew rein close to Kelso, the sheriff nodded down to the body ahead of his saddle. "We'd better use that rope of yours," he said soberly. "I nearly lost him back there."

He and Bill dismounted, Bill loosening the coil of rope thonged to the horn of the saddle. Cathy sat staring at them dully while the lawman gingerly slid Streak's loose bulk off his horse and stretched it out on the ground.

As Bill started across to the sheriff's pony, Cathy spoke abruptly: "What's that?"

At first Bill didn't catch her meaning, for she was looking down at Streak, who lay face up on a matting of pine needles close by. Then he saw the torn pocket of Streak's shirt, the deputy marshal's badge sagging from the inside of its ripped front, and understood.

"Streak was a federal officer. He came in here to look for a partner of his who disappeared a couple weeks ago," he told her.

"Then he wasn't . . ." Cathy's voice caught before she could go on. "He wasn't really this Kincaid?"

Bill shook his head, playing out a loop through the hondo of his rope. "No. His handle was Mathiot, Ned Mathiot. We called him Streak." He sensed the intensity with which the girl was taking in his every word and explained further. "He didn't know who to trust when he drifted in. Couldn't figure how Kelso stood in this mess. So he thought up that dodge of using Kincaid's handle to get busted out of jail."

Cathy's face went pale. "Why was he fighting Dad? Why did he help bring in the sheep?"

Bill shrugged. "Buchwalter told him a fancy story about your old man hiring the drygulching of Dallam and Sternes. He was as twisted on things as I've been. Guess he figured he'd wade right in and by stirring things up find out what had really become of Church, his sidekick."

"And did he ever find out?" Cathy asked in a hushed voice.

"No."

Bill had once more started across toward Kelso's pony, intending to toss his loop over the horn of the lawman's saddle, when Cathy spoke again. "I know what happened to him."

Bill stopped in mid-stride, swung around on her. "Happened to who?" he asked flatly.

"Streak's partner. He's dead. Pete killed him."

"Dallam?" Kelso put in. "Who told you that?"

"No one. I just know. There has to be someone else down there in Pete's grave."

A look quite plain in its meaning passed briefly between the sheriff and Bill. "Why don't you get down and rest a spell, Cathy?" Kelso said mildly.

"But I know I'm right!"

"Sure," the sheriff drawled. He limped across and reached up to offer her his hand. "You can sit over there under that tree while we do this job." When she didn't move, he went on as though explaining a simple known fact to a child: "I was down there when they buried Dallam, girl."

"So was I," Bill put in.

She looked at them angrily. "But you've got to listen." Her voice rose even though she tried to speak calmly. "It was Pete who shot Streak Mathiot. Shot him and carried him into the forest, then set the trees afire. I was up there on the rim and watched him do it."

Again, a glance passed between the two men. Only now it was unsure. "Say that again, Cathy," Bill said tonelessly.

"Pete shot Streak's horse from under him and Streak was knocked out when he fell. When Pete rode away, I climbed down to help Streak. I got down too late." Now her voice was calm, matter-of-fact, heightening the effect of her words on the two men. "His legs must have been hurt somehow. He couldn't stand, couldn't help me when I threw him that rope."

For a brief moment they were wordless. Then Bill breathed: "Dallam alive?" He looked at Kelso, whose startled expression betrayed hesitant conviction.

"Don't you see, Fred?" he went on suddenly, his voice raspy with excitement. "Dallam isn't dead, never was. It's been him all along. He's the one that made the try at Bishop, that slugged Streak up there at the hide-out yesterday. It wasn't him we buried down there at Agua. She's right, Fred. It was Streak's partner."

"But that can't be," Kelso's voice was hoarse. "I was there. I helped nail Dallam in his coffin, watched 'em shovel dirt onto him."

"How do you know it was Dallam? He had his face shot away, all of . . ." A low, startled cry from Cathy cut in on Bill's words. She swung aground in such haste that she stumbled and went to her knees. In a moment she was up again and ran across to where Streak lay and knelt beside him.

"He's alive," she cried softly, almost prayerfully. "I saw his hand move. Streak? Can you hear me?"

Bill let out an incoherent shout and ran over to go down beside her. Together they began working over the unconscious man.

Once, Bill queried, his tone edged and sharp: "You're sure he moved?"

"Yes! Yes!" she sobbed frantically, as though the assertion would bring about the fact of Streak's living. Meantime Kelso watched in mute wonderment, still too stunned by the impact of what he had just heard to help.

Not quite five minutes later, Streak opened his eyes to stare at them in a look of pain-dulled panic. For, briefly, he didn't understand what he was seeing and his whole being was filled with the sound that had roared an accompaniment to his approaching death in his last conscious moment.

Then Cathy spoke to him, quietly, tenderly, again calling him by the name she had heard Bill use. "It's all right, Streak. You're safe now."

His look at once became more natural. He took in Bill and Kelso, really seeing them for the first time. A hint of his contagious smile played over his lean, blackened face and he drawled in a

282

surprisingly strong voice: "Won't this make Dallam sore."

"It's true what she's been tellin' us?" Kelso said hoarsely. "Dallam's alive?"

Streak had momentarily closed his eyes, his face grimacing in pain. But he managed a nod that sealed the lawman's belief of the seemingly impossible truth.

"Lay off the talk, Fred," Bill said. He looked down at Streak. "Just take it easy, fella. We've got all the time in the world to get you away from here now."

Streak opened his eyes. "How bad is it?"

"Nothing to cry over," Bill told him. "I've et beef a lot rawer than you are right now, but that's nothing to worry about. You're too damned tough to cook clear through. Lie here until you feel better. Then we'll get you in to Doc Swain."

"I don't mean that," Streak said impatiently. "What about the fire?"

Bill shrugged. "No use worrying about that, either. It's caught. With this wind, it'll cover the slope before the day's out."

"Here, give me a hand." Streak abruptly pushed up onto one elbow and held a hand out.

"No, you don't." Bill drew away. "You couldn't stand if you had to."

Streak reached out, put his hand on Cathy's shoulder, and sat up. They could see that the effort cost him acute pain. Cathy choked back a cry of alarm and did what she could to steady him.

He looked at her, trying to smile as the pain eased off. "There isn't much a man can say to thank anyone for . . . for pulling him back out of the grave, is there?"

"Don't try, Streak," she said.

"You didn't have to stay there, working to get me out," he insisted. Then, lifting his shoulders in a faint shrug, he reached for her shoulder again, adding: "You've got me this far. Finish the job."

He tried to stand. Bill, convinced there was nothing he could do to fight this rangy man's ingrained stubbornness, took him by the armpits and lifted him erect, an arm around him.

Streak's glance went down to his legs. His blackened face was tight and strained as he lifted his right leg and took a halting, feeble step. Surprise was in his eyes as he moved his left leg next. Then, with a low laugh, he looked at Bill and said: "You never know how handy your legs are till you need 'em real bad."

"What good's this doing you?" Bill growled. "Sit down. Let me and Fred think about getting you in to the sawbones. We can rope you onto a hull if you can't sit one."

"We're not headed for town," was Streak's answer. "How much time have we got before the fire hits the creek?"

"Not much," Kelso said. "An hour, maybe two. But there's nothin' we can do, friend. Like Bill

284

says, you better sit and let us do the worryin' about gettin' you in."

"But there is something we can do."

"What? Hell, the whole slope's goin'! Nothin' on earth can stop that blaze, Streak. Nothin' but rain. There's clouds off to the south and it may rain tonight. But that'll only turn what's left into a stinkin' sorry mess after it's over."

"We could get the dynamite Bill lugged up to the hide-out. We can at least blast a lane through that neck of timber along the creek above Bishop's. It ought to save his layout. Maybe by the time we get to work up there we'll think of something else."

The lawman's glance swung quickly around on Bill. "We could try," he said in a moment. "That is, you can, Bill. You get down there after the dynamite while Cathy gets on home to gather Frank's crew. Tell your dad to hitch up a light rig and haul up axes, buckets, and some gunny sacks, girl. With luck they can keep that fire from jumpin' the creek there. With more . . ."

"And what're we doing all this time?" Streak asked. "You and me."

"We're headed for town."

Streak shook his head. "And miss the fun? Unh-uh. Bill, you get started. You, too, ma'am. Kelso and I will meet both of you up there along the creek."

"Mathiot, you got your head screwed on back-

285

ward," Kelso growled. "You can't do this. You wouldn't be on your feet an hour." He saw the look on Cathy's face and asked: "What's wrong?"

"I just remembered that the crew's gone," she told him. "Dad's there alone."

"Then that settles it," Streak put in. "You'll need all the help you can get, even if I am a cripple. Get going, Bill. And you could go on ahead and get me a horse, miss."

The urgency in his tone had its effect on them. Bill went into saddle at once, Cathy following him shortly. But something made Bill hesitate to leave. He reined over and looked down at Streak. "What about Dallam?"

"He'll keep until we've finished this other," was Streak's level reply.

"I'd give a lot if this hadn't happened, Streak. It's tough about Church."

"Ed was doing a job."

Those sparse words did more than anything to ease Bill Paight's worry over Streak as he abruptly touched his pony with spur and ran down along the narrow aisle of the trail. For in that reply he read a grim resolve he knew would carry Streak through this day, would keep him on his feet until he could find Pete Dallam. What was to happen after that he didn't know.

Chapter Twenty-Three

When Pete Dallam struck the timber footing the rim from which Cathy watched, he had been undecided for the first time that morning. The thing that brought on his uncertainty was that he, too, had his memories of that old meeting spot, and they were memories too pleasing to fit in with his bleak and vengeful mood this morning. Even with this long run of unbelievable luck, he felt a strange lack of something. He'd been a little drunk down there at Agua that night when he planned the killing of Sternes and that stranger who looked so much like him—a little drunk and more than a little angry at Cathy for her mentioning his drinking there in the hotel dining room. He had blamed Frank Bishop both for Cathy's attitude and for his own impossible circumstances. Bishop had made him an outcast, denied him his rightful place in the affairs of the valley. So his sole object in that double killing had been to disappear completely, to become officially dead so that when Bishop, in turn, met a mysterious death the law couldn't possibly discover who had killed him.

The following day Pete had been sober enough to see other possibilities, chief of which was the

287

bringing in of the sheep. When he arranged with Buchwalter to take over Fencerail, to bring in the girl to pose as his sister, he hadn't known exactly how he was to accomplish all this. Luck had been with him in the coming of this stranger. Mathiot had miraculously figured a way to bring in the sheep. Dallam had himself stood well beyond the light of the fire at the camp below the needle that night and heard Mathiot tell Buchwalter and the rest how to bring in the sheep. In that moment, after the failure of his attempted bushwhack of Bishop during the preceding morning, he had again suddenly seen himself as a growing power on this range.

He wondered now if he'd made a major error as far as Mathiot was concerned. No, he decided finally, he hadn't. Mathiot seemed to have played his hand alone. He doubted that Mathiot had told anyone else of the hide-out up the cañon, for Mathiot was looking for the stranger who lay in Dallam's grave down at Agua. He would naturally think the stranger had been the man at the hide-out. Dallam sensed that Mathiot had been no man to ask help in hunting down the stranger. He would keep quiet about the hide-out. Buchwalter's visit to the hide-out this morning had put Dallam in a seething rage. The loss of a large portion of the sheep band wasn't so important as his belief that he had Bishop to thank for the stampede. Believing that, he had started out on this vengeful errand that had halfway been Buchwalter's brain child. Tom had wanted him to go over and burn out Bishop, and Dallam had improved on that original idea himself. Luck had been with him in discovering that Mathiot was on his trail.

For nearly forty minutes there it had looked as though Mathiot would uncover his secret, that Mathiot might even kill him. But he had seen the man in time, his first shot there below the rim had been phenomenally lucky, and the chances of his secret coming to light had died along with Mathiot back there in the burning timber.

For the last hour an awesome realization had sobered Dallam. The complete and wholesale ruin of the east-slope outfits was now certain. Tomorrow those solid bulwarks of this country's affluence and respectability would lie crumbled in the ashes of a holocaust, their power and their money gone. Fencerail would be the valley's biggest outfit. Buchwalter would operate the spread, in theory for the girl who posed as Laura Dallam. There would be enough money to increase the outfit's holdings. And all the while Dallam would he managing things from the obscurity of his pretended grave. He would assume another name, live elsewhere. He would have money, lots of it, wealth, and untold power.

This picture of his future would have been completely satisfying but for one thing. Of all the things he had ever wished for, Cathy Bishop was the ultimate, the prize without which all the rest would be as nothing. Dallam had known many women, but of them all Cathy was the only one for whom he had ever held any real depth of feeling. He loved her. And now he knew that his long fight to accomplish these material gains had been waged only so that he could say to her: *I'm a big man, Cathy! I'm rich! I can give you anything you want! Will you have me?*

In these last few days Buchwalter had told him much about Cathy, chief of which had been her continuing and stubborn defiance of her father. She had even gone so far as to condemn him publicly there in Ledge on the morning of the ambush. Last night Dallam had lain awake in his blankets at the hide-out thinking of that, wondering what advantage he could take of Cathy's loyalty to him. He'd thought out a plan last night. Then, this morning, he'd cast it aside in his mad desire to revenge himself on Frank Bishop.

Sight of the rim, the memory of the many meetings there with Cathy, sobered Dallam out of his vengeful mood to the point where his thinking once more followed the groove it had traveled last night. Cathy undoubtedly loved him; her defiance of her father, her blaming Bishop for the Agua shoot-out, were proof of that. Once more convinced of this, Dallam became at once almost happy. The moment he realized again that Cathy still cared for him, a pressing urgency was in him. What he had last night planned he would have to do at once. There could be no waiting.

He spoke to the grulla as he used his sharp-rowelled spurs cruelly. "Move along, big boy! We're goin' places!"

He knew well this lower stretch of timber and made good time riding it. A glance at the sun, now shining brassily in a cloud-hazed sky, showed him that it was late morning, close to 11:00. Sight of the darker bank of clouds building before the wind in the south brought a smug smile to his face. There would be rain tonight, he judged. Only it would then be too late to save the timber on the east slope. The rain would only increase the misery and discomfort of men who had worked all day to save their stock and their homes.

He passed Schoonover's layout, which lay north of the creek, keeping to the timber as he rode by. It would be another hour or so before that man knew of the ranch's certain destruction. The Lazy S would be the first layout to go, for it was closest to the fires.

Three miles above the Lazy S, Dallam crossed the creek and traveled a southward-flung spur of timber for a mile, and passed one more cluster of buildings set in a pocket of the timber. This was Borden's. He felt a faint regret at what he was doing to Chuck Borden, for Chuck had long been his friend and hadn't sided with the rest of the

Association members in voting him out. But, he decided, this was no time for sentiment and he put Chuck's approaching ruin from his mind as the layout dropped from sight through the trees.

Twenty more minutes brought Dallam into sight of the Crescent B, sprawled across the creek in the downward distance. He had circled far to the south. It was a ticklish job to approach the Bishop headquarters without being seen, for the buildings sat in what would have been an immense meadow but for scattered clumps of trees, jack pine, aspen, and a sprinkling of spruce. By carefully screening himself from sight of the buildings behind the intervening tree clumps, he managed to cross the open grassy stretches without too long exposing himself. Presently he was out of the saddle, the grulla tied well back in the trees, and looking down across the creek to the barn lot less than two hundred yards away.

He was at once struck by the deserted look of the outbuildings. The bunkhouse door was in plain sight, yet in ten minutes of watching he saw no sign of life there. No smoke came from Pinto Sanders's kitchen chimney at the house on this near side of the stream. The corrals were empty, the pole gates down. Something he had no knowledge of had drawn the crew away this morning. Perhaps they weren't back yet from the raid of last night.

The first impulse that struck him was that now

was the time to make sure of his revenge on the man he hated most of all his enemies. Bishop wouldn't be here to see the fire sweep across the upper eastern slope and work its way down to this layout; in fact, with luck the Crescent B might be saved. That possibility occurring to him, Dallam saw where it would be easy now to go down there and touch off the buildings, even the house, as Buchwalter had suggested this morning. But seeing Cathy was much more important than the other. What he had to say to her would be made a mocking untruth if she even suspected that he'd had a hand in what was happening to the north of here right now. Firing the buildings down there would be a foolhardy act unless he failed in seeing her. So he contented himself by waiting.

Presently it occurred to him that Cathy might be in the house, alone. Hardly had that thought come than he was walking off through the trees in the direction of the house. He knew the approach well, had often used it in his clandestine meetings with Cathy after her father had forbidden him to set foot on the layout. He followed the thicker stand of trees down as far as he could, worked his way in farther through the wide-spaced spruces growing behind the house, and finally across to the ice house set close to the oldest end of the building. From here it was less than forty feet to the window of Cathy's room, which stood halfway open.

Listening there for a full minute, being careful not to expose himself, Dallam's feeling that the house was deserted became stronger. His mood had become a reckless one in which he dismissed the possibility of his being seen, of the mask of his supposed death being ripped away. That recklessness prompted him to whistle loudly the three-note call that had in days past been his furtive summons to Cathy. If she was anywhere about the house and heard it, she would come.

He moved out so that he could see her window and leaned carelessly against the corner of the ice house. Minute upon minute passed and still nothing happened. His restlessness mounted. Then, rashly, he decided he would go into the house.

Cathy's bedroom window lifted noiselessly and within fifteen seconds of the time the idea came to him, Dallam was inside. He had never been here before and now his bold glance took in the intimate details of Cathy's recent presence—the turned-down covers of the bed, the nightgown embroidered at the neck that lay over the bed's footboard, the silver brush and comb on the big-mirrored dresser, and the bottles and jars there. The window was curtained with a fine mesh lace and at the doorway to the closet hung printed chintz. Everything about the room was so utterly feminine that Dallam experienced a feeling of intrusion. He took off his Stetson, then, angry at himself for the impulse, clamped it on his head again.

When he crossed soundlessly to the hallway door, he drew his low-slung .38 from its holster. The hinges of the door *squealed* faintly in protest as he swung the panel open. He had a bad moment in which he stood frozen in complete wariness, the gun held pointing toward the hall at waist level, his breathing shallow. But for that feeble sound of the door opening, an utter stillness lay through the house.

Finally he moved on into the hallway and across to the half open door of Bishop's room. He stepped into the room far enough to make sure it was empty, then went on down the corridor to the living room entrance. The cold ashes of a recent fire lay on the broad hearth. Across the room, the dining table was littered with the remains of a breakfast set for two places. Convinced now that he was alone here, Dallam stepped boldly to the center of the room, his glance for a moment enviously taking in the glass-fronted gun cabinet in the room's far back corner between two ranks of filled bookshelves. He had heard about Bishop's fine hunting guns and was tempted to go over there and look at them. But first he would have his look at the kitchen.

There he saw evidence of Pinto Sanders's desertion. For he knew that he would have found more than a small unwashed frying pan and a quart-sized coffee pot on the stove had Pinto cooked a breakfast for the crew. The fact of Pinto's not having been here this morning intrigued him far more than the absence of Bishop and Cathy. What was going on here? Where was the crew? For a moment a strong panic was in him at his first guess—that the crew might even now be burning Fencerail and the other west-slope layouts to the ground. Then he remembered that Buchwalter had left guards at Fencerail and felt easier. Still, the emptiness of the house gave him a feeling of uneasiness.

He pushed open the kitchen door, stepped back into the living room, and started over toward the gun case. He was halfway there when a light quick step sounded on the portal beyond the big front door. As he wheeled, the door opened.

Chapter Twenty-Four

Cathy had begun that hard, punishing ride from the rim trail to the ranch feeling heartsick and without hope. She ended it with the certain conviction that somehow Streak's plan would save the lower slope. She became aware of something else as this new hope strengthened. Streak had come to mean a lot to her, more than Pete Dallam ever had. It meant a great deal that Streak was alive. She hardly knew the man, yet she saw in him the casual but real embodiment of all those qualities she had so wrongly imagined Pete possessed. It didn't enter her head that she might love this comparative stranger, for there was no time to weigh her emotions. All she knew was that the big rangy man could stir her deeply, that she had faith in him, and that even now she was eagerly looking forward to being with him again.

From across the pasture she saw the horses that had been in the corral earlier but were now out on grass. That meant her father had gone to see Jensen. She would have to go to the barn for a *moral* and some oats to catch up a horse for Streak. But first she would go to the house for bandages and salve and the can of tea in Pinto's kitchen. Tea, she remembered, was good for burns.

When she opened the front door and saw Pete across the room, sheer surprise wrung from her a startled cry. Then sudden paralyzing fear hit her.

Pete was smiling. "It's really me, Cathy," he drawled. "Not my ghost."

Through her whirling senses struck a warning note, a knowledge that she had a part to play here against this madman. Whether or not she was equal to it, she didn't know. After that first moment of panic, a strange calmness settled through her. She heard herself breathing: "Pete! You're alive!"

She must have put exactly the right note of pathos and tenderness in her voice, for he crossed the room quickly to her. All at once he gathered her in his arms. At the last moment she dropped her head away from his kiss and felt the pressure of his lips on her hair. She shuddered, revulsion in her, and for a moment doubted that she could stand this physical contact. But again came that utter calmness in the face of her terror. If she could deceive him long enough to get away, she would never again be alone so that he could be near her.

Shortly she pushed against the pressure of his arms and moved back away from him. The violence of her emotions, the fear that was in her, must have showed, she felt. There must have been tears in her eyes, for Dallam let go his hold on her and took the handkerchief from the pocket of his denim jumper. He held it out, laughing easily as he said: "Now's no time to cry, girl. Here, dry your eyes. Then we can talk things over."

"Talk what over, Pete?" she asked as she touched the handkerchief to her eyes. That gesture gave her a better grip on herself. So far, it seemed, he hadn't guessed her real feelings. This knowledge gave her even more courage and she added: "I can't believe it, Pete. I . . . I've . . ."

"Of course you can't," he said easily. Then with

stunning abruptness: "Cathy, you're coming away with me. Right now. We're going to ride clear of this hellish thing. You and I, together, Cathy." Never sensing that added fear had turned her mute, he went on: "There's lots I have to tell you. But you must believe in me, Cathy. I've been hunted like a wolf, living like an Indian in fear of my life. Cathy, I'm through here. You've got to come away with me."

Because of the revelation the morning had brought, she sensed the lies that were coming. Even though she still feared him with all her being, she felt the urge to know just what kind of a story he'd invented. It took her a moment to think of something to draw him out. She used that utterly feminine trick of burying her face in her hands in the hope that her voice would sound as though choked with a sob, saying: "But you were dead, Pete. We saw you buried. It couldn't have been anyone but you."

"Cathy, listen." He tilted her head up and looked into her eyes. "I can explain it all. But not now. We've got to hurry."

"I want to hear it . . . now," Cathy breathed. "No one will find us here. Dad's gone. So are the men, even Pinto. Tell me, Pete. Who was it they buried in your place?"

"A stranger," he replied without hesitation. "A stranger with hair the color of mine, built a lot like me. Maybe you remember him, Cathy. He came in on the stage with you that night."

She nodded. "I remember. But . . . then you killed him?"

He laughed softly, a brittle edge to his voice. "I did." His face went bleak, hard. "But not the way you think. That night, while I waited for you, he came onto the porch of the hotel where I was waiting. Told me he had some information to sell but that I'd have to meet him out beyond town before he'd talk. Don't know why I didn't suspect him from the first. But I agreed to meet him and rode out about five minutes after he left."

Cathy was beginning to understand and cut in with: "Then he tried to kill you?"

He nodded at once. "Him and Mike Sternes. I was lucky. They must have made a mistake in the way they planned it. Sternes bungled the job by opening up on me too soon. Naturally I went for my gun. Sternes went down at my first shot. It was so dark the stranger couldn't tell which of us had fallen. He called out to Mike and let me know where he was hiding. So I circled and told him to throw up his hands. He opened up and I cut him down, hit him in the head." He gave Cathy a direct look that seemed to go beneath the surface of her defenses. "Wouldn't you have done the same if two men tried to kill you?"

"Of course, Pete. Then this stranger was working with Mike?"

"That's the only thing it could've been."

"You mean . . . you mean he was hired to kill you? By . . . Dad?" Cathy was genuinely horrified at the callousness of the indictment against her father she knew was coming.

"Either Bishop or Sternes hired him," Pete said, misreading the look on her face. Then he blurted out the reason that backed his being here. "Tom Buchwalter's told me what a hard time you've had since you came home, Cathy. Frank Bishop is a cold-blooded devil if ever there was one. But you know that. He's had men out hunting me since I made my getaway from Agua. It's been hell for me, Cathy. I thought I could stick it out. But today Prenn and Buchwalter lost their heads. Last night your father's crew stampeded a bunch of cattle into that sheep band. This morning Buchwalter and Prenn decided to burn the east slope and get even with him. Maybe you saw the fires on your way in here."

Cathy gasped, seeing now more than at any time in these last minutes the satanical cunning of this man. And once again Dallam misread her response, thinking she was horrified by the seeming truth of his lies. He said, speaking softly, almost meekly: "So here I am, Cathy, asking you to come away with me and forget all this. You're all I have left. Together, we can make a new start."

Out of the whirlpool torment of stark fear that was in her, Cathy found a slender straw to hold to.

It was the only thing she could think of and she had to clutch at it frantically for she knew her life depended on it. She raised her eyes, hoping there was tenderness rather than hate in them. "I'll come away with you, Pete," she said quietly. "But not now, not in broad daylight. We want to leave without anyone knowing. Dad will stop us if he can. I'll meet you tonight."

He frowned, hesitating in his reply. Then: "Tonight'll be too late. That fire's headed this way. This place will be burned to the ground."

"Then I'll come to town and meet you wherever you say. Can't you see that we might be caught, might be seen, if we tried to get away now? Pete, this is my chance to find happiness. Our one last chance. Don't be careless with it if you love me."

"Love you?" He was suddenly in good spirits and gathered her in his arms again. Once more Cathy turned her face away and his kiss touched her cheek. "It's tonight then, in town. I'll wait behind the hotel. We'll catch the morning stage out of Agua and be across Dry Reach before anyone knows you're gone."

Cathy went suddenly rigid and pushed away from him. "Did I hear someone crossing the bridge?" she asked in a hushed voice.

He swung about quickly, drew his gun in one smooth, swift motion, and went to the broad window to look out. The tautness went out of his face and he smiled easily. "Not a soul, Cathy. You're on edge."

"Pete, you've got to get out of here, get to a safe place, and stay hidden. So much depends on this."

"This is the last place they'd look for me . . . if they knew I was alive. No one knows, Cathy. Only you and Tom Buchwalter."

"But I'm afraid, Pete. Please go. Hurry."

He hesitated a moment, but then nodded. "Anything you say. Tonight, then."

Cathy stood rigidly as he went to the hallway door of the bedroom wing. His parting smile was easy, meant to reassure her. Yet the rigidness didn't go out of her even as she heard him cross her bedroom and caught the *jingle* of a spur as he climbed out her window. Only when the muffled footfall of his pony sounded down from the timber that backed the house did she dare to take a full breath again.

She felt faint. She wanted to scream. But the utter stillness of the house seemed to hold some lurking threat that would materialize if she offended the heavy silence. Abruptly she turned and ran out into the yard. Once in the saddle, she put the black down across the bridge at a run.

Only when she was at the head of the lane did she get a hold on herself and realize that she was acting foolishly, that in this headlong flight she might be betraying the truth of her feelings to Pete if, by chance, he was watching from the timber behind the house. So she swung off toward the corral and there let the black drink at the trough. She even got down to tighten the cinch, hoping that from a distance she would give the appearance of unconcern.

She thought of Streak and was instantly and wholly taken by one mad desire—that of mounting and riding to him as fast as the animal would take her, of putting distance between her and the terror that had held her back in the house. But even as that impulse took her, she remembered. Streak needed medicine. It was impossible to take him a horse, but she would get the other things she had decided to take back to him.

Never in her life had she forced herself to such a frightening task as reëntering the house. She didn't know but what Pete would have come back. Yet she played her part to the end, not hesitating as she followed the hallway back to her father's room, nor as she entered Pinto's kitchen. She wrapped the whiskey, a can of baking soda, and a tin of tea in a newspaper, and left the house, resisting the impulse to look behind and make sure Pete wasn't there in the door, staring at her, watching. She walked the black into the head of the lane. There she put the animal into a trot.

She wanted the assurance of Streak's nearness, wanted it so much that she trembled. Yet even thinking of Streak calmed the riot of her fear. She could swing over to Jensen's place and get a horse for him. She would see her father at Jensen's and take him with her to help Streak and Kelso in their fight to save the Crescent B. What was she to tell Streak about meeting Pete? With that thought came a new fear, greater than the one she was now gradually leaving behind. If Streak found out that Pete would be in town tonight, wouldn't he naturally get a gun and go to meet the man who had only an hour ago tried to kill him? And wasn't it possible, very possible, that Pete Dallam would be the man to come away from that meeting alive? Cathy knew in that moment that she could share her secret with no one. The very thought of sending Streak into danger put a new fear in her. No, Streak had done enough. She would be the one to meet Pete tonight. She would go alone to meet him. And she would take a gun with her.

Chapter Twenty-Five

During the midday hour, the wind that had been sweeping down from the Arrowheads slacked off in a series of fitful gusts until finally the air hung ominously inert over the valley. Southward, the clouds banked heavily and high above the desert moved in slowly over that horizon. With the let up of the wind, the ragged sheets of flame that had raced along the slope mounted skyward in funnels of orange topped by mushrooming umbrellas of smoke. That dense smoke pall blotted out the hazed light of the sun and brought a premature dusk. The pulsating roar of the fires became clearly audible, a vast but low undertone of deep sound heightening the mockery of this taunting easing off of the elements. Instead of encouraging the men who were fighting to stave off their ruin, this weather change drained them of the last of their hopes. For the slow throbbing sound of the raging fires made it seem that destruction was descending on them even more swiftly than before, and the failing light brought hint of a nameless terror to come with the deeper darkness. As the light gradually faded, as the distant roar of the oncoming inferno mounted, men lost heart and ceased their struggles.

Jensen had spent the last three hours working his five-man crew in a desperate attempt to round up and drive toward the valley the two hundred head of yearlings and two-year-olds in the timber above his place. As the awesome stillness settled down around him, as he caught the throbbing echo of the distant fires, he miserably eyed the result of his labors—sixty-nine gathered animals—and gruffly told his bone-weary riders: "To hell with it! If I'm goin' bust, I'll go whole hog. This piddlin' bunch wouldn't even pay half a year's interest on my note. Get on down and gather up your possibles and hightail. If you see anything you want around the layout, take it along." He turned in the saddle to face Frank Bishop, who had come along to help as much as he could. "You comin', Frank? Anything we can do down below for you on the way out?"

Bishop gave a sober shake of the head, too appalled by this momentous but unavoidable gesture of Jensen's to find words for an audible answer.

At the Rafter B, lower on the slope, Chuck Borden took a last long look at the peeled aspen pole cabin he had last year built for his bride and turned to speak to his hired man, who lay on a blanket atop the loaded spring wagon.

"Feelin' better, Jake?"

The answer he got came in a voice coarsened by emotion, for Jake Bigelow had been no help that morning, lamed as he was by a rebellious boot-rubbed boil on his ankle: "I'm all right. But what's Jennie goin' to say?"

Borden himself wondered what his wife would say. She was over in Johnsville, visiting her folks. She'd taken an inordinate pride in that two-room shack, in the new bureau, and the calico curtains now lying mussed and dirty somewhere deep in the load behind. She'd wanted to have the first baby right there in the bedroom and Doc Swain had promised to ride up when her time came. Yet none of Borden's sorrow or regret showed as he gave his even reply: "She always said that front room was too small. Next time I'll build her a bigger one." It went without saying that Borden would have to spend many more years as a top hand before he could save enough to make another start on his own brand.

Schoonover, east of the creek and his place doomed as the first that would go, loaded his wife and kids into an empty buckboard, saying— "Helen, you know there ain't a damn' bit of use cartin' them packin' boxes and pans away from here."—and laid the whip to his scrubby team. Two hours later he was in town, roaring drunk.

When the whine of the wind eased off and that other sound took its place, Kelso and Streak, riding the sheriff's horse double, were within half a mile of their goal, the patch of timber cut by the creek above the Crescent B. For the last hundred rods they had ridden close to the stream, and now Streak said: "This wind slacking off will give us some time. I could do with a little of that water."

He reined in and Kelso slid to the ground and helped him down before he took his cane from the thong on the horn. The sheriff purposely avoided offering to help Streak walk across to the near bank of the creek but followed closely, his limp exaggerated because he was stiff from not having had the saddle under him.

As Streak went to his knees and scooped some water into his face with his cupped hands, Kelso announced: "Here they come, Bill and the girl together."

Streak looked back down the trail to see Bill, with the two cases of dynamite roped to the cantle of his saddle, leading another rider and a third horse out of a clump of trees close below. "Made good time, didn't he?" he said, and turned back to the painful job of washing some of the grime from the seared flesh of his upper arms.

Kelso was silent a long moment. Then he spoken truculently: "Mathiot, you've got a brain and it ain't misfired on you so far. But what you're aimin' to do up here is nothin' but wasted time. With the help of twenty or thirty men, we might do the job. But between the three of us we'll be like three beavers tryin' to dam the Colorado. I say to forget it. Hell, you're bad enough off without . . ."

Suddenly Streak straightened and turned with such violence that Kelso was brought up short. Streak was staring up at him in wide-eyed amazement. Then: "The dam! That's it, Kelso! Why didn't we think of it before?"

"What dam?"

"The one above . . . at Elbow Lake. We've got dynamite. There's a million tons of water back of that dam. Blow it out and what'll happen?"

As comprehension dawned in Kelso's eyes,

hope replaced the dull despair of his expression. There was something awe-inspiring and frightening in the very thought of unleashing the power of a million tons of stored-up water against the raging fires, but if anything could save the east slope from utter destruction, this was it.

Chapter Twenty-Six

Elbow Lake Dam filled in the crotch between two rounded hills, a broad-based wedge of earth and logs some sixty feet high. It held back a dog-legged mass of water that was narrow but deep and over half a mile long. Working its way toward the valley, the twisting bed of the stream cut through occasional broad bands of timber beyond the series of rocky barren hills that flanked it for better than its first descending mile. Far below the timber was meadow land broken only by an occasional patch crossing to the south bank. The crests of the hills to either side of the dam had recently been flattened, the dirt and rock pulled into the gorge between them.

Streak, Cathy, and Sheriff Kelso, standing on the shoulder of the hill to the north, were only slightly above the crown of the dam as they scanned the downward distance and for the first time saw the full enormity of Pete Dallam's intended revenge. Even this high the overcast of smoke had dimmed the day's brightness to a feebleness resembling dusk. Far below, a vast, rosy ring of fire marked the spot where the second and third blazes had joined and were now spreading fast, so fast that even at this distance the mushrooming destruction of the flames could be seen in slow and relentless motion. The southward margin of that lower fire was already closing in on Schoonover's place and would before long threaten the timber right above Prenn's, whose layout marked the northernmost working limit of the narrow upper valley.

Much higher and still farther to the northeast, the blaze Dallam had first touched off as Streak lay across the glade from him had spread south and east, gutting a huge triangular swath in the carpeting of emerald aspen and darker pine. It now crept out from its wide borders and, unless the threatening rain finally came tonight, would eventually climb to timber line and travel that margin all the way across to the east pass, up and beyond the vast reach of the Association's summer meadow here above the lake. If the dark mass of clouds to the south didn't fulfill their promise, tomorrow would see this high fire become a real threat, for it would gut the pass and, catching in the high timber, work down from above and behind to finish what the lower fire had left of the bottom slope.

Streak, seeing this, thought—*One thing at a time.*—and turned to Kelso. "How much longer, Sheriff?"

Kelso had just lifted the first case of dynamite from behind his saddle. He straightened and took out his watch. "Twenty minutes," he answered, "and he'll need all of it."

He referred to the errand Bill Paight had set out upon, a ride that might mean the difference between life and death to a number of people. Bill's first goal had been Jensen's, where he hoped to get a fresh horse and recruit part of the outbound crew to spread the news of what was coming, and to get others to clear the trails that would be threatened. Even more important, he was to find men to fight any jump fires that would later threaten that vast expanse of rangeland to the south of the creek. Lastly he was to get down to town and let the people there know what was coming.

Down below, as Cathy bandaged the worst of Streak's burns and finally helped him into his ragged shirt, they had talked it over and finally agreed to Streak's verdict, which had been: "We can spare you an even hour, Bill. No longer."

That hour, they realized now, would crowd their luck. For the fire below was traveling with such speed that the next twenty minutes might completely circumvent things they were doing to make good their last desperate chance. Twenty minutes might see the flames spanning the creek below Schoonover's; that was the danger point, for once it crossed there the outfits to the south were as good as gone.

"We didn't figure how long it'll take this head of water to travel that far," Kelso said as he pocketed his watch.

Streak nodded. "Then we'd better get started. You're sure the tools are down there?"

"They'd better be."

Kelso shouldered the case and, leaning on his cane, started down the short slope toward a small slab shed that squatted on the near shoulder of the narrow crowned dam. In that shed, the water mason's, they should find the tools necessary for doing a quick job, a shovel and certainly a big crowbar for the turning of the big wheel to the water gate set low on the dam's face.

As Kelso walked away, Streak stepped over to the lawman's pony and began working at the knot in the rope that held the second case of dynamite to the saddle.

"Don't. Let me, Streak," Cathy said at once, and came over to him.

He stepped back, smiled, and looked down at his blackened hands. "Maybe you'd better," he drawled.

All the way up here Cathy had marveled at the stoicism and the seemingly untouched reservoir of tough strength this tall, rangy man had. Instead of slowing them, Streak had urged Kelso to ride faster. He had ridden well, with seeming ease. But once or twice Cathy had caught a sudden sharp cast of tight pain lined across his lean face and had realized the intense anguish the hard ride was costing him. She had seen his shoulders draw back against the pull of the burns showing through his torn shirt along his ropy, muscled back. His blister-mottled face, dark in the beginning, darker now with the stain of the wet tea leaves, glistened whitely where she had smeared the worst of the burns with baking soda. She had bound the seared channel along the side of his head with a bandage, and the streak of gray hair showing over it against the black only heightened his look of having undergone unbearable agony. But outwardly he had given no sign of anything but an urge to get this job done.

Cathy worked loose the knot that held the case tight and the rope suddenly came apart. She reached out and tried to catch the falling box. Streak was a fraction of a second before her, his shoulder touching hers with a hard pressure. For a moment they stood that way, each with a hand grasping a corner of the case.

Streak gave a low laugh. "Let me get under it," he said, and moved away from her, putting both arms about the case, hugging it to his chest as he straightened and turned away with it.

In those few seconds something happened to

Cathy. She felt a constriction in her throat and her heart seemed to stop its beat. She was deeply aware of Streak's nearness and the firm pressure of his shoulder; she knew that quick move must have pulled at his sore muscles and hurt him to the bone. Yet he had laughed, scorning the pain. All at once there was an emotion in her that was a blend of tenderness and pity, of something else, too. Something that reminded her of that earlier resolve never to let Streak know her feelings toward him. Now there came the almost irresistible urge to tell this man her innermost thoughts, to tell him how wrong she had been yesterday, how hard she was trying to make amends for that shallow betrayal of her father and even shallower loyalty toward the man whose bestial cunning had nearly cost Streak his life.

The next moment a shot sounded up from the shack as Kelso broke the padlock on the door. Cathy saw him push open the door with his cane and disappear inside. Then, shortly, he reappeared. He looked up at Streak and called: "We're out o' luck! Except for a busted shovel, the damn' place is empty!"

Streak's stride slowed. He stopped, the move eloquent of the shock the sheriff's words held for him. Suddenly Cathy remembered something that laid a paralysis of apprehension through her. As soon as it was gone, she hurried down to him.

"Jensen sent a man over here on his way down

from the pass yesterday," she said breathlessly. "I should have remembered. He was clearing stumps from one of his new fields and asked Dad if he could borrow the tools for a few days. What . . . does this mean we can't . . . ?" She couldn't speak for a moment. Then: "Oh, Streak! I'm to blame for not thinking of it!"

He caught the rising note of her voice and said: "Easy, Cathy. Come along." He led the way on down the slope.

She saw the glance that passed between him and Kelso as he set the case down. "Why don't you say it?" she said lifelessly. "It's my fault! I'm nothing but . . ."

"Cathy!" Streak said sharply. Then, more mildly: "Let's go out and have a look."

He must have sensed her utter misery, for he reached out and laid a hand on her arm and made her join him as he started out the narrow path along the crown of the dam. Kelso, silent, followed.

When they stopped at the big gate wheel at almost the exact center of the dam's span, Cathy felt a moment of near panic as Streak's hand left her arm. Far below, the water foaming from the wide concrete apron of the water gate arced out and splashed into a lower rock pool, its roar remote and subdued by the distance. The gate marked the near bottom of the lake, some forty-five vertical feet, and even for the outsloping face of the dam the height was awesome. Cathy looked away toward the lake, and her uneasiness over the sheer drop eased at the friendly nearness of the still water only four feet down from the solid earth under her feet.

Streak stood with hands on the big wheel that operated the gear of the steel gate far below. He leaned over and looked down the long round-tiled shaft that ran through the heart of the dam to the big gate's gear box far below. Feeble light coming in through the concrete mouth of the gate down there disclosed a few hazy details. He could catch the oily sheen of the water rushing down the apron and above it the gear box with its four sturdy arms bolted to the top of the thick steel slab that held back the water. At three points between the gate and the wheel, big double brackets held rigid the bearings of the wheel shaft. The wheel itself was waist high, supported above the crown of the dam by a broad-based standard that was capped by a big bearing to hold this upper limit of the shaft rigid. Around the wheel the water mason's boots had flattened a circular footpath, the mark of his countless openings and closings of the gate below. When water was plentiful, he lived up here in the shack, but during the last month the Association members had agreed on a permanent setting of the gate, and the water mason had gone down to fill a riding job.

Kelso, standing behind Cathy, said: "I could

climb down a ways and you could let the stuff down to me with a rope. It'd take some time, but there's enough loose rock down there so I could pile it up and take a chance on the blast pushin' through."

Streak straightened and shook his head. "That's too much earth to move. You couldn't pile enough rock over this much dynamite in a week to push the blast in. We'll have to try something else."

The lawman nodded toward the water's edge, close below. "We could use that busted shovel and bury the stuff here at the top. In time, the water that came through would eat deeper and do the job."

"Then there wouldn't be enough water going down the creek at one time to do what we're after," was Streak's answer.

Kelso let out a long slow sigh and shrugged. "Then I give up."

"What about using all the dynamite we've got, tying it to one long bundle and dropping it down along this shaft on a rope? We let it lie on one of those supports and set it on a long fuse. Save out two sticks on a short fuse and let them down ten feet or so to blow in the top of the hole first. Then, when the main blast comes, it'll rip out the middle of the . . ."

"That's it! Man, you've got it!" Kelso cut in. He swung around and headed back toward the shack, his broken stride hurrying as he leaned heavily on his cane.

Cathy looked at Streak, caught his seriousness, and asked haltingly: "Will it . . . have we a chance?"

"We aren't licked until we try," was his answer. Still, she could see that he was worried.

It seemed an interminable time before they were ready. Kelso had to make one trip up the hill to the horses after the coil of capped fuses, several rawhide saddle thongs, and the rope. When he came back with them, there was another delay when Streak had to remove several of the copper caps and tie lengths of fuse together. Cathy wondered at his careful handling of the small copper cylinders until Kelso stated: "You've worked with this stuff before, Mathiot."

Finally Streak came erect. "That'll about do it," he drawled. Lying at his feet was a long cylindrical bundle of dynamite sticks with the black lengths of their fuses gathered at one end and wound to the main fuse, a scant two feet long. Near the head of the bundle one end of the long rope was secured. Three other sticks on a shorter fuse were tied to the lengths of rawhide the sheriff had taken from the saddles.

"Got a match, Sheriff?" Streak asked, looking up.

Kelso's answer surprised Cathy. "No."

"Come on," Streak drawled. "You're wasting time. This is my baby."

The sheriff shook his head stubbornly. "Maybe

so. But I take over from here on. Whoever lights them things is goin' to have to drop that bundle sure and fast and get out faster. That means me, not you."

Cathy understood now. They had used all the short lengths of fuse. Still, the man who stayed behind to light them, first to lower the big bundle down along the tiled shaft by the rope and then tie the small one so that it hung only eight or ten feet below the crown of the dam, was to be in real danger. Kelso's insistence on doing the job himself, Streak's equally insistent refusal to let him, was proof enough. They regarded each other a moment in stubborn silence. Finally Streak shrugged and reached into a pocket to bring out a silver dollar. "Call it," he said, spinning the coin in the air, catching it, and covering it with his other palm.

"You call it," Kelso growled.

"Heads."

Kelso leaned over to look as Streak uncovered the coin. He cursed softly when he saw what it was. Then he nodded to Cathy. "We'd better get out of here."

Cathy looked back when she and Kelso were halfway across to the shack. Streak was beside the wheel lighting the fuse of the big bundle. She stopped, watching him suddenly lift the bundle and drop it down the opening of the wheel shaft, the trailing length of black smoking fuse snaking after it. Then he was lighting a match and holding it to the fuse of the smaller bundle.

Beside her, Ledge's sheriff breathed: "There's a man, Cathy."

They saw the short rope that was to hold the smaller charge in place play out through Streak's stiff hands. He stood up, holding the end of the rope. Blue smoke fogged up out of the shaft hole as he deliberately reached over and began tying the end of the rope to the wheel rim.

"A single knot'll hold!" Kelso shouted. "Get out of there!"

But Streak made sure, doubling his knot. Then he turned and started running toward them, waving them back.

As the lawman and Cathy turned away again, hurrying on, a hollow explosion marked the instant the earth trembled under their feet. Cathy cried out, tried to stop. But the sheriff pulled her on.

"He's all right," he said brusquely. "That's the small one."

They were abreast the shack, past it, and then several paces up the slope. Cathy pulled her arm loose and stopped. Streak was halfway to the shack.

She saw him suddenly stumble and fall to his knees. He was up again before she felt the ground under her shake with a violence that threatened to throw her off her feet. The muted yet terrific blast echoed in a concussion that hurt her ears. She saw a billowing mass of earth geyser out from the creek face of the dam, saw the path behind Streak drop out of sight into a cavernous break. Then she cried out as the very ground under his boots seemed to fall away.

Sensing his peril, Streak gave a lunging leap that carried him onto firm ground. For a moment it seemed that he would fall back onto the huge water-moved mass of shifting earth the blast had torn in the dam. Then, abruptly, he was standing straight, running across the last twenty feet of the dam's crown and in toward the shack. He paused momentarily beside them, breathing deep gasping inhalations of air, his glance going to the awesome scene below. Slowly, majestically the center of the dam gave way, hung outward and seemingly motionless an instant, then started dropping with gathering speed before a solid wall of water.

"Run for it!" Streak called over the roll of mounting thunder. He took Cathy's arm and started up the shoulder of the hill. Kelso stayed abreast of them, his choppy stride as fast as he could make it.

Streak saw one of the horses, the sheriff's, wheel nervously and toss his head, whipping his trailing reins clear of the ground. He left Cathy and ran across to catch the animal's reins, then managed to catch up the other two as the thunder of the tons of cascading water welled up out of the gorge in a deafening inferno of sound.

Cathy and Kelso came up to him and the three of them stood speechless, watching. A solid wall of water a little lower than the dam itself had already filled the narrow notch downstream and was plummeting toward the valley, tearing out loose boulders from the hillsides, uprooting the few towering yellow bark pines along the slopes as though they were slender twigs. Where the dam had been, only an oily glistening mass of water showed, flowing so swiftly that the shack, floating away, seemed to travel out of sight with the speed of an express train.

"That'll do it!" Kelso shouted over the thundering roar that was gradually increasing in tone.

Half a mile below, they saw a scattering of huge boulders and outcrops mowed off the face of a hill by the roiled and foaming wall of water. In a short time they saw that mass of water flatten slightly as it reached a broader expanse of ground. It struck the first thick stand of timber and bowled over the trees like matchwood, the giant boles of the pines upending and wheeling along with the swift current. Close downward, the lake had fallen twenty feet, and still that relentless solid mass of water flowed over the crumbling lower sections of the dam, eating its foundations away. Now the roar had increased to a treble note, like the sound made by a high wind, a silky rush of overtones that became almost a shriek, with the distant thunder of the water wall far downward adding depth to the terrific note.

Kelso put a hand on Streak's shoulder, squeezed it and shouted: "It's good you're here, boy! I couldn't have made it."

Streak looked at Cathy, his expression sober with a strong amusement in his eyes. He reached into his pocket to bring out the silver dollar he had used in deciding the issue down there on the dam. It lay in his palm, showing heads. He showed it to Kelso. He turned it over. It still showed heads.

Chapter Twenty-Seven

Tom Buchwalter was scared. He was getting out, leaving this country fast. He took his last unregretful look at Fencerail shortly after 2:00 that afternoon and cut quickly into the friendly cover of the timber trail, his blanket roll tied to the saddle behind him. Too much had happened today for him to keep his usual peace of mind, and his confidence, supreme when he held the whip hand, had been shaken mightily by things he didn't understand. He had read the signs and had decided that he was finished in this country, that his luck had run out.

Back there at the hide-out, Buchwalter had regained consciousness with a tender scalp, a splitting headache, and the flash memory of Mathiot striking him down. How Mathiot had escaped jail a second time he had no way of knowing, nor could he guess where Mathiot had gone on leaving the hide-out. But below the slitted entrance to the cañon pocket he had found two more sets of tracks besides that of his own strangely missing pony and realized with sudden numbing apprehension that someone besides Mathiot now knew his secret. Still, when he walked back to the camp in Prenn's meadow, he'd had no thought of leaving, for he could easily explain being there in the hide-out. Hadn't he as much right as anyone else to be curious, to have gone in there for a look around? But when the fires were spotted high in the timber in the east, when the word came that there was not one fire but three, some inner sixth sense told Buchwalter that he had reached the end of his rope here, that it was only a matter of time before his murder-fed intrigue with Pete Dallam would come to light. He had always been a man to look out for himself first and the other fellow afterward. Making Prenn an excuse of having to ride across to Fencerail on business, he had left the west slope crews as they began moving the sheep to the far side of the meadow.

At Fencerail he had spent some minutes burning a bundle of papers and gathering only his necessary belongings to roll in a ground sheet and blanket. He seldom carried a gun, yet one thing to which he now gave careful attention was the strapping on of a shoulder holster under his coat and an inspection of the short-barreled Colt in it. While he worked, Buchwalter thought back on the morning, on Pete Dallam's all-consuming rage at learning of last night's raid on the meadow. Buchwalter himself was partly to blame for those three fires raging on the east slope for, as he left Prenn there at the meadow shortly after dawn, he'd had the idea that Pete could even the score with Bishop by that day putting the torch to the Crescent B. However, Pete had amplified that idea. The sheer magnitude of his revenge impressed Buchwalter as nothing he had ever had a hand in.

Except for knowing that at least one other man besides Mathiot was on a warm trail that might eventually lead to Dallam, Buchwalter would have seen in those fires a sure way for Dallam to become kingpin in this country and a secure future for himself. But there was that very possible chance that Dallam's secret would soon be exposed, and himself with it. So, reluctantly, he went to the big iron safe in the office and took from it $2,300, what remained of the $4,000 Laura had collected on Pete's insurance. It wasn't much, he decided, but it would give him some kind of a start in a new country.

Only when he had put the banknotes and gold coins in a money belt and strapped the belt about his waist under his shirt did real fear begin to plague him. He was stealing money from Pete, and of all the men he had ever known, Pete Dallam, in one of his late half-insane rages, could be the most dangerous. For this reason Buchwalter felt keen relief once he was well into the trees along the town trail. He would follow it a few miles and then strike a little-used side trail that would eventually put him onto the Agua Verde road well over the hill hump that marked the western limit of the valley. He had better than four hours to get to Agua and take the stage out. Not bad, he decided.

Life for Tom Buchwalter had been a series of just such happenings as this. He had known cards and used them professionally before he was fifteen. By his twentieth year his real name, Shropshire, had graced Reward dodgers posted on all the Mississippi and Ohio riverboats and he'd had to move on. In Montana he'd had some brief success at cattle rustling and selling stolen beef to a crooked Indian agent. Then the Army caught up with him, forcing him into the business he had stuck with ever since. He knew sheep, knew the men who worked them, although he hadn't ever owned any himself. A shrewd and brainy man, he had more than once realized that he might do better on his own than in working for someone else. Still, there was in him a warped sense of values that turned drab the prospect of years of hard work to build an honest stake. He had been tempted to try it but had never given way to the temptation. Now, at fifty-four, he knew that it was too late. So he played with what goodness was left in him by showing a benign and gentle face to the world, using it as an outward mask behind which to hide his truer self.

He was unhurriedly riding a section in which trees were sparse as these thoughts of the past came to him. He was so absorbed in his thinking that the quick wary lift of his pony's ears passed unnoticed. Only when the animal whickered nervously was he aware of anything wrong, and by that time it was too late.

Pete Dallam, elbow leaning on the full swell of his saddle, sat his grulla horse squarely across the trail only fifty feet ahead. Buchwalter's look was so openly amazed that Dallam laughed.

"Sort of spooked, ain't you, Tom?" he drawled.

The older man's recovery was quick and sure. He smiled broadly. "You're a damned cat the way you get around," he said. "Sure I was spooked."

His casualness didn't quite carry, for Dallam had caught him an instant unawares, when his face was without its guarded expression,

"Goin' somewhere?" Dallam asked, staring pointedly at the tarp-covered roll laced to the cantle of Buchwalter's saddle.

The Fencerail foreman did some quick and straight thinking. No use in trying to lie his way out of this, he decided. So, for once, he put his trust in the truth. "I'm on my way out," he said. "Mathiot gun-whipped me up there at the hideout. When I came to, I found he wasn't the only one that had been there. So I figured we'd about played out our string."

Something he said laid a sharp graven cast over Dallam's face. "You're tellin' me someone else besides Mathiot knows about this?" he queried flatly.

"Looks that way."

Dallam's look turned ugly, then eased as he sat a moment in deep thought. Then: "Tom, we've got to find out who this other jasper is, get to him before he can talk. Any guesses?"

"If I was you, I'd worry about Mathiot first."

"He's dead."

That answer, hardly surprising, started Buchwalter on a new line of thinking. If Mathiot was dead, and if, as Pete said, the other man could be found and silenced, then there was still hope of a future for him here. He cast back over the happenings of the night before and that day, and said finally: "Paight sort of took to Mathiot from

329

the first. But he's been up at the needle rock since before sunup waiting for word from me to blow that channel clear. So it couldn't have been . . ." He paused abruptly, then breathed: "Kelso. He must be the one. Mathiot was in jail last night. No one I know of busted him out. Riggs sure didn't. I didn't. So he must've talked Kelso into letting him out and siding him to the hide-out. There's your man, Pete."

"That could be," Pete drawled. "Fred never had much use for me. Bishop's one of his best friends. Tom, it's up to you to get him."

"Why me?" Buchwalter was quick to ask.

"I sure can't. And you don't dare send another man without a reason. That leaves it up to you."

"What if he's talked?"

"How could he? Mathiot was alone when I got him. That much I'm sure of. I'll lay you two to one Kelso hasn't got his answers yet. He hasn't had a look at me. With all the hell poppin' up there on the slope he likely hasn't had a chance to think much about this if Mathiot gave him anything at all to go on."

"You sure pick me some nice jobs, son," Buchwalter drawled.

"Do this one right and we're set," was Dallam's answer. "I've seen Cathy. She's leaving with me tonight. You'll hear from me in a week or so. By then we ought to have things goin' pretty much our own way."

"You've seen Cathy." Buchwalter whistled softly. "You burn out her old man and she's still for you?"

"Just like she always was."

"Pete, I'll have to hand it to you." Buchwalter's tone was tinged with an honest admiration.

"Then you'll hang on and see this through?"

"Think I'd throw a thing like this away?" Buchwalter's laugh was gentle and for that reason all the more packed with meaning. "Hell, yes, I'll hang on."

Bill Paight wondered if he was going loco. He stood on a tie rail in front of the Emporium, bracing himself with a hand on an awning post and stared belligerently down into the faces of the crowd below him. Ledge's street was packed walk to walk except for a small cleared space halfway across where Bill's dead horse lay. He had run the animal to death, killed him getting here to warn these people of what was coming. And now they wouldn't believe him!

Someone on the far walk shouted: "What good will two cases of dynamite do Kelso? If he had a wagon load, he couldn't blow enough of that dam away to fill my back pocket!"

Loud guffaws greeted this remark and another man called: "Kelso could pick it away with his cane!"

Bill waited out the laughter and the ribald

side remarks. He was reaching the end of his patience, feeling a white-hot anger. At the same time he sensed the half hysteria that had taken the townspeople; all they could do was watch the smoke-fogged east slope, the orange glow of the fires there, and imagine the slow dying of the town after the big outfits, which were the chief source of trade in this country, lay in ashes. When he could make himself heard, he shouted: "All I'm asking is that you empty those houses down by the creek and carry whatever can be moved up here onto the street where it's safe! Those people down there don't deserve to be flooded out and lose everything."

"You do it, Paight. We'll look on!" came a raucous voice from the middle of the street.

There were some more laughs. Bill knew then that he was wasting his time. He looked down, about to jump aground, when Harvey Strosnider's voice boomed all over the others. "Quiet, you jug-headed fools!" the owner of the Pride Saloon yelled. "Is it goin' to hurt you to do a little work? Suppose the dam does go out?"

"Supposin' it does, Harvey. Your place is safe." This time no one laughed at the poor wisecrack. The saloon owner's word bore some weight.

"Who's goin' down there with me and help clear out those houses?" Strosnider yelled again.

Instead of waiting for answers, he moved through the crowd, making for the path down the passageway between his saloon and a neighboring store. The path led down to the flat along the creek. Several men followed him, but not many.

Bill sensed in the hush that had fallen over the crowd his last chance to drive home the small doubt Strosnider had put in his listeners. He called scornfully: "The least you can do is stay off the walks and give us room to pile things!"

He jumped down off the rail and, using his elbows roughly, began shoving his way across toward the passageway. Men moved sullenly out of his way. Whenever Bill saw a face he knew well, he glared at it before going on. Three shamefaced men fell in behind him and followed. By the time he reached the far wall seven others had joined the first trio. Still, but for those ten, the rest held back. Yet they no longer shouted their taunts; they were silent before a stubbornness against being bulldozed into doing something they wouldn't do.

Bill was stepping into the head of the passageway when a faint earthy concussion pounded over the barely audible roar of the distant fires. Faces turned upstreet, all eyes traveling to the rosy-tinted east slope, beyond it, and up toward the pass that was hidden by the billowing clouds of smoke there. The crowd stood hushed, not a man moving.

Then a strident shout rang along the street: "There she goes!"

For a moment longer a paralysis of uncertainty held the crowd. Had the blast broken the dam? Suddenly a man bolted for the mouth of the passageway. Then, in near riot, others were after him. They jammed the narrow opening and ran down it toward the shacks below. At the foot of the alleyway, Bill stepped aside and watched them go past, a bleak smile graven on his square-shaped face.

Within the next two minutes the shacks down there began disgorging their furnishings: sofas, beds, barrels of dishes, piled bed clothing, chairs, crates, a hundred other items. Two men fashioned a stretcher of broomsticks and an old overcoat and carried a sick woman up to a house on the street. Most amazing of all, eight others got to work axing out the end wall of one house and, through the opening, lifted out a grand piano. They lugged the heavy burden up the alleyway as carefully as though it had been stuffed with eggs and didn't set it down until it was in the back warehouse room of the Emporium. Up off the flats and into the lower mouth of the passageway alongside the Pride trudged an unbroken line of men stooped under heavy burdens. They climbed the slope singly, in pairs, an occasional quartet grunting under the dead weight of a horsehair sofa or a big walnut bureau. On the street, Bill kept order, gathering together the belongings of one household, piling everything in under the walk awnings.

All at once a series of shouts echoed up the passageway. Bill caught the words: "She's comin' down!"

"Jumpin' Jehoshaphat, look at the trees!"

"It's too late! The fire's jumpin' the creek!" He understood at once and wheeled to look out along the murky distance of the east slope. A fierce joyous shout welled up out of his deep chest.

There, barely in sight through the murk, a thick gray shadow moved slowly down along the twisting line of the creek. It was a wall of water so wide that the broad ribbon of the foaming flood behind it took up half the expanse of the Crescent B's lower meadow. Bill caught his breath at imagining what the raging torrent had probably done to Bishop's house. What looked like twigs and branches, in reality huge uprooted trees, rolled on the crest of the first high and foaming wave.

Bill looked below and groaned as his hopes instantly died. The ring of fire had spread around the small cleared pocket that marked Schoonover's place and the rosy line of flames had already crept beyond the line of the creek. In his frenzy of work Bill had forgotten to watch that critical point. Now he knew that all this work was for nothing, that the east slope was doomed as certainly as it had been before Streak thought of that last desperate way of saving the big layouts. For now, with the fire spreading on the creek's south bank, nothing could keep it from gutting the timber of the lower slope.

He sat down wearily on an overstuffed chair beyond the walk, unable to take his glance from the oncoming wall of water. It appeared to be moving no faster than a man could walk, but Bill realized its great speed in the face of seeing it, at this distance, in motion at all.

After what seemed an eternity, it reached the upper end of Schoonover's clearing. The small dark square that was Schoonover's house disappeared under the gray mass. Then the water wall was cutting through the lower line of fire, erasing it. But when it had swept lower, beyond Schoonover's, a minute speck of livid flame still remained on the south bank. Bill sat in that lifeless posture of lost hope as the roar of the oncoming water mass filled the air. Presently the sound became deafening. Majestically, more slowly now, the oncoming flood surged down across the lower valley. Its mighty roar made the air tremble, rattled windows in the stores along the street. Finally it was abreast the upper end of the street. The *crash* of the crushed buildings along the lower flat was drowned in the voice of the raging water. Twenty feet high, the giant boles of uprooted trees turning lazily below its crest, it picked up the shacks and houses below the street level, ground them, crushed them into splintered boards, and passed relentlessly on.

Then came the main mass of the flood, a boulder and tree-strewn river of white, foaming water littered with all the débris of its twelve-mile flow. Its roiled borders struck the foundations of a few of the higher buildings. The lean-to at the back of the Pride was swept away and for half a minute sailed majestically along until it tilted over and was slowly crushed. A wagon bed floated in the middle of the current, turning around and around as though its lost wheels were trying to find a secure footing.

Then the main flood was gone, its roar receding as it struck southward along the lower line of the creek. Toward nightfall it would hit Twin Forks, far below at the edge of the desert and sometime tonight would spread out across the sandy waste of Dry Reach to spend itself in running the countless dry washes there.

Men gathered along the alley behind the stores to look down on the destruction that lay along the still overflowing creek. Nothing was left of the settlement down there, nothing but a few broken boards, the mud-filled brick foundation line of one cottage, and a few littered scraps of metal marking the spot where the hardware store's junk pile had been. A layer of clay-colored silt covered everything. And up to the south of Schoonover's a bright pinpoint of live flame marked the gloom to make a mockery of the awesome destruction these men had just witnessed.

When nothing but the fading, far-off roar of the flood disturbed the silence, Bill got up out of the chair and stared along the street. Other men were doing the same, their glances stunned, helpless. They didn't talk. They were too miserable for words.

With a lifeless shrug, Bill faced halfway around and started toward the Pride, feeling the need for whiskey. He had taken only three steps when he came to an abrupt halt. Up the street from the lower end of town came a rider, his horse at a trot. That rider was Tom Buchwalter.

Bill's glance whipped around to a trio of men standing nearby. One wore a gun butt foremost in the holster at the left side of his waist. Unceremoniously Bill went over and jerked the gun from the man's belt, saying: "You'll get this back." He stepped down off the wall, ducked under a tie rail, and, the gun hanging in his hand at his side, waited there as Buchwalter approached.

Buchwalter was barely thirty feet away when he saw and recognized Bill. His face lighted up at sight of his crew man and he reined over toward Bill, saying: "What happened? Who blew the . . . ?" Abruptly he reined his horse to a stand. The look on Bill's face was unmistakably hostile, and now Buchwalter saw the gun.

"Get down, Buchwalter," Bill drawled.

Fencerail's foreman sat silently a moment, making no move to dismount. Then: "What's eating you, Bill? What have I done?"

"Get down," Bill said tonelessly.

There was a veiled wariness in Buchwalter's look now. His glance wouldn't meet Bill's directly. He looked beyond and asked the men on the walk: "You know anything about this?"

Before they could reply, Bill's voice rasped out: "Blast you, light and take your licking!"

Buchwalter's glance swung on Bill an instant. Then he looked down at his waist. "You can see for yourself I'm not packing an iron," he said.

"That makes it all the easier." Bill tossed his Colt away. It skidded into one of the shallow wheel ruts a few feet out from him.

A cold smile came to Buchwalter's face. "You always were a trusting soul, Bill," he drawled. And suddenly his right hand lifted from the swell of his saddle and stabbed in under his coat.

For the split second it took Bill to realize his mistake, he stood motionlessly. Then, as Buchwalter's arm swiveled down, Bill made a sideward lunge that became a rolling fall. Buchwalter took deliberate aim and fired. Bill, rolling over, clawing his gun from the dirt, went rigid as the bullet struck him. Then, arcing up the gun, he got in a shot that blasted out at the exact instant Buchwalter's second bullet came.

The Fencerail foreman stood up in stirrups as his

second bullet kicked up a geyser of dirt that sprayed in Bill's face. Then, his horse shying, Buchwalter toppled off balance. Bill's next three shots jerked the man erect in three separate solid blows. But finally he was so far off balance that he fell. He struck the ground on his head and right shoulder. In the momentary silence the breaking of his shoulder bone made a small but plainly audible sound.

Bill came to his knees and, his gun held before him, crawled the twelve feet across to where the other lay. Men were running along the walks but Bill ignored them. When he was within reach of Buchwalter, he twisted the smoking gun from the dying man's hand and threw it aside. He took a hard hold on the shoulder of Buchwalter's coat and gave it a savage pull.

"How did you drag her into this?" his voice grated. "Damn you, talk! What were you holding over that girl to make her come here and back your play?"

The very intentness of his tone seemed to bring Buchwalter back to consciousness. He opened his eyes.

"What have you got on Laura?" Bill repeated. "How did you get her to come here?"

Blood flecked Buchwalter's lips and his white-shirted chest was splotched with spreading crimson. Still, no pain showed on his face. When he spoke, his voice bore the kindly gentle lift Bill knew so well. "You'd like to know, wouldn't you, Paight?"

"You're going to tell me."

While Buchwalter took a gasping breath, the onlookers who by now had gathered close listened in wonder to this play of words they couldn't understand.

In a moment Buchwalter said: "She's a good girl, Bill, sound clear through. Her father was my partner once. I . . . I had something on him. She threw in with us when I threatened to . . . to send him to Yuma. She . . . she . . ."

They saw life leave him. His eyes remained open but his head rolled loosely to one side, lying against his twisted broken shoulder.

Bill stared up bleakly at the circle of men. Then, slowly, a smile played against the pain written on his face. He reached up, grasped the belt of a man standing close by and pulled himself erect. Now the watchers could see the red stain low along his side at waist level. A man said quietly to a youngster at his side: "Run down and get Doc Swain."

Bill shook his head. "No. What I need is a horse. Who's going to lend me one?"

"You're hurt, Paight," the man who had helped him to his feet protested. "Where you want to go?"

"Agua. Where's a jughead?"

"You couldn't ride a mile if you had to."

"Damn it, I want a horse!" Suddenly Bill's glance went to Buchwalter's pony, standing ground-haltered in the middle of the street. Pushing aside a man who blocked his way, he walked over to the animal, spoke to it gently when it shied, and caught up the reins.

He managed somehow to get into the saddle and thrust his boots in stirrups. So amazed were the watchers that no one thought to try to stop him. He was sitting straight when the horse took him out the lower end of the street at a run.

Chapter Twenty-Eight

Streak walked his pony into the upper end of Ledge's narrow street a few minutes short of 9:00 that night, his borrowed Stetson tilted against the slant of the downpour. Along his back the cold feel of his soaked shirt—borrowed, too—gave him keen relief from the bite of the burns there. But for the rawness of the rain-washed night air, he would have slept in the saddle, for now the nerve tension that had kept him going since mid-morning had drained out of him and he was feeling bone-deep the nagging exhaustion that made even the weight of the gun at his thigh a bothersome burden. He fought his weariness with a restlessness that wouldn't let him alone. He could explain that uneasiness no better than he could his feeling of having left something undone, or than he could the sense of incompleteness he had felt on leaving Cathy Bishop some five hours ago.

Common sense told him that he should look up a doctor, have his burns treated, and turn in at the hotel for a night's rest, but a subconscious urging kept him from doing this. That urging was a blend of several emotions—an emptiness that hit him each time he thought of Ed Church lying in that mistakenly marked grave down at Agua, cold anger at the realization that Pete Dallam was still very much alive and very much a threat, and, most irritating of all, a reluctance to ride out of this country now that his job here was done. Guilford had sent him in to find out what had happened to Ed Church. He had found that out and there was nothing to keep him. Certainly the affairs of the men and the one girl he had met during the past four days were no longer any concern of his.

This last thought brought Streak to a decision and he made up his mind to act on it before he gave way to those more personal urgings. He would leave tonight, ride to Agua Verde, pay Snyder to return his borrowed horse, and take the morning stage across to Johnsville and start back home—well, not home exactly because he didn't have a real home. Rather, he'd report back to Guilford. Maybe Guilford would keep him on now that he was shy a deputy.

Streak wondered if he were foolish in starting on a thirty-mile night ride as played out as he was. But then his stubbornness ruled out any thought of changing that decision. and he lifted the pony to a trot as he went on down the street. He saw the lights of the Pride and didn't fight the welcome idea of turning in there. He excused this brief delay by telling himself he would be better off for a drink or two of whiskey and a light meal with plenty of coffee; actually, in turning in to the saloon's tie rail, he was making a small concession to that inexplicable reticence he felt at so abruptly leaving.

Before he went in through the swing doors he took the bandage off his head and tilted his hat so that it would cover the spot where the hair had been burned away. He was thankful at finding the place nearly empty and at the way the half dozen customers politely ignored him and went on with their drinking and their small stake game of draw at a table in the big room's back corner.

There was a reason for the Pride's near emptiness. Late this afternoon close to forty men had come up from town to the stretch of timber across the creek from Schoonover's where Frank Bishop, Fred Kelso, and Jensen's crew were already fighting the fire. Streak had come down there after leaving Cathy at the Crescent B; luckily the flood hadn't damaged Bishop's house, sitting as it did high above the creek, except for the foundations of the portal being undermined and a little water having come in under the door onto the front end of the living room floor. It had taken just short of half an hour to organize those forty men to do a job that had any hope of checking the fire. Bishop and Kelso between them had finally thought out the best way.

A mile to the south of the creek a fairly large clearing centered the thick neck of the timber stretching southward, the trees running around it on its upper and lower sides. The final plan had been to cut a wide lane through those two segments of the timber that joined beyond the clearing. The townsmen and Jensen's crew had worked their guts out and managed to cut those two lanes by the time the fire had spread to the northern edge of the clearing. Then, thinking they had won their battle, they had seen the fire cross the west lane by burning underground along the tinder-dry roots of a big dead ponderosa pine. As night fell, those men, Kelso working with the rest, had madly fought this jump fire, checking it as best they could. Then, when it got out of hand and the exhausted men faced the threat of losing all they had gained, the first misty drizzle of the rain had come down out of the night sky. Within ten minutes, the downpour started. Men had shouted crazily, gone flat on their bellies beside the quickly gathering and blackened pools of rain water, and cooled their parched throats and burned faces. The Baptist preacher, who had worked so hard he could barely stand, had offered to say a prayer of thankfulness. It was while those men knelt shadowed in the feeble light of the dying fire that Streak had quietly gone to his horse, pulled himself up into the saddle, and ridden away.

He would never forget that last glimpse of the valley, men kneeling there, humbly thanking their God for the blessings of the rain that had saved them while the parson's low voice droned a prayer. Bishop, Jensen, and old Fred Kelso, their faces lined with fatigue but now relaxed out of the grim set of hopelessness, had been on their knees close to where the preacher stood. As Streak had ridden away through the trees, he had taken a last look at Kelso and Bishop and himself came as near as he ever had to praying. But his prayer wasn't in thankfulness over Nature having taken a hand in saving the valley; it was that Frank Bishop and his daughter would find the happiness denied them these past months, that they would all forget the hates and blood lust that had become the scourge of the valley, that they would find peace in the days to come.

Streak now forced himself to eat the cold over-cooked beef and bread the bartender brought him when he asked for food. He had coffee, too, four steaming big mugs of it that put new strength and warmth in him. Leaving his half dollar in change on the bar, he nodded to the bartender and said—"So long."—feeling that it was his final farewell to this valley and all it had come to mean to him.

He went out, spent a moment pulling tight his cinch, and had lifted a boot to stirrup when he saw a rider cross the street up ahead from a side alleyway to the one flanking the hotel's far side. The rider's outline was made shapeless by a yellow poncho. The horse was a dark one, white-stockinged. There was something strangely familiar about the animal's markings. Suddenly Streak knew what it was. The black Cathy had ridden today had been marked exactly like this animal, both forelegs white to the knee joint, the left hind leg white to the hock. Streak wound his reins to the tie rail again, putting down the spark of excitement in him at the thought that he might see Cathy a last time. Reason told him that that rider probably wasn't Cathy, yet he couldn't ignore a sudden strong hunger for a last word with her, for even only a last glimpse of her. Because she might possibly be the rider on the black, he crossed the street and started for the opening into which the rider had disappeared, feeling the cold and the wetness crowd in on him once more, knowing he would be disappointed in having followed this foolish urge.

The passage was totally dark except toward its head where the light coming from the side window of the hotel lobby was reflected from the gray, weathered siding of the adjoining building. Beyond that, the blackness closed in until Streak couldn't see the hand he held outstretched before him. The rusty gutter two stories overhead leaked a continual thin sheet of water that quickly soaked him to the skin. Far back, he could make out the rectangular opening of the passageway's lower end and the hazy cobalt outline of a building across the back alley.

He was within two strides of the end of the passage when he heard voices. Cathy's he knew at once. The other was a man's, vaguely familiar but still unrecognizable. Streak abruptly understood something. Cathy had ridden all this way to town in the rain to meet someone. Her wary crossing of the street from a passageway opposite spoke of a furtiveness that was distasteful to him. He knew at once that he was an intruder and, feeling a slow let-down, turned back up the passageway. Then he heard the man's voice say sharply, clearly: "You little hellion! Drop that gun!"

In the instant he recognized Dallam's voice Streak wheeled and in three lunging strides was out of the foot of the passageway. His hand stabbed to holster. Then he saw them, indistinctly, Cathy's shape recognizable only by the lighter shade of her yellow poncho and because it was so much shorter than Dallam's. They stood barely twenty feet away down the alley, Cathy with her back turned, Dallam beyond and facing Streak. They were almost within reach of each other.

Streak heard Cathy say sharply—"Stay where you are!"—as Dallam took a step toward her. Dallam drew back at her quick warning and she went on: "Pete, Streak Mathiot is still alive. I wanted you to know that."

"But I left . . ." Dallam stopped short. Then: "What's Mathiot to you?"

"Everything I once thought you were, Pete. He's fine all the way through. He's kind and gentle, and . . . I love him."

"Who got him out of there?" Dallam queried in a rasping voice.

"I did."

"So you've already picked up another man now that you're through with me."

"Pete, you're loathsome," Cathy said in a trembling voice. "Raise your hands and turn around. I'm taking you to jail."

"No, you're not." Again Dallam took a step toward her.

Through the soft undertone of the pelting rain, Streak caught the sharp *click* of a gun falling in cock. He lifted his Colt quickly into line, then froze in fear of his shot hitting Cathy. He knew she was going to shoot and called out sharply: "Don't, Cathy!"

The sound of his voice brought her head around and in that instant Dallam lunged in. Cathy's gun exploded deafeningly, but the stabbing flame of the shot lined downward, away from Dallam. Streak saw Dallam jerk the gun from her hand and arc it up at him. A split second before Dallam fired, Streak side-stepped and his shoulder hit hard against the hotel's back wall. The flash of Dallam's shot blinded him for an instant; at his back he felt the shock of the bullet hitting a board of the wall. Then his momentary blindness was gone and he made out Dallam's shape towering over Cathy's, behind it. Dallam was using Cathy for a shield.

"Mathiot!" Dallam called when a moment's silence remained unbroken.

Streak breathed shallowly, not moving.

"Mathiot!" Dallam called again, more sharply this time.

Cathy gave a choked cry. "You've killed him."

"If I haven't, I'm going to," Dallam's voice snarled.

Suddenly Dallam half shouted a curse and Streak saw him move as Cathy twisted sideways and nearly out of his grasp. For an instant the pale outline of her poncho left Dallam's tall shape clearly outlined, open. Streak squeezed the trigger of the Colt he held hip high. He saw the impact of that bullet as he once more lunged sideways and closed in. Dallam jerked back half a step. Then in a powerful sweep of his arm he was holding the girl in front of him again and his gun laid a blazing crescendo of fire in at the wall where Streak had stood. Streak counted the shots. There were three of them and they splintered a board of the wall only two feet to his right.

Cathy called—"Streak!"—and her voice was edged with terror.

Streak was about to answer, then checked himself. For he realized what an advantage he had over Dallam; the other couldn't see him.

Now he could hear Dallam's rattling breathing and knew that his bullet had hit the man where it counted. Still Dallam stood his ground, Cathy held squarely before him in the powerful clutch of his left arm.

There was another brief moment in which no sound but the rhythmic drone of the rain on the tin roof of the hotel broke the stillness. Then Dallam was saying in a choked, thick voice: "Want some more, Mathiot?" When Streak made no answer, Dallam added: "I'll count up to five. Either show before I finish, reachin', or I put this last slug through Cathy's back!" There was a moment's pause. Then: "One . . . two . . . three . . ."

Streak deliberately brought his gun up to eye level. He could see the worn, shiny back of the front sight in the notch of the rear as he targeted the dim outline of Pete Dallam's head. He didn't for an instant doubt that Dallam would carry out his threat. Barely below his sight Streak sensed a lower target, Cathy's head. Panic gripped him as Dallam called: "Four!" He was using a strange gun, one of Frank Bishop's that Cathy had loaned him there at the house this afternoon on his way down from Elbow Lake. He didn't know how it was patterned. As he sensed that Dallam was about to make his last count, he lifted his sights almost to the crown of the man's hat and put a firm, even pressure on the trigger. The gun's hard pound against his wrist surprised him.

He saw Dallam move backward, saw Cathy's vague shape melt toward the ground in a fall. He knew then that his bullet had struck her. A blossom of gun flame winked above Cathy, at the level of Dallam's chest. A blow on Streak's shoulder drove him hard against the wall. Then he was emptying his gun into Dallam, three swift shots that laid a roll of thunder along the alley.

Dallam lurched to one side in a wide-stanced step and stood solidly against the last bullet. He tried to come in at Streak, but his off-weight knee bent as he moved and he fell in a slow wheeling drop, to his knees and finally straight out on his face.

An aching throb pounded in Streak's shoulder as he walked slowly out to where Cathy lay. He didn't want to look. But he didn't have the will to keep himself from it.

Cathy moved when he was two steps from her, seeming to rise up out of the shadows.

"Streak!" she sobbed. "You're alive!"

Then she was in his arms, her own hugging him close to her. And he was gently kissing her upturned face.

The next morning Fred Kelso was standing on the bottom step that led down off the hotel verandah lighting his after-breakfast cigar. Hank Snyder saw him and reined in off the street to the rail beyond to ask: "Know where I can find a gent by the name of Mathiot, Sheriff?"

"Sure," Kelso said. "He's in there havin' breakfast in bed." The lawman jerked a thumb to indicate the hotel. He was curious over Snyder's being here in Ledge instead of down at the stage corral at Agua.

Snyder gave him a sour look. "I'm in too much of a hurry to listen to any of your wisecracks," he drawled. "Maybe I better ask someone else."

"I'm tellin' you the truth," Kelso bridled. "Mathiot's in bed havin' breakfast. He couldn't be any place else. He's too weak to walk. Why you want to see him?"

"Paight sent me. I got something to tell Mathiot."

"Paight!" Kelso tossed away the match, forgetting to pull on his cigar to get it going. "What about Paight?"

"He wants Mathiot to get down to Agua today if he can."

"Well, he can't, he's laid up."

"So's Paight," Snyder said.

"I wondered. They say he had a hole through him when he left here yesterday. Is he hurt bad?"

"Not too bad. His wife's lookin' after him."

"Wife?" Kelso echoed.

Snyder nodded. "They was married last night, him and that sister of Dallam's. Only she ain't Dallam's sister."

Kelso thumbed his Stetson onto the back of his head and said slowly, deliberately: "I'm damned." Then, when he became aware of Snyder again: "Well, what is it you want me to tell Mathiot?"

"What I been tellin' you. Ain't that enough?" Snyder said testily.

"Plenty," Kelso said. He turned, let his cane slip down from the crook of his arm, and started up the steps. Halfway up, he stopped and faced Snyder again: "You might tell Paight the same thing about Mathiot you were supposed to tell Mathiot about Paight."

"What?"

"What you been tellin' me. He's married."

"Who is?"

"Mathiot. And you can tell Bill for me he'd better get healed up and back here quick. Mathiot's goin' to need a straw boss to help him run Fencerail. He's buyin' it from the bank."

"That so?" Snyder said. "Things sure happen fast around here. Who did Mathiot marry?"

"You just tell Bill he's hitched. He'll guess who to."

About the Author

Peter Dawson is the *nom de plume* used by Jonathan Hurff Glidden. He was born in Kewanee, Illinois, and was graduated from the University of Illinois with a degree in English literature. In his career as a Western writer he published sixteen Western novels and wrote over 120 Western short novels and short stories for the magazine market. From the beginning he was a dedicated craftsman who revised and polished his fiction until it shone as a fine gem. His Peter Dawson novels are noted for their adept plotting, interesting and well-developed characters, their authentically researched historical backgrounds, and his stylistic flair. During the Second World War, Glidden served with the U.S. Strategic and Tactical Air Force in the United Kingdom. Later in 1950 he served for a time as Assistant to Chief of Station in Germany. After the war, his novels were frequently serialized in *The Saturday Evening Post*. Peter Dawson titles such as *Royal Gorge* and *Ruler of the Range* are generally conceded to be among his best titles, although he was an extremely consistent writer, and virtually all his fiction has retained its classic stature among readers of all generations. One of Jon

Glidden's finest techniques was his ability, after the fashion of Dickens and Tolstoy, to tell his stories via a series of dramatic vignettes which focus on a wide assortment of different characters, all tending to develop their own lives, situations, and predicaments, while at the same time propelling the general plot of the story toward a suspenseful conclusion. He was no less gifted as a master of the short novel and short story. *Dark Riders of Doom* (Five Star Westerns, 1996) was the first collection of his Western short novels and stories to be published.

Center Point Large Print
600 Brooks Road / PO Box 1
Thorndike ME 04986-0001 USA

(207) 568-3717

US & Canada:
1 800 929-9108
www.centerpointlargeprint.com